Gaia, Queen of Ants

Middle East Literature in Translation
Michael Beard and Adnan Haydar, *Series Editors*

For a full list of titles in this series,
visit https://press.syr.edu/supressbook-series
/middle-east-literature-in-translation/.

GAIA, Queen of Ants

Ялмоғиз Гея ё мўр-малах маликаси

Hamid Ismailov

Translated from the Uzbek by
Shelley Fairweather-Vega

Syracuse University Press

The section entitled "The Dervish and the Mermaid" in the "Water" chapter
originally appeared in *Image*. Reprinted with permission.

First Edition 2020

20 21 22 23 24 25   6 5 4 3 2 1

∞ The paper used in this publication meets the minimum requirements
of the American National Standard for Information Sciences—Permanence
of Paper for Printed Library Materials, ANSI Z39.48-1992.

For a listing of books published and distributed by Syracuse University Press,
visit https://press.syr.edu.

ISBN: 978-0-8156-1115-8 (paperback)   978-0-8156-5489-6 (e-book)

Library of Congress Control Number: 2019950578

Manufactured in the United States of America

Ἦ τοι μὲν πρώτιστα Χάος γένετ᾽, αὐτὰρ ἔπειτα
Γαῖ᾽ εὐρύστερνος, πάντων ἕδος ἀσφαλὲς αἰεὶ
ἀθανάτων, οἳ ἔχουσι κάρη νιφόεντος Ὀλύμπου,
Τάρταρά τ᾽ ἠερόεντα μυχῷ χθονὸς εὐρυοδείης,
ἠδ᾽ Ἔρος, ὃς κάλλιστος ἐν ἀθανάτοισι θεοῖσι,
λυσιμελής, πάντων δὲ θεῶν πάντων τ᾽ ἀνθρώπων
δάμναται ἐν στήθεσσι νόον καὶ ἐπίφρονα βουλήν.
          —(Ἡσίοδος, Θεογονία)

First Chaos was born,
but next wide-bosomed Earth, the ever-sure foundations of all
the deathless ones who hold the peaks of snowy Olympus,
and dim Tartarus in the depth of the wide-pathed Earth,
and Eros or Love, fairest among the deathless gods,
who unnerves the limbs and overcomes the mind and wise
counsels of all gods and all men within them.
          —(Hesiod, *Theogony*, translated
             by Hugh G. Evelyn-White, 1914)

Contents

Translator's Note

My job as the translator of this tale is to provide you, curious reader, with as accurate and intimate a view as I can of a place that for most of you is far away and quite unfamiliar, in a language in which you can, nevertheless, feel at home. For someone who learned Uzbek only as an adult, this is a risky undertaking. It could very well be that the clouds here in Seattle this October are obscuring my view of Central Asia just as much as the drizzle of Eastbourne and our hero Domrul's own scarred past obscure *his* view. I suppose that's only fair.

Since you are relying so much on my words to get a glimpse of this world, you deserve an extra word or two about language: both the one in which this novel was first created, and the one in which you are about to read it. Hamid Ismailov wrote *Gaia, Queen of Ants* in Uzbek, as Ялмоғиз Гея ё мўр-малах маликаси, something like "Gaia the Witch, or the Queen of Ants and Insects." This is one of three Uzbek novels by Ismailov to have the luck to be translated into English directly from Uzbek, rather than getting squeezed and filtered through Russian on the way.

Russia, whether in its imperial, Soviet, or post-Soviet forms, has been squeezing and filtering Uzbekistan for some time, of course. One effect of that relationship is visible in the Uzbek language (a construct made up of Persian poetry, Arabic vocabulary, Turkic grammar, and Soviet bureaucracy) and particularly in the alphabet. Uzbek was once written, by those who could write at all, using Arabic characters. Later a Latin alphabet was created for it, then a Cyrillic one. Since 1992, soon after Uzbekistan's independence from the Soviet Union, a change back to a modified Latin alphabet has been perpetually in progress. The changes in alphabet have had to accommodate differences between the sounds of the two languages. For example, Uzbek needs to depict vowel sounds that Russian does not: it has the long /u/ represented in Russian by the Cyrillic letter y, but also a rounder version written ў in Uzbek Cyrillic and *o'* in the newer alphabet. Our characters O'rhon and Bo'riboy have this sound in their names. Uzbek itself, as a matter of fact, is written "O'zbek" in the current version of the alphabet (but since you're so used to seeing it with a U, we'll stick with that).

In the dialect of Uzbek most often considered the literary one, the written vowel *o* is not pronounced with a long sound like "oh" in English, or like a stressed Russian "o," but more like "ah." This means words that Uzbek shares with other languages may not look quite the same when it comes to representing this sound. I have preserved this spelling difference, so you'll need to keep in mind that the Uzbek *non* and the *naan* you pick up at the Indian buffet come from the same linguistic kitchen, probably baked in the same linguistic *tandir* (or *tandoor*) oven.

In translating, I've applied that rule to everything you might see on the menu at an Indian restaurant, but I've used a different rule for words you've seen on a map. The capital city where Emer gets into so much trouble in the book is "Toshkent" to the locals, but since most of us reading this aren't local at all, we'll call it "Tashkent," the way we've seen it written before. That's assuming it really is Tashkent, of course, because Ismailov never really tells us for sure. And if the word "Uzbekistan" ever appeared in this novel, we'd have written it like that, rather than "O'zbekistan." As you read, you'll see that Gaia herself can also be identified in various ways, all thanks to that first *a* in her name. You'll also learn how to say "Emer." Whatever problems that name poses, though, are not Uzbek's fault.

Gaia, Queen of Ants

Introduction

A son of the Turks, around thirty years old, was lying in bed with an old woman two and a half times his age, and he wiped the cold sweat off his back with a swath of linen cloth, truly hating himself. Through the open window, the sea breeze carried in the ceaseless shattering sounds of the waves on the gravel, and those lustful noises increased his misery, and he did not know whether to get up or to go on lying there wrapped in his disgust. Whatever had he done? Did he have any sense at all, to be propelled toward this shame? They'd fire him for sure! Or things could get even worse. Now the young man thought of his own, distant love: how could he ever look her in the eye now? Shame, shame, shame! What if he just strangled the old witch to death right here? That thought hitting his brain was enough of a blow to make the young man tremble. Was the old woman even alive? When the fluids of passion were still spilling onto the white sheet, when she was yelling her lust out loud, could she have choked herself dead? No, there was a slight trembling in her clumpy, frumpy henna-dyed hair. Her crotch barely covered by the sheet, and the beady mole on her scrawny waist, still seemed to be trembling. God damn it, if only this son of the Turks had known that even at that age women could be so lustful . . .

The young man was in torment. Now what was he going to do?

Earth and Fire

In the sad twilight of her life, Gaia Mangitkhanovna, Gaia in her youth, found herself condemned to be abandoned and alone. If you had put it to her in those words, then out of misunderstanding, or half understanding, she might have just shrugged a shoulder. "*Nabliueshsia!*" she would say in her most scornful Russian, cutting you off. "Not a lick of truth to it! You're just giving them something to wag their tails about!" With her seeming so indifferent, getting those words turned around and interpreted just right would have to be our responsibility, and we would end up thinking, "Fine, with this nagging old woman as stubborn as ever, let's just get this job done ourselves." So you'd do the translation, into your own, more reliable, tongue, and discover that this is what she meant: "Shrink, my heart! That's a bright-red lie! You asses just like waggling your you-know-whats around!" And later, after drilling down to the heart of those words, one by one— against the "twilight of life," "sad and abandoned," "condemned"—she would shove her own merciless and pointed arguments back in your face.

For that reason, it would be kinder of us not to say those words at all and just to state that Gaia Mangitkhanovna lived in Apartment 38 of the tallest building in the city of Eastbourne at the edge of the sea, in Sussex. On three sides, in the adjacent apartments, lived English pensioners, while the roof looked out at the sky, and a glass-walled balcony looked over the sea. In more majestic places, such elegance might have been called a "penthouse," wouldn't it? But for this building full of old folks, it's better for us not to express it that way.

As her name might have told you, Gaia-khonim's distant roots and her heart were in other, far-off lands, and if we were to ask her neighbors, they would tell us she was from one of what her neighbor Beryl called "the stans" (it definitely wasn't Pakistan; Gaia Mangitkhanovna made that exceedingly clear), where her father was renowned for being descended from the Barlos or some other respected old clan like that; and we would hear that her mother was allegedly from the most ancient tribe of all, and if we ever laid eyes on her blue diplomatic passport, we would see only half a word, "-chka," in the nationality section.

By now, you must be asking how it came to be that Gaia-khonim was in the twilight of her life and condemned to this sadness and this lonely abandonment. Everything in its time.

◈

Gaia Mangitkhanovna put the deep iron skillet on the burner, and immediately, she froze, no idea what to put in it. She did not like this one bit. She had never been so distracted and ill at ease. She used her fat fingers to abruptly twist the dials on the oven, and she shut off the gas. Her rings clattered and collided against each other. She left the skillet on the stove, pulled a cloudy-green jacket off its peg and heaved it over her shoulders, took her gray beret in one hand and a ring of keys in the other, and stepped resolutely outside. She pulled the door shut and locked it. Her eye fell on the window looking out from the common corridor she shared with Beryl, which gave such a satisfying view out of the building, and she pressed the button for the lift.

Bringing with it the smell of mouse, the lift came for her, moving as ponderously as the old folk it carried. Old lady Gaia pressed the G button and peered into the mirror. Her hair stuck out in clumps, and her eyelids were swollen. But what truly broke her heart was that her mustache had thickened. Or had that place just grown darker under the shadow of her swollen, reddish nose? Her thin lips seemed a bit blue. Last of all, she looked herself in the eye. Gear ground against gear, and the mirror cracked—oh, no, that was just the lift settling at a particular floor with a bang. The door opened. There at the lift stood another old woman with three dogs on leashes.

"No!" pronounced Gaia Mangitkhanovna, in a tone allowing no debate, and she pushed the G button again with resolve. And the doors closed, leaving the dogs whining and the old woman stammering, confused. The lift shuddered one more time and started to descend. Gaia

Mangitkhanovna's mood was irretrievably wrecked. She stepped outside the building, cut across the street, and set off toward the little path along the sea. If only that crazy old woman would mind her dogs more closely! Gaia Mangitkhanovna hurried up her bent old legs with their knots of veins.

Around her, as usual, a light rain was falling, or was that just the waves from the sea, being pounded against the gravel of the shore till they were nothing but froth and dampness? Rising up behind her, to the left, toward the ocean, a noisy pier loomed over the sea on its iron legs, but she walked on, along the wet sidewalk leading off to the hilly area on the edge of town. Just fifty or sixty paces from the pier, her face buffeted by the inescapable gray wind, she caught sight of an old Indian woman wrapped up in her little garden, and the back of her neck stiffened. "A Hindu, passing herself off as an Englishwoman!" What was her name again? Mrs. Chori? The old Indian woman seemed to sense Gaia Mangitkhanovna's acrid glance from the direction of the sea, and with one hand she propped up her decrepit old waist, using the other hand to shoo her away. Gaia Mangitkhanovna pretended not to see her and continued on.

Sitting for a bit outside the summer theater, her eye fell on her downstairs neighbor Irving. The fussy old fart's granddaughter had come from London, and the clueless old man showed her to a wet chair, while he himself clowned around on stage. "Old fool!" Gaia Mangitkhanovna muttered to herself, and she felt like spitting on the ground, but her mouth had gone dry after her brisk walk, and the glob of saliva seemed to be stuck to her lip . . . Or was that the raindrops growing larger?

The sky had darkened to take on the same hue as the sea. Were those misers going to turn on the streetlights? They would not! They always waited right up till seven o'clock. Gaia Mangitkhanovna's mood felt heavy as lead. Was she too out of breath to walk to that castle-looking restaurant up the hill? If she made it up the hill, Antonina Ivanovna would come, pushing that old woman professor in a wheelchair. She was in no mood to talk to them! It was bad enough that the professor was always dozing off. That Antonina was like a bat, couldn't see a thing four paces away without her glasses. Gaia Mangitkhanovna took cover under the stone wall. The damp tops of her boots had started to sag. Could she escape them, now, sitting down at the castle-shaped café with that ancient couple of communists Lucy and Pete? What the hell were they doing anyway, chasing after her? Did they know something?

Now Gaia Mangitkhanovna tossed the hood that flopped over to one side of her mud-green jacket up over her head and hung her head low. Her soaked beret slipped down and lapped over her brow. That made her forehead drip, too, and two streams of water ran down from it. Gaia Mangitkhanovna drew the cord on her hood. The howl of the wind had become a roar. The tamarisks over the sidewalk were struck by the storm and wiped clean, and when a gust of wind in front of her tore a rubbish bin away from the lamppost it was tied up to and smashed it into a bench installed nearby in memory of someone or other, Gaia Mangitkhanovna knew for sure that today's walk would unravel right there.

❖

Now that we've gotten acquainted with Gaia Mangitkhanovna, even if only superficially, let's share a couple of words about the young man named Domrul whom she hired to care not so much for her physical ailments, but for her spiritual scars. Keep in mind, meanwhile, that everything that we know and can say about Gaia Mangitkhanovna comes from this young man. The English like to call people providing certain health services "social carers," and Domrul was one of these. Of course, this awkward-sounding name is just the homemade translation Domrul himself provided us. "He must be an Uzbek," you might say, but that's not right; Domrul is a Meskhetian Turk. When he was nine years old, he left with an aunt of his from the Ferghana Valley, where mobs had set their house ablaze, and after a great many other ordeals he ended up coming to England. Since he still retained some traces of the Uzbek and Russian languages from his childhood, he never had bad feelings toward them, and he studied those languages at university in his new country, hoping to become a real expert. For that reason, the Uzbek he spoke was a little bit bookish, a little bit of pasture grass mixed in with the rice, and we have to say in all honesty that you will need to forgive the occasional Turkish phrasing mixed up in his Uzbek speech.

If the occasion were to arise, he would tell you that everything that had happened this past year made it quite fitting that he should start his career as a "social carer." First of all, he was the one who cared for his old, war-wounded aunt right up to her very last days. Then he helped usher his Irish girlfriend Emer's ninety-seven-year-old grandmother to the hereafter. So he had landed like a bird in this little city of old people by the sea and gotten quite used to it, and perhaps that is the reason that, one day, he got a call from the office: "A rich old woman has been asking around, and she wants to hire you!" they said. "In these uncertain times, if I can get a few pennies more, I'll do it," he told them, and put his next Paris rendezvous with Emer off for another time, because he had this new job to do now.

◆

The next day Gaia Mangitkhanovna decided to take advantage of the morning sun and walk to the hills in the place called Beachy Head. The knots in her legs gradually loosened as she went. Who knows, maybe it was because there was no gravel or cement here, just young grass trampled into the earth. Maybe it was because the lazy old folks were still lounging about everywhere. But as she trudged on this time, not one of them caught her eye. There were a lot of young people there walking their dogs, too, but that crazy witch was nowhere to be seen. Gaia Mangitkhanovna crested one peak and came upon a rugby pitch in a low spot between two hills. At the edges of a miniature valley, autumn weather aside, all sorts of branches were blossoming like wild cherries. "Such improper seasons in this land!" thought Gaia Mangitkhanovna to herself, frowning, but the strange vastness of her thoughts carried her away to a different place and time, to the valleys of her childhood. The ancient woman remembered the tulip festivals, but that did not make anything easier; very soon her mood slumped. She had a few hills to crest yet. Her goal was still far off, and she couldn't let herself overflow like white lumps of rising dough . . .

Halfway up the second hill there was a little bench put up in memory of someone or other, pressed up against a bush buffeted by the wind, and she sat down there until she had her fill of staring at the sea under the light breeze. Her heart grew calmer, quieter. Her thoughts grew clear again. She stood up. She walked some more. There was a steep downhill, then she slowly climbed to the crest of another hill. Below, there was a sharp cliff and a drop to the sea. Now there was no oasis between the pairs of hills, and after walking across a flat place atop one of the rises, Gaia

Mangitkhanovna started to climb again. Those might be more wild cherries, a thick grove of them sticking out this way, though maybe because the wind met them from all four sides, they were all bent over, kneeling nearly to the ground. It wasn't just their flowers that were missing, but all the leaves too. The naked, crooked twigs rubbed and pressed against each other, coming together fortuitously, crowding together as if they were thankful to be alive here. Just like those old English people from her building, thought Gaia, and from that steep hill she looked out over the city. There it was, the old fortress of a building, rising into view.

Thudding against her heart was the Turk's word for his job, *g'amko'r*, and the old aunt the carer had mentioned who spoke that language. The aunt who had sat drooling for a year, who had become nothing but a vegetable . . . No, Gaia Mangitkhanovna would never, ever put herself on that road! With some new dose of passion and authority, she started out on the path leading to the next hill. By the time she emerged on the top of this new hill, it felt like her lungs were up in her mouth, but as hard as she was biting her lower lip, Gaia Mangitkhanovna did not stop. Her steps slowed bit by bit, to just the length of her foot, until she reached an iron stake with ten or twelve arrows all pointing different directions, said "Uff!," and stopped.

From this place, Gaia Mangitkhanovna stood at a stone-throwing distance from what she had come to see, and now there was no need to hurry. This woman of advanced age stood gazing at how many kilometers it was from this luckless point to any of the other cities of the world, as if trying to even out her breathing. For instance, just fifty or a hundred meters across the way was the evil place known as Suicide Peak. Now Gaia Mangitkhanovna would let her mind collect itself, and then she would walk off toward that point.

From the sea a cold breeze blew, and her loosened hair blew out from under her beret. She was afraid of catching cold, with her head bare, if she took the beret off. Setting the beret on straight again, she started off, at a measured pace, for that wicked spot. Just after a small rise, the horizon opened up, and at the horizon, the eternal sky met the eternal sea. At her feet, the stunted grass tossed in the wind. Gaia Mangitkhanovna flattened that grass with vigor, moving against the wind. Just a few days ago, a young man and wife, with two little children, had thrown themselves down to their damnation from that unhappy place . . . There was nobody around . . . Well then, old woman, what have you come to this place for, all by yourself? Nobody was shouting that question.

Gaia Mangitkhanovna took another step toward the steep slope to the sea, and two paces away from the sharp cliff, she stopped. The wind gusted, pushing back against her, and feeling at that moment that she would not fall even if she wished to, the elderly woman looked down fearlessly. How many dozens of suicidal heads had reached the sea down the face of this chalk cliff? But of course, it seems they always smashed not against the sea, but against the rocks at the bottom, she thought gloomily. Then the rescue teams walked through, collecting their bits and pieces . . . Gaia frowned. No! She turned back from the drop, as if accepting the will of the wind, and her steps decisive, she went into a local pub, made the Polish waitress understand her Russian and call her a taxi, and rode back home.

Now she knew, even more firmly than before, what she must do.

◈

Domrul would never think to call Gaia Mangitkhanovna an old woman. We felt the same way ourselves. No, this was not out of a sense of duty, but rather because she was part of a whole newly developing subgroup of humankind, as one writer has put it. That group is not growing old, just getting obsolete. Gaia Mangitkhanovna's doings and dealings, but also her outward appearance and attitude, had taken shape when she was forty years old and had stayed the same ever since. He never called her "Gaia Mangitkhanovna" either. Instead, Domrul cast about for something shorter, but still never settled on *kampir*, "old woman." Calling her *khonim* was a path closed to him, too old-fashioned; and while the Turks had the title *khonim-afandi*, which was maybe more appropriate, it seemed a little sarcastic, to his unaccustomed ear, even for her. If he had found anything usable in the old literature he had read that was suitable for her, he would have said that. There was *begum* . . . yes, begum! Not *begim*, not *bekim* or *bekachim*, but just that, begum.

The thing was that, as Domrul found out at the office, before Gaia Mangitkhanovna showed up, there had actually been a Mumtoz Mehal-begum, and Jahonoro-begum, and Nodira-begum, and they were all modern respectable ladies. Before Domrul's first time at Gaia Mangitkhanovna's place, his boss told him, "Your task is not so much to assist with her MS, but to be more like an entertainer, bringing her joy." ("What a vocabulary they've learned in their spare time!" thought Domrul when he heard that.)

"Make an effort to capture our lady customer's heart, nudge her toward the life going on around her, get her out into the neighborhood. Be as creative as you can!"

Domrul's boss was well acquainted with the story of Domrul's aunt. Before his aunt had been completely paralyzed, she had felt, while under their care, that her needs were more spiritual than physical. So Domrul had added Scottish dance groups, poker games, walking clubs, and tai chi classes to his arsenal. To which his all-knowing boss told him, "Everything is up to you!"—and he meant every one of those things.

But as soon as he met this begum for the first time, it was clear how much trouble Domrul was in. He still remembered how he had stood there pressing the buzzer on the gate of Eastbourne's tallest, most mountainous apartment building, receiving no answer for a long time. Domrul's finger was getting tired, and he was just thinking he'd come back later when an old woman pulling three dogs on leashes swished up like an octopus and told him, "You're pushing the roof button. Push 38 if you want that philandering immigrant woman." She pulled the dogs toward her, banged the door in his face, and disappeared inside. Domrul pushed the 38 button, and silence fell again.

While he was still thinking idly about that unceremonious old woman, a strong-willed voice rang out over the speaker. "Who's there?" the voice demanded in Russian. The interrogation had begun.

Domrul started to explain hurriedly, in his nearly forgotten Russian, and got to the part about his title "social carer," and no reasonable word came into his head, and he was left speechless. The begum, maybe to chase away his speechlessness, opened the door, and while the door was opening, she asked him, "How do you come to know Russian?" She was continuing her interview. As the door below was opening, and as he answered five or six merciless questions, Domrul blushed, then paled, then started to sweat.

As he rode up to the very top floor in the lift, which smelled of dog and mouse, he asked himself, "Do I really need this? Or should I just stay unemployed and go to Paris to see my Emer?" He worried, undecided.

The old woman kept him waiting there at the door to the apartment too. Time passed, and just when he thought she'd have to open up, from inside, a rough voice said, "Let me get ready!" And Domrul was made to stare at his long-uncleaned shoes, trying to comb a couple strands of his thinning hair with his fingers. Finally the door opened, and in front of Domrul emerged the khonim-afandi herself—as if straight from the bath, no makeup, some fashionable clothing just tossed on. To Domrul's mind came a phrase from the Turks, who call that race of people "reddish," but for some reason, the Uzbek word *malla*, for pale yellow, appeared on his tongue instead. This uncoiffed, thin-lipped woman drilled into Domrul with her eyes, and inside Domrul's heart, her merciless reckoning made its mark: "Tall, a bit thin, nice big eyes, thinning hair, looks educated, but simpleminded—in short, the maggot of a golden fly!"

She did not show Domrul in, but continued the interrogation on the doorstep. She asked who he was, where he was born and raised, what kind of schooling he had, where he learned Russian, how he had heard about this job, and what kind of prior experience he had. And the whole time, she might as well have been saying, "Don't play the fool. I know exactly who you are!"

At the end, as if visiting hours were now over, she announced her verdict. "If I have a need for you, I'll call your agency!" she declared. And with that Domrul, awed and ashamed, never having gotten past the doorstep, was sent away from their first meeting. He knew he was a very patient and tolerant person, but still, as he descended in that malodorous lift ride from the heavens to the earth, from the distant tongue of his childhood a curse came to him. F . . . yes, *fuck* her, even if she is a begum!

Angels bless both good words and bad, as they say, and this absolute shame indeed came to pass at their second meeting.

◆

The begum herself called Domrul's office. She first told them in her halfhearted English that she needed that Turk who spoke Russian, apparently she could handle that much; and when the call was put through to

Domrul, Gaia Mangitkhanovna told him herself, "I have given it some thought and it seems that I need you." In tone, this was not a request, but an order. We might have mentioned that in her old life, the begum had gotten used to her slaves and servants, and in resorting to Domrul's services it seemed to him that what she needed was not "care" so much as having maybe a kind of secretary by her elbow, or a gopher on her tail. If only he had heeded that feeling! No, he wasn't upset, it didn't bring him down; on the contrary, compared to his sufferings with his aunt, it seemed to him he had discovered a secret, uncovered a mystery.

The fact was that Domrul was a young man harboring secrets of his own, and as we said at the start, he and his aunt came to this country after a great many trials and tribulations, sometime in the early nineties. Are you wondering about his father and mother? In the butchery of 1989— though his tongue was unable to say it—his mother had been burned alive. As for his father, due to his work as a sculptor, he had been in some capital city for some exhibition, or visiting some friends or loved ones, and had been spared the frenzied mob. Two or three days later, he must have driven home—and found his house in ashes, not a single member of his family there. Searching for them, his soul embittered, he ran over two people with his car.

Because Domrul's aunt had married an Uzbek man, they hid their surviving family members among the carrots stored in the cellar, but soon the aunt's husband was slaughtered, too, because he had a Turkish wife. Five endless days later, when the army came to save them, it became clear that Domrul's father had also disappeared without a trace. They spent several days huddled at the airport, then made it to Kazakhstan; from Kazakhstan they went to Stavropol, and their travels were underway.

Now, as they say, "I can wipe my eyes with the hand that slaps me," and maybe his heart had gotten left in the abyss of his childhood, but by and by Domrul learned Uzbek to make it his career. And now he was running, so fast his lungs could hardly keep up with him, toward that cold-faced witch Gaia Mangitkhanovna, calling her "begum." Domrul thought about it quite a lot, and it seemed he had discovered the reason: The emptiness left in his parents' place would be sucking him in, like a whirlpool, his whole life long. No matter where he was going to live or what he was going to do, he would always be clinging to his aunt's linen skirt on that summer day in that pitch-black cellar, among the smells of damp and carrots, his eyes pleading for help. Maybe that was why he seemed to see his mother in every ray of light, and his father in every shadow?

◆

For some reason, her childhood home had constantly been penetrating into Gaia Mangitkhanovna's dreams. True, if she were to go back, at her age, to those old houses in the valley, any mother, father, or uncle of hers she would meet would be even older than she was now; but in any case, while she dreamed, she knew nothing of this mismatch, and she troubled nobody with the things she did or the path she took, just like goldfish in an aquarium, swimming along past one another unhurriedly through the water; they, too, crisscrossed peacefully among themselves through the somnolent waters.

Maybe that dream and those silhouettes were brought on by the sea fifty paces outside her window, and its crashing waves drawn back again and again, coming and going; in any case, in the lonely luxury of her apartment, for some reason the sleepy Gaia Mangitkhanovna remembered the war years, and the top of the blanket covering the duvet reminded her of the rough Uzbek cotton fabric out of which her mother's skilled hands had made her a school shirt. Hanging at her side was that little satchel sewn so long ago, and inside the bag, her Russian Language textbook and a clump of flat corn bread. Or was this all because outside the window a lump of cloud had come into view, looking to her sleepy eyes just like that cotton bag, and didn't the moon, pursued by that cloud, look just like the old flat corn bread?

Still the waves of the sea rolled on ceaselessly, and whether in her memory, or in her dream, Gaia made her own tiny, tiny steps, ceaselessly, and turned to look over the road to the center which joined the village to the city from its outskirts; but now, those roads could lead back to neither her mother, nor her grandmother on her father's side, nor her suddenly absent father . . .

◆

The second time Domrul went to serve Gaia Mangitkhanovna, she met him in a way that was not warmer, exactly, but more businesslike. She let him into her apartment. Her apartment, as far as Domrul could tell, must have been purchased from rather rich foreigners, because what caught his eye most were the furniture and things originating the farthest from where the begum lived, and differing the most from her nature. No, we won't say that the things filling that home were poor or worn out; on the contrary. The hundreds of dusty little china plates hanging on the dining room wall had been put together every which way, one of the rugs thrown on the floor was from Iran, another from Afghanistan, and another felt mat seemed clearly to be Mongolian, and Gaia Mangitkhanovna had no connection to any of them. "Brought these things in from all over the damn place!" Domrul remembered her saying with a shake of her disheveled head. From the entryway, she led Domrul into a living room, passing by the kitchen. From that grand room, the windows looked toward the sea, stretching to each end of the balcony. The balcony held some low-slung seats and scarlet flowers blooming in pots. But all of this . . . Maybe it was the sun shining above the sea, like the very heart of the blue sky, and pleasing their own hearts, too, which made such a remarkable picture for the young man's eye?

Gaia Mangitkhanovna pointed Domrul to a long narrow table, then sat down across from him, nodding her head to one side. "My own rooms are over there," she said. Domrul sensed a certain apologetic tone in those words, as if she wanted to say that all of these awkward household tools and decorations here had nothing to do with her, or even, seeing the admiration in the young man's eyes, as if she meant she had just as many rooms "over there" and she aimed to impress him—maybe that was it. She offered him nothing to eat and no tea to drink, and she had him write down the kind of work a social carer was supposed to do and then briskly stood up. Looking out toward the window, and toward the blue-green sky far above the azure sea, she spoke suddenly. "By the way, do you know if they sell dry yeast here?" she asked him. That sentence, that tone, that look, that landscape took Domrul's thoughts far, far away. He had just begun processing the question when the begum announced, "I've got some good Armenian cognac and some Qoraqum chocolate candy. Come, let's celebrate our first day together!" and she took a crystal cup for each of them out of the cabinet nearby and set them on the table.

The Armenian cognac had no effect on him, but when the Qoraqum candy, which Domrul had forgotten, touched his mouth, his heart grew warm and suddenly overflowed. Both his tongue and his soul spread their wings. He told the begum about his childhood. They drank some more, the begum brought out some Russian caramels, and another teacup later, she served up more Russian treats: gingerbread and wafer cookies. That did it for Domrul. When he was recalling how, on his first day of first grade, his mother had given him a Rot-Front chocolate, the begum suddenly clutched at her heart. Stopping his story halfway through a word, Domrul sprang up to help. The begum spit something out and seemed to be gesturing toward the bedroom. Domrul guided her, one hand at her elbow, the other at her waist, toward the bed. The begum leaned toward him too. You may think that an old woman's body is too flabby to have any character, but Domrul, somewhere in the back of his mind, could certainly sense the begum's strong frame and catch the scent of her sweet-smelling skin. Domrul put the begum down carefully on a blanket on the narrow but comfortable bed, eased the slippers off her feet, lifted her legs up, one after the other, and helped her lie down. The begum asked for some water. By the time the young man brought some water from the kitchen, the begum had turned over onto her stomach. "Why don't you massage my arms and back!" she whispered. The young man started from high up on the Begum's plump arms, and then with a kind of childlike joy, as if he were pounding out a massage for his aunt's rheumatism, he worked with his hands on the begum's neck. "Such healing power in those hands of yours!" she said, and a moment later, she ordered him to give her a nice massage under her robe. Domrul lifted the begum's skirt. Drunk as he was, his blood boiled. "Your hands are on fire!" the Begum gasped. "Lower," she told him, "lower . . ." Domrul's burning hands touched the Begum's tail bone, and his breath trembled. The begum moaned, and shook, and her buttocks danced.

◆

To put it another way, Gaia Mangitkhanovna had Domrul nicely impaled on her hook. Now she knew exactly how to manage this naive carer of hers. Next time he'd have to walk into this room filled not so much with inspiration and enthusiasm, but rather with honest regret. Too ashamed to lift his eyes from his paperwork, he'd probably invite his "client" either to an old folks' Christmastime get-together, or a charitable lottery for pensioners, or some other similarly stupid thing. And that time Gaia Mangitkhanovna might even agree, and if she lost an hour or so, so be it. But like the perfect student she had been so many years before, in her long-ago school days, she had done her homework this time, too, just as diligently. When Antonina Ivanovna had brought over a pile of Russian-language papers from churches in this city, and *London Info* and *Pulse UK*, Gaia Mangitkhanovna rifled through them, looking for the medical advice columns. What You Need to Know About Euthanasia. Legal Regulations on Euthanasia in Europe. Euthanasia: For and Against. She read all of them top to bottom, underlining the parts she needed in red ink. Certainly, she would not show any of them to the young man. Assuredly not. He would have to be warmed up and cooked, slowly and circumspectly.

The young man would have to be shaped and tuned just right. Gaia Mangitkhanovna could see how he lived his life, sleeping like a dog and walking like a master. He had taken up this ugly land as his home, and he thought he was a free fellow countryman here—but these old locals didn't think him worth a yellow penny. Gaia Mangitkhanovna could clearly see their haughtiness and indifference. Whenever the lad spoke, they would knit their brows, purse their lips, and tease him. "What on earth is that Oriental boy talking about?" they'd ask. She had already hooked him. She would try to persuade him, coax and cajole him, and if he didn't agree she would threaten him, tell him she'd have him fired or arrested. I'll reveal your shame! she would say. Think well before you refuse! He had never washed his linens in Gaia's soap. She would show him how it was done.

But the next time the "caring young man" didn't show up at all. Gaia Mangitkhanovna's patience was now spent. There was no thought she had not thought. Earlier, when there had still been half an hour left before his visit, she had aired the rooms, and then Gaia-khonim sat down on her rocking chair, deep in thought, looking to the sea. The young man had been in this country since childhood, right? So he had clearly grown up knowing little about real life. What could this generation know! Gaia looked her carer over mentally with her merciless heart and remembered her war years again. How could they know what it was like, when she was a little girl returning hungry and tired from school one day, when she came across a group of countless people in tattered and torn clothes of all sorts of colors, being driven like herds of cattle by regiments of armed soldiers and three or four local policemen? Gaia had never seen such a riffraff of people in her life. Besides the handful of hunched-over old men in fur hats, it was mostly women and little children, dirtying the street with dust, some in shoes and some barefoot, bumbling and stumbling off one another when the soldiers or policemen barked at them.

On that day, when little Gaia returned home, the whole neighborhood and all the neighbors were buzzing like a hive full of bees, or maybe a hill full of ants, in confusion. The new unrest was just like before the war, when from time to time the Gypsy camps made all the wild horses neigh and made their filthy children dance and play and cause chaos. That evening the old folks in the neighborhood went visiting, house to house. "We found out they're Muslims too, and they even talk like the Tatars," they said, pacifying their audiences. The people were all sent to live in some little huts built on the desolate steppe at the outskirts of the city. At first the grown-ups warned off the children and scared them from getting close, but a week or a month passed, and the new women started coming in, first to bring little trinkets they had hidden in their bosoms to the rich housewives, to see if they might sell them or trade them for something. As they got used to one another with time, their old women started teaching the younger Uzbek women cheese-making, and the old men taught the coppers the ins and outs of homemade wine. In exchange the local *mahallas* built ovens for those living in the tents and baked bread for them, dug some canals, and shared the water.

The quick-witted Gaia watched all of that happening while she did her lessons with a new classmate called Sakina, or helped the grown-ups, or, rarely, while she enjoyed the rope swings or played with clay. Before they had come here, the soldiers had shot Sakina's father, as Sakina and her older brother watched.

These kids today—which one of them had seen, which one of them would know any of that? Now this one would be coming in, hemming and hawing . . . But half an hour had now passed since the scheduled time, and he hadn't come. There was no ring after an hour, either, and then two hours passed, and there was no sign of him. Then, angry, Gaia Mangit-khanovna picked up the telephone and called the care agency. They said he had suddenly taken ill.

◈

Domrul truly was sitting in his tiny, windowless, rented room, not know-ing what to do, and he lay in his bed a long time without getting up. In his mind, the whole world knew about his shameful act, and if he were to lift his head from under the blanket covering it, the phone would ring, and first the agency director would inform him of his dismissal, and then Emer would call from Paris and break it off, and finally he would turn on the television or the radio and dozens of reporters would be buzzing like flies around shit, reporting on the scandal surrounding the young social carer. A little past eleven o'clock, the telephone really did ring. Should he pick it up or not? From under the blanket, one hand moved toward the night-stand, and he gave the telephone cord a sharp yank. The phone knocked into a flower vase, and the vase fell and crashed into pieces. Swearing, Domrul looked at the phone number. It was the office. Oh God, here we go, thought Domrul, blasphemously, and pushed the button. "Hello?" he said, but his still-sleepy voice sounded ruder than usual. "Who's this?" asked the agency director unceremoniously. "It's me, Domrul," said the young man, stiff-necked and irritated. "Why haven't you come in to work? Your old lady is asking for you." (They're the senior carers! But they talk like street tramps, thought Domrul to himself.) "I'm sick," said Domrul, in the appropriate tone of voice, and instead of listening to what his boss said next, he hung up.

His mood was irretrievably wrecked. The only good part was that nothing had been said about him being fired (if they didn't fire him for this recent rudeness, of course). So the old woman only asked them why I didn't come, and apparently she's expecting me, the witch! Is there any way for me to go and make some arrangement with that old devil? Any way to be sure she'll keep the secret? But what kind of contract would that deceitful woman ever agree to?

At that new thought Domrul sat up in his narrow bed, stepped onto the floor, and cried out impatiently in pain. A broken piece of that vase had stuck into the sole of his foot, and the blood was erupting like lava from a volcano. A mountain peak of glass shard shoved into his heel, Domrul hopped on one foot into the bathroom. He had a corner of the vase stuck deep in his flesh, and getting it out hurt so much that he cried out in pain. He finally managed to wrest the piece out and settle his foot in the warm water. The blood flowed, spreading in all directions. "There, I really have turned out to be sick," was the thought that crossed Domrul's mind. He had taken a first aid course, right? So he wrapped a towel around his shin as tight as he could, pressed another towel to the open, still-bleeding wound, and went back to his bed, where he lay down flat on his back with his foot up. A little while later, though the wound throbbed, the bleeding seemed to have stopped, and Domrul remembered a Turkic word he had forgotten: *kasofat*, a calamity. The kasofat with the old woman struck him hard. If only his aunt were alive, he would spill out his heart to her . . .

Before he had been pierced with that broken glass, there had been one profound thought in his mind. He wanted to talk with Emer. He felt for his phone, left lying next to the pillow where he lay, picked it up, and pushed the button for a video call. It chirped like a quail, then rang. Domrul's face shrank into the corner, and Emer's face materialized. "Hi!" said Emer, her voice happy as always. (So she doesn't know anything, thought Domrul immediately.)

"Hi!" he answered. They continued with their hellos, and when he heard unruly voices of some sort behind Emer, he asked, "Where are you? I can hear someone talking in the background."

"I'm at home. Did you know, Kuyuk-baxshi just got here! The Homer and Hesiod of today! I told you, remember? He brought some Armenian cognac and a little candy, and we're celebrating his arrival."

Domrul's tongue stuck to the roof of his mouth, and he wasn't sure why he had gone dumb, from some hidden hint or from the real meaning of the words she had said.

Not hearing any response from him, Emer went on. "How's your old lady?"

"I, uh, I hurt my foot," Domrul found himself blurting out, but Emer either didn't hear him or didn't understand, or maybe she was a little bit tipsy.

"Is she a cripple? What did you say her name was? Gaia, was it? Kuyuk knows a woman named Goia from way back, calls her a real pill. Hope she's not the same one." At that moment the telephone in Domrul's hand told him he had another call, but that, too, somehow brought down on the young man's chest the weight of some adolescent grudge. "Sorry, someone's calling me, we'll talk soon," he said, and he shut off the video.

Whether it was a grudge, or suspicion, or jealousy, it made no difference; Domrul threw the phone down on the floor, and the wound in his heel gaped wide open.

❖

Here we will need to say a few words about Emer. Domrul had met the girl not at school or university, not at a club or someone's birthday party, and not even at work, but at an evangelical church. Actually, if we are to stick to Domrul's thoughts about it, we should call it an *injilchi* church, rather than evangelical. You may or may not be aware, but using once again Domrul's own description, we'll need to call this evangelical church a church of hand-clappers and foot-hoppers. You've probably seen young Christians on the television or in the movies or in photographs, their arms reaching for the mountains or the heavens, swaying from side to side just like in an Uzbek folk dance. That's where the two of them had found each other.

You must be wondering: If Domrul was a son of the Turks, then what was he doing there? You could ask the same thing about Emer. Aren't most Irish Catholics? In centuries past, didn't Ireland revolt against Britain, and in the ages that followed, wasn't most of Northern Ireland in rebellion because of that? Emer's family had in fact come through the millstone of these conflicts.

Emer had been born in the district of Bogside, in the city named Londonderry. Her resolutely Catholic family, of course, called it Derry rather than Londonderry, and Bogside prided itself as the birthplace of the latest revolts against Britain. Emer's father Sean was known by his household as a secret member of the National Liberation Army, but when Emer was five years old, nobody would have ever imagined, not in their wildest dreams, that it would not be the British troops or the loyal Unionists who would kill him, but rather a gang of bandits who called themselves the Irish People's Rescue Organization, who had split off from the National Liberation Army.

In the wake of that tragedy, Emer's mother Bryher buried her husband and took her young daughter with her to Sarajevo in Yugoslavia, where her older sister Boudicca taught English at a university, and took refuge with her. Little Emer went to school there, learned Serbian, adapted to Sarajevo, and came to think of it as her home town.

But that peaceful life did not last long either. Emer had just barely turned twelve when the war started, and Sarajevo fell under siege. No matter how hard they tried, they were unable to leave the city. For one year, they lived with no respite under bombs and bullets, separating them from most of their friends. Emer's best friend Dušica took a bullet in the head and died in her arms. Nearly one and a half years later, with help from Aunt Boudicca's former student, who had reached a high rank in the Serbian army, Boudicca sent Emer and her mother first to Belgrade, then to Budapest and Vienna, then Paris, and from there, with true irony, they traveled straight into the bosom of their worst enemy: London.

Naturally, once they were installed in Brixton in London, Emer did not make friends with any English girls, only Jamaicans, Indians and Bangladeshis, Turks and Tamils. It was them she grew up with, and while in college she happened to visit an evangelical group, and she liked the way they danced and chanted, and she joined them.

◆

Domrul's first encounter with Emer happened at an interreligious gathering. Among the dozens of people there, Domrul wouldn't perhaps have paid any attention to her in particular, but after a break, as Domrul stood drinking coffee in the churchyard, and wondering whether or not to go rejoin the rest of the gathering, he saw her sitting at a table not far away from him, peering this way and that in some sort of indecision. "Looking for something?" asked Domrul, moving naturally in her direction.

"I lost my phone," said the girl, not turning his way.

Domrul's eye was caught by the girl's helplessness, on the one hand, and her indifference on the other. Addressing one or the other of these things, he said, "Hold on, I'll give you a call, and we'll find it!" And that made this girl finally look at him. She turned to him silently, apparently not sensing any trick.

"What's your number?" asked Domrul, getting out his own phone. She told him. Domrul dialed. Soon a ringing sound came from far off. Not a ringing so much as a noise like a wasp buzzing around inside a gourd. They both perked up their ears, searching for the sound.

"Over here," said she.

"No, I think it's that direction," said he.

"I turned the volume down on purpose . . ."

At that, the buzzing sound went silent, and in Domrul's telephone, a recording of the girl's clear voice rang out. "This is Emer Finnegan. Leave a message, and I will return your call as soon as possible."

Having unintentionally gotten an introduction, Domrul introduced himself too. "And my name is Domrul," he said, extending his hand. His voice got recorded, and the girl took his hand in her own, and she suddenly let a smile break out on her face and laughed. (Later, they listened to this recording on Emer's voice mail over and over again together.)

"Look, our phones have gotten to know each other without us," said Emer, and she laughed again. Her smile was so wide-open, so transparent, that the churchyard and garden suddenly brightened up right along with it. Whether because he had forgotten himself, or because he wanted to make this moment last, Domrul picked up his phone again, and again he punched in the number he had just dialed. This time they could tell the buzzing and vibrating were coming from the middle of the yard, and the phone was revealed in a playful sunbeam tossed onto the black trunk of an oak tree there.

After these adventures that had brought them together, they didn't attend the last part of the conference, instead leaving from the little gate in the church garden to walk to a café in the next street. Who knows what they talked about, but by the time they got back to the church, the event was long over, and everyone had left. Emer had driven there in her car and offered her newfound friend a favor. "I'm going south, toward Brixton. I can drop you at the tube," she said.

"I need to go to Eastbourne, from Victoria Station. My aunt and I are living there right now," said Domrul, and he agreed to join her.

Happily for Domrul, as packed as the traffic was on that route, they had time to talk as much as they liked in the nearly unmoving car. Meanwhile, it had gotten dark. Whether taking advantage of that or inspired by it, at one stop, Domrul placed his own hand on Emer's hand on the gearshift. Emer did not flinch. Instead, she turned her head smoothly toward Domrul, and face to face, her lips sighed at him. Domrul closed his eyes to the countless red lights outside, and the hustle and bustle of the city, and leaned in to meet her . . .

That evening, Domrul did not go back to Eastbourne. She turned the car down a narrow street, and the two young people took a walk together along the Thames, and standing on one of the bridges, they pondered romantic thoughts, like, "Are we flying, or is that the river flowing under us?" And they shared their secrets with nighttime London. In that shivery early morning, on the side of the road to Victoria Station, they burnt their fingers eating some roasted chestnuts, cooked over the open stove of a black man who had just set the fire. Here, Emer spoke to Domrul. "If I ever become a mother, I'll raise my children to be great and glorious as a chestnut tree, driven and determined, polemical and poetical," she said, playing with her words. That's how Domrul remembered it, though in English, of course, all those words would have had to be set up differently; it was later on, after Domrul had learned about the Emer of Irish myth and her six notable traits, that he would take up those words and translate them for himself into this set of six.

Yes, those words remained stamped on Domrul's very heart.

◆

We have a saying: You know a child by his shit. Here the accent gets placed mostly on "child" and "know." In other words, the child's "shit" gets elevated to the level of the "knowing." But there must be a reason the shit made it into this proverb. Children may also be known by their wisdom, or perceptiveness, or seed, or this, or that, or whatever good and pleasant things you like, but have you ever thought why the grimiest, vilest, foulest attribute possible was the one chosen?

Someone might say that conflict strengthens a quality, someone else might prefer the newer term *kontrast,* and another person would choose the old-fashioned way and call it simply a contradiction in terms. They are all partly true. But there also must be another side to the saying.

We spoke of how Gaia made friends with Sakina during the war. Sakina's brother O'rhon, who was one year older, either because he could not find a friend as mischievous as he was or for some other reason, was always hanging around them. One day the girls were coming home from school—and it was a long way—and maybe because of those unripe green apricots they had eaten, they felt the urge and went out to the barren place on the outskirts to take care of that urge; and here that O'rhon spied the two girls from far off and started hooting and hollering, and he wouldn't leave them alone. No matter how fast the girls ran, or what shelter they found behind the little hills, he followed them.

Then the girls decided to trick him, and at the mouth of the main irrigation ditch that cut through the field, they agreed on a plan. "You run to this side of the canal, and I'll go over there to the opposite side. We'll finish our business and meet by that poplar over there!" Each ran to her own side. First, O'rhon truly was confused, and perplexed; he could not determine which side he should pick. Then he decided against his little sister and started off toward Gaia.

Before he reached her, Gaia had managed to empty herself out, and from a little hollow behind a hillock at the side of the big canal she took a few steps to one side, then tripped over something and fell down. Panting now, O'rhon took off running at his target, and he jumped into the hollow where he had seen Gaia, swore suddenly, and came out again. He looked and saw Gaia stretched out on the ground ten or fifteen paces away— shaking off her clothing. "Help!" she screamed. Wiping his shit-covered feet relentlessly in the grass, O'rhon stumbled in her direction. What had tripped Gaia, you see, was an anthill. Gaia had accidentally broken off part of it and brought the fury of the ants down upon herself.

O'rhon was confused again. He didn't know whether to go first to the canal to wash the filth off his boots or to go to Gaia to help. But finally, hardly able to stand the stink of the shit he had stepped in, he came up to the place where Gaia was and started pounding away at the ants that had swarmed her layers of clothing. With the ants for an excuse, O'rhon

groped at the girl's skin from head to toe, his hands infused with a somehow unfamiliar but unforgettable feeling, and this feeling was not just in
his hands, but would be preserved forever, throughout his body, from that
day on.

Gaia wasn't the only one disgusted by that stink. The ants, too, instead
of continuing the attack, fled in all directions. At that, when O'rhon saw
the grimace on the face of the smartest girl in her class, he left her to
one side and hurried off to the canal. He washed his boots and his hands
and face.

He returned to Gaia with two boots full of water, and as if wanting to
surprise her, he said, "Look!"—and he dumped the water onto the anthill.
"Now we'll make their queen come out, and we'll take our revenge!" he
announced in a conspiratorial tone. O'rhon was at least one grade above
Gaia and Sakina, and he had already learned quite a lot about birds and
beasts, bugs and beetles. The ants indeed were flowing out by the hundreds, spreading out bewildered in all directions. The mischievous child
was not satisfied with that, and again and again he poured more water
from his boots onto the ants, and onto their nest, flooding it. The hundreds became thousands, beset by trouble and terror on all sides. And
finally, from inside the nest, a huge, winged ant really did emerge. She
cast her majestic gaze in all four directions, shook her wet wings out and
straightened them, and climbed up to the top of the pile of her chaotic
subjects, stretched out those wings, and flew off in a direction known only
to herself.

And at that, Gaia, bitten head to toe, understood very well who she
was going to be.

◈

Later Gaia Mangitkhanovna got a call from the social care agency again,
and they said her carer had hurt his foot. "Shall we send one of our other
employees instead?" they asked her, but Gaia Mangitkhanovna replied
with a firm "No!" and slammed down the phone.

She was angry on the outside, but remained calm on the inside.
"He only cut his foot, not some other appendage! Or he was trying to
escape! Now that cut-up foot will make it harder for him to get away." She
snickered.

While Gaia Mangitkhanovna's lust had not dissipated, right now her lust was a minor companion to the idea that was her central focus. From now on, while her body had the strength and the lust that was its reflection, she would need to be ready! At that thought, Gaia Mangitkhanovna closed the door to the balcony, which scattered the rays of the autumnal sun so deceptively, and walked off toward her own private bedroom. She paused at the doorway to the room where that deed had been done. She wanted to shut the door, and pulled it toward her. The bedsheets there had still not been changed, and they stank with memory. She pushed open the door across from that one, entered her room, switched on the light, and drew the curtains over the window into the common hallway with the lift. Then she took a suitcase with two heavy locks on it from the corner and flung them open energetically.

First she took a piece of paper, folded into four sections, out of the suitcase's side pocket, and spread it out. The top of the page was inscribed with "Government Clinic No. 1" in Russian, in big Cyrillic letters. Gaia Mangitkhanovna stared at this paper for a long time, then folded it up again and put it back in the pile where she had found it. Then she took out a thick album, covered in red velvet and sprinkled with little jewels, and she shut and locked the suitcase, then stepped out of the room, the album pressed to her bosom. As soon as she closed the door to her room, the door to the opposite room opened. The rank smell hit Gaia Mangitkhanovna's nose. With one hand, she pulled the door shut again, hard. The door closed with a bang, and the doorknob detached with a click and remained in her hand. "You old idiot!" she cursed herself. Now she'd have to call a handyman, and what would the handyman do when he discovered those putrid sheets? Angry, she hurled the thing onto the floor, and the iron doorknob unexpectedly bounced and broke the glass in a low-hanging picture frame with a crack. Now Gaia Mangitkhanovna paid no attention to the broken door, nor to the cracked glass, nor to the doorknob lying there on the floor, but instead walked, lips clamped tight, into the kitchen.

There, she put the album down on the table, thudded the big iron skillet down onto the stove, and then pulled one chair over to the oven and sat down upon it, taking the album back in her hands. For some reason, she opened the album up at its end, rather than its beginning. She tossed a passing look at a pile of photographs of just herself and threw them into the skillet. From the back of the album, she turned some pages and ran her eyes over the photos taken with her husband, one after the next. Mostly visits, entertaining guests. In one of them, her hair was messy, she was getting out of a car. In another, she joined in with her husband's fake smile, his smirk, and in another, the two caustic, narrow eyes expressed surprise and astonishment, and she clutched a bouquet of flowers . . . Gaia Mangitkhanovna tossed every one of them, with hardly a pause, into the skillet.

We were going to say that Gaia Mangitkhanovna looked at the next pages and pictures in a rush, but it would be more precise to say, rather, that in a rush, she didn't look at them. Her eyes scanned those pictures slantwise without ever getting stuck, and her hands were even more dexterous than her eyes, ripping and plucking those photos out of the places they had sat for years and flinging one after another into the frying pan. Any time one of these shadows fell out of Gaia Mangitkhanovna's driven, grabbing hand and onto the marble floor, whoever it was casting shadows in those pictures might have remained dark to us. But in *this* brightly colored picture there is Gaia Mangitkhanovna's little boy, and a baby girl in her husband's arms, and seeming frightened of landing in the skillet, they kept their faces turned innocently toward the ceiling. As if a secret had suddenly been exposed, Gaia Mangitkhanovna quickly stomped down a foot on that picture, then leaned over and pulled it out from under her sandal, flipped it over, and put it in the pan.

The album had been emptied from end to end, while the cauldron had grown full. Gaia Mangitkhanovna stood up, her legs barely back in working order after going numb, her knees still bent, and she walked to the rubbish bin in the corner and tossed the album into its black depths. Then she returned to stand before the stove, picked up a box of matches, plucked out a match, and set on fire three or four pictures at one edge of the frying pan. The pictures hissed, breathed out an acrid smoke, and started to burn. Gaia Mangitkhanovna turned on the ventilation fan over the stove. The bitter smoke started to rise. She picked up another bunch of photographs lying there and tilted them in. They too went up in flames. Whether from the breeze from the fan or the chemistry of the photos, the shadows instantly went up in a blaze and began to burn. The fire rose toward the fan. At that moment, Gaia Mangitkhanovna's heart cracked open. "I'm dead! The building will catch fire!" she thought, racing in fear to the tap nearby. She ladled up some water and tossed it on the frying pan. She got more water and soaked it again. After the fourth or fifth ladle, the fire in the pan died out.

The ashes and corpses of the half-burnt photographs rose toward the top of the pan. Gaia Mangitkhanovna added more water to the skillet, nearly filling it, and then, with her hands shaking, she turned on the gas under the skillet, and put a match to it.

◆

Gaia had never met her father. If she hadn't been a resolute atheist or materialist, she might have believed that she had been born without a father's interference at all. According to her mother Rohila, her father Mangitkhan worked for the militia, and when little Gaia was just learning to toddle about, he shot someone, was put in jail, decreed an "enemy of the people," and exiled to the North. But in the winter of 1940, a captain from the military command brought what they called a "black letter" to their home. In that letter, which Gaia saved her whole life, confirmation was delivered that Private Mangitkhan, fighting against the Finns near the village of Suomussalmi, had perished heroically in a battle with the enemy. With that, yesterday's family of enemies of the people was transformed, in one breath, into the family of a war hero.

In this state of heroism, since Gaia had grown up in the Stalinist spirit of the Pioneer and Komsomol organizations, she started subjecting her mother to severe criticism from a very early age. "What were you doing giving lessons to the whole school while you couldn't cope with your own husband, telling everyone that he was an enemy of the people? Good thing that once the war began he cleared his own name. You would never have done it! And I would have been the daughter of an enemy of the people my whole life! From now on, not you, but I myself will be choosing, and securing, my own destiny," she said, introducing a slogan of the times into the family.

She really did take herself in hand . . . like tempered steel. When she was just barely sixteen years old, the party was beginning its fight against rootless cosmopolitans, and in her fiery work for the Komsomol, she wrote a letter of seven pages indicting her own mother and sent it off to the highest party organs. In that document, Gaia mercilessly exposed her mother for every kind of filthy cosmopolitan evil, from hypocrisy right down to failing in her upbringing of the younger generation, caught in the trap of petty-bourgeois psychology.

One by one, investigators appeared in the school where her mother Rohila taught Russian language and literature. In the end, Gaia's mother was sentenced neither to execution nor exile nor arrest, but was only fired from her job, denied the pension she had been receiving in her husband's name, and called a rootless cosmopolitan, nonstop; and with this filth and misfortune piled upon her, her mother could not last long and finally died of a heart attack.

But the party of Stalin and the country of the Bolsheviks appreciated Gaia's selfless deeds, and this daughter of a war hero, with a Komsomol recommendation and a government stipend, was sent to Saratov State University to study biology, with a concentration in invertebrate zoology.

◆

Three days later, leaning on a crutch, the limping Domrul came in. He avoided her with his eyes, and instead, maybe because his foot hurt, he constantly looked down. Gaia Mangitkhanovna, immediately sensing the young man's state, spoke in a serious, very flat voice, as if not a thing had ever happened between them. "I have something very important to discuss with you," she began, in Russian. The young man wrinkled his brow. "But this conversation is strictly between you and me!" Domrul, who had not even received permission to take off his coat, started to sweat, and his cheeks blushed. "Do you people have a vow you take, like the doctors have the Hippocratic Oath?" Gaia Mangitkhanovna asked. Feigning ignorance, and not expecting an answer, she went on. "What's important to me isn't your pledges and promises. I need your word!" she said, suddenly calling him "ty" in her Russian, when just the sentence before, she had used the more formal form of address. But it wasn't the arrogance in the "you" she used, but the secrecy behind it, that scared the young man at first, because now he clearly sensed the element of intimacy there. "Yes. *Your* word!" continued Gaia Mangitkhanovna, as if underlining that feeling. Domrul stammered a bit. It would be a bit vulgar to say "What?" so he thought he should carry on with his polite silence.

From under her swollen eyelids, Gaia Mangitkhanovna's two diamond eyes pierced into the young man's face, and they looked as if they would penetrate straight through and enter inside him. He wondered what intrigue the sorceress was weaving. As if Gaia's eyes had picked up these words passing through his mind and transported them to her own ears, she was watching to catch any change, perceptible or imperceptible, in the young man's face.

"I have decided to pursue euthanasia." Gaia Mangitkhanovna noted the young man's bewilderment and continued. "No, not today, and not tomorrow either. When the time comes. But the important thing to me, the vital thing, is that *you* will be by my side when it comes."

Domrul started to say something, but Gaia Mangitkhanovna put a stop to it. "I know, euthanasia is illegal in this country. But in Holland you can do it, and France is moving in that direction . . . If you need to, you can go and investigate. I'll make it worth your while. We'll write my will together! But as I said, nobody must know." The young man moved to speak again, but Gaia Mangitkhanovna interrupted him. "Now go! My head hurts, I can't bear any more noise," she said, and she stood up and went to her room.

Domrul, not knowing what to do, gripped his stick of a crutch and limped to the door.

That crutch was just a prop for Domrul, defense against a certain truly inexcusable offense. Once he got outside and made it out to his own narrow road, he tossed the crutch over his shoulder like an old spade, lost in thought. So that's what the old woman was up to! Like a fly who had suddenly landed in a spiderweb, Domrul did not know which foot to drag free or which wing to pull loose first. He was dumbfounded. If that stick had been Domrul's protection against Gaia Mangitkhanovna's lust, a way to fight off any passion or fondness, then she had used the other end of the stick to flummox him with her plans for death. That witch's love was death for Domrul, and her death would be death for him too! If her love were to be discovered he would obviously be arrested, and if her death were to be discovered, the result would be the same. But bewilderment cannot plan ahead, and if you flap your wings like that fly, you'll just continue floundering in the web.

Domrul came out on the town's High Street, intending to disappear in the crowd, and he went into the busiest *creperie* he could find. As usual, he ordered a lemon-sugar crepe and a milk tea and sat down next to a glass wall. If he could find a way, he needed to get rid of the old woman. What was it she had said? "I'll make it worth your while! We'll write my will together!" At least he needed to get rid of her temporarily! In order to regain his senses . . .

Or maybe it wasn't the old woman, but her opposite. Was it Kuyuk-baxshi eating away at him? Whereas these thoughts about the old woman might be a distraction, a way to forget? Should he take the excuse of investigating euthanasia and get himself to Paris?

Just then the Polish or Slovakian waitress brought Domrul the crepe and thick English milk tea he had ordered and put it down in front of him with a counterfeit smile. "They're all witches!" thought Domrul, without meaning to, and as if he now knew what to say to the old woman, he faked a grin.

The next day, near noon, Domrul rolled in on the Eurostar to the Gare du Nord in Paris. Half an hour later, he got off the metro at Place de la Republique, and without bothering to call ahead, he walked over to the flat Emer had rented on rue Charlot and rang the bell at the street entrance. There was no answer at first, and Domrul thought, as he stood there, that they must have gone into the city on business, but suddenly he heard Emer's seductive voice from the door, asking, "Who's there?"

"Me!" answered Domrul, his own voice suddenly gone tight. Who knows whether that tightness of voice was due to the fact that he was trying to hide his suspicions, or because when he heard Emer's beloved voice all his doubts were forgotten?

Emer opened the door herself and froze for a moment; either she hadn't expected Domrul, or the unexpected was standing there in front of her . . . "You?" With a certain loose gentleness, she embraced Domrul, but didn't kiss him, and she sniffed, nuzzling her nose against his neck. "It's you."

Domrul started to lead her inside. They walked into the palm-size courtyard, and then Emer noticed that Domrul was lagging behind. "What happened to you?"

Domrul was startled by the question. What was she asking about? He hesitated.

Emer didn't prod him, but opened the door into the building. The place was a square studio apartment, with nobody inside.

"Where is he?" asked Domrul, unable to conceal his feelings.

"Who?" asked Emer, honestly confused.

"Your bard. Kuyuk-baxshi."

"Oh, right!" Emer laughed. "He's set up in a hotel. Frederique is looking after him now."

Domrul deflated with a whoosh, like a playground ball suddenly pierced with a nail, and collapsed with a plop onto a stool. "You're all alone?" he asked again, awkwardly.

"Yes," chuckled Emer again, as if understanding something, and sitting down on Domrul's knee, she hugged him again and whispered, "Oh, my Turkish Othello . . ."

They spent a long time talking things over together. On top of a burgundy wine, Emer offered him some of the Qoraqum and Alyonka chocolates that Kuyuk-baxshi had brought, and together they sipped from their glasses. When we say they talked, it was more Emer telling him what she had been doing and what she would be doing next. From time to time she asked Domrul questions, too, but Domrul would answer mechanically or lazily, with phrases like, "Yes, you know, not bad," without offering details and descriptions, so the conversation would always go back to Emer.

"You haven't told me about your old woman!" Emer finally decided to prod him. "What's she like? Is she a chatterbox or a bore? How does she dress? Does she still use makeup?" Simple little questions, without any pretext, just like that. But Domrul seemed to see provocation and intrigue in every one of them, so he was stingy in his answer.

"Oh, she's so haughty, a real witch. She is the type who turns even her requests into orders." And he tried casually to hand the reins of the conversation back to Emer. "What about you? You're using Coco Chanel now, too, are you?"

In fact, Domrul's heart felt dull, as if his insides were going to crack open from rot and fill the clear blue sky. But one thing made him bitter, and he acknowledged to himself that the closer a person is to you, the deeper you hide your secrets away from him or her. If Emer had been just a friend, rather than his girlfriend, he would have let out the words inside of him—about how the old woman had taken him to bed, with her cunning and conniving, and then used that as an excuse to wager that he would serve as her executioner . . . But how could he say all of that to Emer, with his own heart, face, and tongue? That's the kind of graveyard Domrul felt he had entered at that moment.

Luckily, under the influence of the wine, Emer's questions finally ran out, and she settled down on Domrul's lap again, cuddling close. The two lovers had not seen each other for almost two months, and in the tipsiness from the wine, combined with their intoxication at meeting again, they clung to each other tightly. They kissed, in silent moments of pleasure, only their meaningless whispers interrupting those moments, and then Emer, like a nightingale landing on a flower, said in her drunken voice, "Now I have a request to make of you—and it's an order!" And Domrul suddenly went limp, just like a ball thudding to the ground when popped with the tip of a nail, completely exhausted.

Later, when the two of them were lying side by side in bed, Emer issued no invitations, made no attempts, and did not try to discuss it. But she ran her fingers through Domrul's thinning hair, caressing him. Whether from that kindness, or out of weariness from his trip, or for some other reason, Domrul fell into a sweet sleep. Emer, getting carefully out of bed, pulled a comforter over his feet. Domrul, half asleep, dragged the comforter up to his chest, then up to his head. And he dreamed he had drifted off to sleep in a cave like the one he had just made. Though he had just been in a swelteringly hot house, suddenly snow was falling on the mountains, and the only place to hide was this cave. The cave seemed to have been meant for travelers, hunters, pilgrims trapped by the snow or avalanches, and inside it, everything was ready: a sleeping bag, a hearth and skillet, and canned food. Everywhere you looked, it was a comfy little house. There were stalls inside too. If you looked to the wall, you would see a door, probably the one you needed to take to go to your own house. Domrul tried to open that door. He looked, and in this house, instead of his cat, there was a little dog running to meet him. No, it didn't bite him, but the dog was heading outside, and he realized that this house belonged to the neighbors. He was confused that he had walked into their house, unasked and uninvited, and he turned right around and shut the door carefully.

In the wall in front of him, there was another small door. Domrul moved to open this one too. He walked through it and found he was in a tiny storeroom: laundry drying, sheets, three or four slips, a barrel of gas, a lamp. That must be for the cave's owner.

Unable to find the way back to his own house, Domrul thought about leaving the cave, but outside, the snow was still falling on the mountains and rocks, wasn't it, and in the cold, the pathways had iced over too. He thought that if he were to go out, he would surely fall over the cliff. It seemed today was his last day. He could not avoid falling into the abyss!

If he were to set just one foot outside, would he fall, crashing to the rocks below? He stuck his head out just for a moment and looked down. An unreliable passageway one handwidth across, and below, the sharply cut-out valley. Is getting out really so impossible, he wondered? After all, I got here so easily—why am I so afraid of going back? In that thought, with no solace and no consolation, he woke up.

◈

Gaia Mangitkhanovna's mood was a good match for this land's damp autumn loneliness. Why had she given that carer permission to go? Fine, he had gone lame, but when he had shown up, shouldn't she have gone on trying to convince him to do the deed? If she went out she'd get soaked, if she sat at home she'd have nothing to do, and it had become uncomfortable for her in her own skin. She had said she would catch that unripe melon on her hook, but had he hooked her instead? "Damn you, at your age" was not something she would permit herself to say. She thought for a moment, then went back into her bedroom, and from one of the drawers next to the bed, she took out a deck of tarot cards. She sat down at the head of the big table in the kitchen, shuffled the deck a little, picked from the middle, and tossed three cards onto the table.

The first one was the sun card. That meant that intellectually she was full of light and love. Yes, intellectually, which was to say that her love and desire were superficial, maybe only at the tip of her tongue, because the second card, the one in the middle, showed the hanging silhouette of a person. In other words, emotionally there was nothing between them. The rope wrapped around him was not love. It was the rope of death. Or to put it another way, the binding rope of business. Like a rope bound around the neck of a calf and nailed down into the earth by a spike. One move from the calf, and where's the rope, and where's the spike? From the deepest recesses of her memory, Gaia Mangitkhanovna dredged up a saying by the Uzbeks, that the calf only knows how to moo at his food.

There was a reason for Gaia Mangitkhanovna's distraction, and it was a horrible reason too. Because the third card was the death card! That meant that actually, if you discounted the outward sunshiny love and brilliance, or the sinister threads inside the secrets, the outcome was death, the reality was death, the fact was death.

For whom had Gaia Mangitkhanovna revealed this prediction? Did she think it was for herself, or was it for that young man who had left her all alone? Or was she purposely leaving that question open, or reinterpreting the private relationship between the two of them? Whatever it was, hadn't the cards shown her things befitting Gaia Mangitkhanovna's sullied heart? She whisked all three cards off the table, put them back in the deck, and shut them back up in the drawer by the bed.

Now from the chest of drawers in the living room she took a few small candles and returned to the big table in the kitchen. She put the candles onto a silver tray, lit some of them, and set two of them close to one another, then joined a third to that pair, making a triangle. She whispered something. Then she lit some more candles, and from them she built a Star of David, and with a sudden passion, she started whispering over them again.

◆

"I will never let my husband get out of control, like my mother did!" That was the motto stamped on Gaia's heart, like a Roman-legion slogan inscribed on a steel plate, practically since childhood. She had gone to school side by side with her husband, and in school and in her social life, she was always competing to see whom she could beat. If her husband used a hammer, she would use a sickle; when her husband became a party council member at the factory, she was elected the chairman of the trade unions council at the institute. Two children came in two years, one after the other—she bore both a son and a daughter—and while she raised her children in the communist spirit of equality, she pushed her husband up and up the rungs of the career ladder.

Though the Communist leaders had ideals on their tongues, they had desire in their eyes and hunger in their bellies, as the intelligent Gaia had long ago discovered. Unwillingly made into a housewife in those years, she suddenly found herself transformed into a kitchen wench and hostess too. Her husband's bosses started coming to their house at all hours, and it was his responsibility to provide them drink, whereas the rest was up to Gaia: *somsa* and soup for the greedy bellies, flirtatious glances for the envious eyes. And for dessert, her children, who had just started to mumble, would recite poems about Grandfather Lenin, sing songs, and melt the bosses' steel-tempered hearts like butter.

As if moving a pawn by bald-faced trickery to the far end of the chessboard to turn it into a queen, Gaia slowly, carefully filled up her husband with airs and importance.

But, as they say, only a sheep can carry fat well, so Gaia's husband, as he became a boss, was plagued by the freedom that bosses have. Now the lust flashed in his eye, too, and the gluttony bloated his belly. How could he possibly hide all that from Gaia, who was thin and tattered, but watchful and awake? Now her husband would make one excuse or another for coming home late, and when she asked where he had been, if he didn't excuse himself with some hearing or meeting which had run late, his eyes would wander, and he would say they had been celebrating the new apartment of one of his secretaries or somebody's new baby.

One day, after one of those feasts, before her husband could open his eyes in the morning, while he still lay in bed, Gaia sent the children off to school, and she told him, "I'm off to the clinic, won't be back till evening!"—and she shut herself up in the hall closet. In about half an hour her husband got up, and without dressing or anything else he went over to the telephone in the hallway and spoke so impudently with someone who was apparently a Komsomol girl—no memory was spared of the previous evening's party, words were even said about flying on the wings of love to her house, right this minute, and her address, which he had forgotten in his drunkenness, was written down again. Later, after he called for a car from the office and got himself all dressed up, her husband, stinking with copious cologne, opened the door with a clatter and stepped outside.

For a moment, Gaia was exhausted. She felt withered. The tears came. But that very minute, she collected herself. She stepped outside, hailed a taxi, recited the address she had memorized, went straight to that ridiculous Komsomol flirt's house, and took her husband and his mistress by surprise.

When she caught her husband with his mistress, Gaia did not claw at her rival's face or pull her hair, and did not even file a complaint with the party committee. She annihilated her, like a cat thrown in the water, and she made those two assholes write down a statement regarding the truth of the incident that had taken place. Her husband, who had once thought of himself as a king and his own shadow as a shield, was now a puppet in her hands.

But Gaia did not stop there. She had not left her old competitive spirit behind, and she found herself infatuated by one thought: "Can't I do the things that you have done?"

In those days, a refined young man named Bo'riboy, from the neighboring republic, was coming to their zoology institute, interested in the extrasensory powers of livestock. Gaia selected him to be her sacrifice. In one month he would return to his own country, leaving not a trace, she thought. That summer her husband went to Moscow for additional training, the children were at a Young Pioneers camp, and Gaia was left at home by herself.

She cooked her plan up well, and one day, Gaia called the institute from her house, and told the departmental secretary, "I was taking out the garbage when the door closed. The key is inside. Can you send one of our young men over here to open a window for me? Maybe you can send that Bo'riboy, he's useless, anyway," she suggested. The secretary did not keep her waiting, but sent Bo'riboy straight to Gaia's house.

When the useless Bo'riboy arrived at his destination, Gaia was sitting in the yard morosely, only half-covered in a nightgown. Her lightweight garment could hardly hope to conceal either her hips or her breasts. "I was trying to get in through that window, but I can't do it," said Gaia, reaching for the window, revealing her beauty in all its nakedness once more. "Maybe if you give me a little boost, I can fit through," she said as she tried.

Bo'riboy took hold of Gaia, one hand at her waist, the other at her crotch, and it was soaked through. Suddenly unable to catch his breath, in a rush, he said, "Let me come in!" and he mounted the windowsill himself. Gaia moved to help him, and now her hands were suddenly touching Bo'riboy's treasures too, arousing him.

Just as Bo'riboy entered that house that day, once inside, he entered Gaia in the very same way. And that was the start of a many-faceted, long-lived friendship that lasted from that day on.

Domrul told Emer nothing about his dream. This was not because he wanted to add to the unspoken secrets between them, but rather because his heart had grown dull, like the bad-mood weather in Paris. They shoved and squeezed through the rain, down the crowded streets, in Emer's tiny Peugeot, and spent almost an hour on the ten-minute drive to the metro. Emer parked the car on one of the narrow avenues of the capital city and headed with Domrul for the Théâtre de la Ville. It was not just that silence and this weather that was making Domrul feel so low. Maybe it could be explained better by the event that now awaited him. They were on their way to see Kuyuk-baxshi in concert, and as they neared the theater, Emer's enthusiasm and passion were growing, while Domrul's mood was quickly heading in the other direction. No matter how indifferent and unconcerned he was trying to seem, the jealousy gnawing away at his insides was casting some sort of sarcastic, pained shadow on his face. While Emer rushed panting toward the theater, Domrul dawdled at the intersections, delaying till the yellow lights turned to red, disappearing into the crowd, making Emer wait despite her impatience, trying hundreds of tricks like a fussy, irritable little child, barely dragging along.

No, they finally did make it into the theater, just at the first bell. They skipped the coat check window, and Emer bought a program along the way; with their special-guest tickets, the two of them walked through the crowds who had just been seated to the very center of the first row, show-ing off. Now they had time to take off their raincoats, and before they had quite caught their breath, the concert began.

Throughout the concert, Domrul's attention was focused surrepti-tiously not on Kuyuk strumming his *dombra*, not on his throaty voice, but on the behavior of Emer, sitting by his side. He monitored her every motion. What he meant to learn is unclear to us, but anguish must lie at the basis of any interpretation. Even as we ask ourselves "What is this?," when we see a "this," aren't we saying "what"? Jealousy is also full to the brim of suspicions and doubts, so where do you suppose there might be any room for reason to fit in? What we are saying is that Domrul was find-ing what he wanted to find that evening, with his intellect worn down by jealousy. In Emer's shining eyes, he perceived the sparks of betrayal, and in her clapping hands, the sounds of treachery. Even during the intermis-sion, she spoke more with the friends she found there about Kuyuk-baxshi and his performance than about Domrul.

Now, after the concert, when Emer had dragged him backstage to glorify the bard, he kept his head tucked into his raincoat, and he felt weak and feeble enough to cry. Would his beloved leave Domrul behind in front of so many people, and split through the crowd of fans, passing through to the innocently grinning Kuyuk, hugging him, old man that he was, and kissing his beardless cheek? Domrul stabbed his eyes like needles into the bard, and the old man went and propped his dombra up so it stuck up between his legs, then took Emer's hands into both of his own and kissed them; and wiping his sly, narrow eyes, he peered through the crowd surrounding him . . . yes, Domrul saw it all, and he was heartbroken, as if he had found proof.

The French are rather a carefree people. After the concert, the organizers led particular members of the audience in a chaotic flock to the Brasserie

Zimmer restaurant opposite the theater, the bard leading the way, and among them was not a single person who could understand the performer's language. Then Emer, guiding Kuyuk-baxshi by the elbow, turned back, and called forth Domrul, who had been unhappily and unwillingly dragged along, and she made Domrul cut through the ranks of the bard's fans till he was seated right at the most important place of honor at the table.

"Mon amour!" Emer tossed the French words out somewhere in between Domrul and Kuyuk-baxshi; and whereas the bard grinned, not having understood, Domrul, who had, blushed all the way to his hairline. Who is Emer talking about? Who is she introducing to whom? he wondered. In any case, the bard extended both his hands to Domrul, took Domrul's hand, kissed it, then passed a hand over his slanting eyes.

In short order, Kuyuk-baxshi was sitting at the head of the table, Emer at his left hand, Domrul at his right side, and all the other riffraff were seated in row after row, and the chaotic French banquet got into full swing. First the chief organizer of the concert, the theater manager, a thin Iranian woman named Sudabe, lifted her glass to honor Kuyuk's ancient craft. Domrul uttered what seemed to be a very dry translation of the grandiose words the bard said in response. That made two toasts, which had little in common with one another.

True, a bard has a good sense of human nature, and he may have sensed a crisis between the two people at his sides, and so making use of how everyone was buried in the commotion, in his own language he praised Emer to Domrul; but it was the kind of praise that, for every one of her virtues, one of Domrul's was also revealed. He recited to the young man his congratulations for having found such a chaste, modest young woman, and he uttered words of praise for her like-minded fellow, for teaching her the art of hospitality and an open heart, and he pronounced blessings over her beloved, who laid the foundations for her, whose smile never left her face.

He was melting Domrul's heart like butter and cutting into him like a knife. "From what I've heard, you are providing care to one of our elders. Her name is Goia, is that what they said?" he asked innocently, leaning toward Domrul. Emer, satisfied that the two of them had found a common language, was now talking with Sudabe, sitting on her other side, about arrangements for new concerts and new performances, and then Domrul's heart relaxed a little, too, and he felt he could confide in this detestable Qaraqalpaq or Turkmen with his little triangular beard.

"Not Goia, but Gaia. Gaia Mangitkhanovna."

"If she is the same I know, then I know her well!" said Kuyuk, slapping his knee. "So, she has fled to Anglistan, the bitch."

"What do you mean fled? Why is she a bitch?" asked Domrul in surprise, not sure what he was defending his client from.

"Oh, there's a great deal to be said about that," mused the bard, as if setting the stage for a long, epic tale.

❖

Though she had done all the fortune-telling she could, Gaia Mangitkhanovna's heart was uneasy. Useless thoughts occupied her, such as whether she had done the right thing revealing her secret to him. She had never been so unsure and full of doubt in her life. Apparently the uncertain, indefinite weather in this place had worked its way into her, changing her very nature. Where was that clear distinction, that no-turning-back?

Look, she had sent her carer to Paris, and now she was sitting buried in her doubts. Maybe, as her partner to euthanasia, she should have hired that Russian woman, Antonina Ivanovna? But unlike the young man, there was the problem that Antonina Ivanovna was an old church lady. People like her, you could never expect them to lend a hand. On the contrary, it's practically inevitable that they will turn the whole world upside down resisting. Gaia Mangitkhanovna knew all about saints like her. She had met so many of them.

Her thoughts were scattered. All her life she had never looked back, instead always striding toward the future. So how had she now become the type of person who was tied up in musings and memories? Was this another effect of the wet weather, or was the ceaseless, endless noise of the waves of the sea driving her mad?

Yes, now she remembered! When she had wanted to hook her future husband, the first woman who was living with him was just like that. A Russian nun in a headscarf. At the time, Gaia held that woman by her most sensitive feather, and she raised burning questions at the labor council, and the trade union, and the party councils, about what kind of innocent nun that bitch really was! Her face grew wrinkled and contorted while she fought over her husband like a cat over a corpse; but since he still craved party membership, her husband divorced that Russian, while with his beloved party, meaning also with Gaia, he maintained his everlasting relationship. One year later, the two of them got married and traveled to Moscow for a professional development course. As for the naive first wife, from the rumors Gaia heard, she lost her mind, shouting all kind of nonsense all over the city. Then she must have gotten arrested, or maybe committed, but in any case, she disappeared.

So, she thought, God save us from pious people like Antonina Ivanovna. When she pushed that Russian professor around in her chair, the chair was always getting stuck in the mud, and any time Gaia Mangitkhanovna happened to come across them, and look at them, the face of Antonina Ivanovna also grew wrinkled and twisted and contorted, looking like an old fox's snout.

No, whether he was an unripe melon or an immature apricot, now that Gaia Mangitkhanovna had chosen her young Turk, she would steam him, stew him, cook him . . .

◈

The next day, Domrul, not having forgotten his business for his client, had a meeting over coffee with a lawyer named Jean-Michel, someone Emer's friend Sudabe had found. Sudabe had named the time and place. Domrul had never in his life seen such a quiet, uncrowded café in the middle of Paris. It was one street down from last evening's Zimmer, and half a block over, on the corner. Domrul arrived there a little bit early and wandered around in front of the café a bit. Then, wanting to demonstrate his politeness and wait for the lawyer rather than be waited for himself, he went inside. He ordered himself an espresso, and next to a huge window, under a real palm tree stuck in a pot, he sat for some time and watched the people go by.

A little past the appointed time, Jean-Michel himself arrived. From his outward appearance, he had no idea he belonged to the posh tribe of attorneys and law. This intellectual-looking man in a suit and tie more resembled a university instructor, maybe even a schoolteacher. His ordinariness and his simplicity made him even more attractive. On his way over he ordered himself a special Irish coffee, and the barista seemed to be an old friend of his. They inquired warmly about each other's health and laughed together.

Jean-Michel and Domrul introduced themselves in a way that felt sincere. They sat down. The lawyer asked about London. "We can speak English, if you like," he offered. Domrul accepted gratefully. That would be easier for him and also keep things at a remove from other people's ears.

He started the conversation right at the point. "Is euthanasia being made legal in France?" he asked.

Jean-Michel gave him a thorough report on the matter, then added, "If your client isn't dreaming of being buried at Père Lachaise, then it would certainly be easier to do it in Belgium, Holland, or Luxembourg." He interrupted the conversation at this point with a smile.

"And what if she is the kind of client who, as you said, does choose Père Lachaise?" Domrul inquired.

"That can be arranged, too, but as you know, in this world, the stranger one's dreams, the costlier the price." After that, Jean-Michel offered Domrul a couple more examples, from what he had done recently for the Al-Fayed family. "If your client has the right kind of power, the path to the next world could be wide open," he said, making a joke out of destiny.

When the meeting was over, Domrul stepped outside with a feeling of elation, but inside, he hesitated. He wasn't sure whether he was glad that Jean-Michel had made light of the painful subject, or on the other hand, if he was terrified to have been told that even tickets to the other world cost money.

◆

Until Gaia Mangitkhanovna's carer came back, she felt imprisoned between her four walls, and finally she had no choice but to call Antonina Ivanovna. Antonina Ivanovna had sent her own client to some relatives for two days, and she was also tired of sitting around with nothing to do. "This evening there's a poetry event at Pushkin House in London," she said. When Gaia Mangitkhanovna probed, she learned that neither Pushkin nor any descendants of his had ever lived in that house, but Pushkin's name had just metaphorically been attached to a splendid building, and evenings devoted to Russian and Soviet culture, literature, and music were arranged there.

It ought to be nicer than sitting around this stinking place, thought Gaia Mangitkhanovna, and an hour later she met Antonina Ivanovna at the entrance to her building. Domrul may have called her "begum," but Antonina Ivanovna thought she had better call the woman she met half an hour later "madame." She had a darling little theater satchel in her hand, and over her shoulders she wore a coat that was not quite black, but more the deep blue color of the night, and on her head was a little cap they called a "pillbox hat" in just the same color.

First they caught a taxi, then rode to Eastbourne Station, and from there took the train into King's Cross in London. With Antonina leading the way—she had been breathing the air of this place for twenty years now—they got on a bus, rode to Bloomsbury Square, and walked into the poetry evening just in time.

We won't give any description of the event that took place there; it ought to be sufficient to provide you the words that Gaia Mangitkhanovna spoke in the empty train car going back to Eastbourne, not to Antonina Ivanovna's face, but rather into the cold air.

"What kind of place did you take me to? It's enough to make you vomit!" she began. "Did you see that note-taker? He's afraid of his own words. They introduced him as a professor. Professors used to be pompous, authoritative people, but this one of yours looked like a mouse fleeing a cat from the other room. Looking around in all directions. Can't even be faithful to what he said! What was that? One poem by Pushkin, translated by him three times? If you can't pull it off, leave it alone! Give it to someone else to fix! And we're supposed to pick out the best one of those three translations! Do you call on someone else to introduce you when you lie down with your wife, too, you idiot?

"And the audience was even worse than him! That old fart sitting next to us hadn't had a bath for two months, he hadn't washed his clothes for half a year, he stank! It was impossible to sit next to him! I could barely stand it even spraying my own perfume under my nose. And that fool they introduced to us as a poet! His hair was falling out, four threads of hair sitting limp on his shoulders, and still not a bit grown up! What about

that other one, who tied up all that rotting white hair in a ponytail? Not
to mention the women. A sixty-year-old one with her legs painted like she
was wearing stockings! That bald poet's lady friend, with the earring in
her nose—every single hole of hers has earrings, she probably has a hoop
dangling from her asshole, too, couldn't even sit calmly in her seat, fidget,
fidget, fidget.

"You could die from that wine they gave us, the kind of wine you
never want another sip of, it's not even wine, it's puke! Don't ever remind
me of that place again!"

Antonina Ivanovna did not know what to say, so she sat there, brooding.

◆

For some reason, the passengers were a little more sparse in the last car
of the Eurostar. Domrul looked at his dark reflection in the window
and entered into a conversation between himself and his own thoughts.
Coming to Paris without a *bismallah*, like his late aunt would have told
him, had been a bad idea. Even if his relationship with Emer was not yet
ruined, cracks had started to appear. In the end, while he seemed to have
overcome his jealousy, his manly potency had been neither upheld nor
confirmed, however hard he tried. Emer had not told him outright to go
see a doctor, just indirectly, managing to drop in conversation that her
aunt in London's current husband was a specialist in that particular type
of weakness and distress, and she diligently wrote down his phone number
and email address for him.

And it was hard to say where his relationship with Kuyuk started and
where it ended. On the one hand, the triangular-bearded old man seemed
to have really warmed his heart, especially when he was talking about
the various misdeeds of his old acquaintance Goia, making the spiderweb
binding Domrul's arms and legs feel a bit more feeble, but when he said
he couldn't tell whether it was her or not until he saw her, the turmoil and
uneasiness in Domrul's heart grew larger and stronger, more indelible.

Kuyuk had gone back home too. They had made a pact that evening.
Domrul would invite the storyteller to come to London, accompanied by
Emer, and once they found an opportunity and the means, Kuyuk-baxshi
could get a glimpse of Gaia Mangitkhanovna and tell them whether she
was in fact his ill-fated Goia or not.

Now, as he remembered Kuyuk's description of that Goia woman's evil doings, Domrul weighed them against those of his client Gaia Mangit-khanovna, and he asked himself a question that could not be answered—could it be that this arrogant woman was actually so sullied by such low deeds? Kuyuk had said his Goia had her own son put in jail and her own daughter made destitute. Could that be the Gaia Mangitkhanovna that Domrul the carer had in his care?

The next morning Domrul, still limping a little, arrived at Gaia Man-gitkhanovna's apartment. While Gaia-khonim did not let her happiness show when she met him in the entryway, he did think he noticed that a few odds and ends in this home had changed a bit, such as the brand-new felt house slippers she had out for him to use. As if making up for his absence, Domrul had brought the kind of Saint-Émilion wine that was sold in a wooden box. After a brief hello, they went into the living room. From the windows facing the sea, the deep blue moved and flowed into the room, and the sea's now audible, now inaudible humming conveyed to them a kind of unsurpassed peace.

Gaia Mangitkhanovna truly seemed to have changed, and it was as if a sort of mildness, a gentleness, had come to shade her expression. Grasping in her hand the bottle that was inside that box, she stopped under a ray of light pouring in from the window, and staring into the fiery clear color of that wine, she recited a poem by Osip Mandelstam, the one about a little red wine.

A little bit of light red wine
A tiny bit of sunny May . . .

No, she didn't open a bottle, and didn't invite him to drink it, but with pride she set down this superior *vin* on the buffet, and looking at the disheveled Domrul, who was left standing on one foot, she asked him, "What is going on with your foot?"

Domrul had no idea how to answer that unexpected question and just shrugged his shoulders.

"Come on, let's have a look!" declared Gaia Mangitkhanovna in the bossy tone she used to make requests, and she gestured toward the couch in the living room. Domrul sat down. Embarrassed, he shook off his slipper and removed his sock. "Take off that bandage." There was no hint of danger in those words, just the tone a nurse might use with a patient. Domrul pulled the bandage off, showing no pain. When Gaia Mangitkhanovna saw the still gaping, dark red wound, she gasped. Thank God she didn't faint, thought Domrul, who was still unable to overcome his own embarrassment.

"You know, I have some stuff they call *shilajit* that will clear that right up," she said, and leaving Domrul on the couch, she went off toward her own room. In a moment she came out, carrying a reddish copper basin, and sat it down near the sofa. "First we'll wash it off with some antiseptic," she said, and pushed Domrul's foot into the warm water. Then she took a soft piece of cork in her hand and began carefully washing the young man's foot. Domrul's head started spinning. No, it wasn't because of this haughty empress's sudden transformation into a gentle maiden, but because his own dead mother, nearly thirty years ago, had used just such a basin to wash her son's bare, pimply feet, and the notion of that had struck Domrul's brain, his memory, his feelings, with a thud.

Gaia Mangitkhanovna wrapped his freshly washed foot in a white towel, not wiping it, but just patting and patting it dry (Domrul's mother had done that very same thing!), and then said, "Roll up your pants and lie down." Domrul, for some reason, obeyed her with no words. Gaia Mangitkhanovna carried away the copper basin and returned holding two teacups instead. In one was a brown medicine, and in the other, something the same color glowed more faintly. She put the medicine on the wound. It started to sting instantly, then all at once tingled sweetly. "Now this one is to drink!" she said, offering the brown fluid. Domrul lifted his head and emptied the teacup in two gulps. The inside of his throat burned. Maybe because of his brisk movement, when he lay down again, his head spun dizzily.

Gaia Mangitkhanovna took what remained of the medicine and rubbed it around Domrul's ankle, then moved with little circular motions up to his calf, then nearly to the place where his rolled-up pants met his knee. Whether from the gentleness of her fingers, the change in mood, or the dizziness that had hit his head, Domrul's cheeks blazed, and the masculine power that had been destined for Emer was now in untimely excess. He had his eyes shut tight, but he saw the begum's merry face leaning right over his treasure, and in his ear, she whispered, "Oh, my silly little fool, it looks as if I've cast a spell on you."

Air

Kuyuk-baxshi had been born in the desert wastelands that cross through Turkmenistan and Kazakhstan and Qoraqalpakistan, and for that reason, through his veins, like the ancient river Jayhun's muddy and fertile waters, there also surged the blood of the Khanate of Khorazm. He came into this world in an aul, an encampment of yurts huddled around the grave of a saint called Qais al-Halabi. His childhood was spent raising cattle in the empty environs of the gravesite, and from those who made pilgrimages to the holy saint's grave, if he showed them the way, or shared with them water from the spring, he could sometimes make a tenge or two. However, he went to the school in the next village, perhaps three kilometers distant, two or rarely three times per week, and as soon as he somehow finished seventh grade, he moved on to a bigger place, and there he learned to drive a tractor.

After that, when he was called to join the army, he became a tank driver in the Russian Far East, and along the way he also learned to drive a car. Returning to that bigger place, Kuyuk began to drive a bus connecting the yurt villages, one after the other, and the most distant cities, along the rough and rocky road through the desert. Once he had saved a little money that way, he started making preparations to marry and have children, but then one day, unexpectedly, disaster struck, and his straightforward life was turned upside down.

In their aul lived a rather simpleminded orphan boy named G'ulli. He used to steal the pieces of cloth bound by the believers to the trees in front of the saint's gravesite and use them as neckties, or fall into the muddy canal, or swoop out in front of the passing pilgrims to show them his rear end. Well, as they say, "every town has its fool, every outpost has its madman," and nobody paid much attention to this harmless creature. That one's hanging around again, is he? So be it, they'd say, and carry on with their business.

When you walked outside the aul, at the foot of the saint's grave, a grand elm tree was growing, and a rumor had passed from generation to generation that big snakes had made a nest in that elm tree, and due to that rumor, while strangers might stop to rest in the shade of that tree, no local person would ever come near the magnificent elm, and though they remained deprived of its shade, they gave thanks that their lives remained safe. On this day, our Kuyuk came back to the aul on his bus. He brought his elderly mother some food and supplies from far away, left some clothes and things, picked up three schoolchildren from the aul, and headed for the neighboring village.

As it left the aul the road curved toward the big elm, and Kuyuk made the dust rise on the road. He did not decrease his speed, and as he whizzed by, the branches of the tree struck the roof. The branches rattled and rustled against the roof of the bus and then suddenly, with a banging sound, the bus trembled. "Is that a snake?" thought Kuyuk, and he stepped on the brake hard, in a flash. Every one of them, terrified, saw how, from the roof of the bus, the body of G'ulli the Simpleminded toppled to the ground, and behind it, there fell down in a tangle not a snake, but a very snake-like rope.

At first they shuddered, as if waking from a bad dream, and then, in their wild fright, they were stunned speechless. Our Kuyuk, who had stopped the bus at the base of the dry elm, was in agony, not knowing what to do. Finally, one of the children on the bus started to scream, and they all came back to their senses. Kuyuk opened the door of the bus and stepped outside. G'ulli the Simpleminded was covered in dust, lying flat on his back, and blood was frothing out of his mouth. One end of the rope lying in a heap next to him was tied around his neck, around his home-made necktie of old clothes and rags . . .

Our Kuyuk, in desperation, would go to lift G'ulli up, and for some reason, the unbreathing G'ulli would slip right out of his hands. With the help of the children he had left behind, our Kuyuk would lift G'ulli's lifeless body onto the bus and turn the bus back to the aul. He would put him down in front of Yo'lli-baxshi, who was reciting a prayer in front of the holy grave . . .

The baxshi watched the bus draw near him and opened his arms for the funeral prayers.

That day, as soon as the red-haired orphan G'ulli was buried, our Kuyuk started to burn with fever, his heart galloped, his breath came hard. He had left his bus where he had stopped, but he did not have the strength to sit at the wheel, or distribute the children to their homes, much less to school, or even to go back to his own house. He found himself lying stuffed in a corner of Yo'lli-baxshi's hut of straw and clay at the entrance to the graveyard. Once a rising din made him open his eyes, and then he saw he was surrounded by all sorts of wolves and jackals, growling and snarling, as if they were moving in on him. "Help!" Kuyuk shouted, covering his head in his quilted robe and cowering tighter into the corner. The wolves and jackals threw themselves upon him, first tearing at his clothing, stripping him, seizing his flesh, wresting the flesh from his bones, gnawing at it. The most imposing one of them waited for Kuyuk's heart, and he charged, snapped up his heart, and then retreated, and the beating heart slid, thump-thump, from his mouth onto the dust, and in front of Kuyuk's terror-filled eyes, his heart started to transform into G'ulli the Simpleminded.

At that moment came Yo'lli-baxshi's strong voice, out of nowhere. "Stand up!" The red-haired G'ulli, lying in the dust, was wrapped up in the clothes and rags that used to hang from the tree's branches, and he stood up, brushed the dust off, and blew a whistle, and every one of the beasts plodded after him out of the room and they left.

Kuyuk realized that all that remained of his own flesh was the tongue in his mouth, and he remembered how he had bitten that tongue.

A moment may have passed, or a day, or a week—Kuyuk did not know. What he did know was that, when he opened his eyes weakly one more time, there was Yo'lli-baxshi sitting in front of him, telling him, "Stand up!" And at Yo'lli-baxshi's side was the policeman Qoyip, the ugly old local dose of wrath and poison incarnate nicknamed Tyson.

What happened then only those two knew for sure, but the young Kuyuk was not put in prison, and he dropped the bus business, forsook material things completely, and ended up in the service of Yo'lli-baxshi.

❖

You must be asking when and how our sister Goia comes into this story. It is right for us to have a little patience. Patience, as Yo'lli-baxshi explained again and again to Kuyuk the Apprentice, is the main post supporting the disciple's tent. When there is no patience, it is difficult to keep one's own yurt erect.

> One who has not built a home in the eyes of patience
> will have difficulty building one on the Jayhun river,

as the master used to say. We ourselves will be heeding this advice and taking our tale down a different road for the time being.

Yo'lli-baxshi's sincere admirers numbered in the thousands. Yo'lli-baxshi never begrudged his assistance to anyone, but healed some, recited funeral prayers for others, and graced the celebration feasts of them all. Yet people with unfounded claims and ambitions also traveled among the pilgrims, and some of them, in a flood of jealousy and envy, were keen to learn his art for themselves, and though they did not stay to serve the baxshi, they frequently came to see him. One of them, a rather yellowish boaster named Qimbat-guppi, from the oasis, remotely reminded Kuyuk of the red-haired G'ulli, and an unexplainable hardness against him was born in his heart. Qimbat-guppi did resemble the simpleminded G'ulli, and he sometimes wore a stone bead around his neck, or would bare his round belly and greet the pilgrim women, and prop himself up under the ill-fated elm tree, and secretly drink from a hidden bottle of vodka, and fall asleep snoring under the tree.

Because Yo'lli-baxshi never beheld any person as an enemy, he placed the boaster Qimbat-guppi at one edge of his soul, wide as the desert, and as others said, since he would never trouble even a tomcat to get out of his way, on the contrary, he looked at even this young man, fool that he was, with loving eyes. Qimbat-guppi had been dropping in to join the pilgrimages for two or three years, mostly in the summer months, and then suddenly stopped. From what people knew from words spoken here and there, he worked supervising the grave of some saintly father in the oasis, and they said he had even taken on the title "Qimbat-baxshi, disciple of Yo'lli-baxshi." When he heard this news, Kuyuk the Apprentice, whether jealous of his teacher, or jealous of all his selfless years in his service, or envious of how shamelessly that title had been claimed, told Yo'lli-baxshi what he had heard, and Yo'lli-baxshi chuckled, and then said,

> The tales you have told are as fragile as you,
> To add like to like is my plea to you.
> Your tales are a dagger straight through my heart.
> Now heal my troubles, Kuyuk, dear heart.

And they never returned to that topic again.

◆

The young Kuyuk spent seven years in Yo'lli-baxshi's service. While the depraved policeman Qoyip would still have liked to put him in prison, in which case he also would have forsaken all material things for the same period of time, as it was he learned the epic tales, and he ran his hands over his *dutor* and dombra, and he memorized the hadith and the prayers. Now he learned how to make medicine out of different herbs, how to heal people and how to train horses, riding them in the hilly slopes, and interpret dreams, and look at every living beast and being and recognize their breed.

After those seven years, a campaign against religious innovations and superstition was proclaimed throughout the land. There was ranting and raving about it from all four directions, and one day the devil's own demon, the policeman Qoyip, stormed into his clay cell. "I will tear down your twisted hut like the yurt of religion!" he declared in disdain. Yo'lli-baxshi hemmed and hawed and was allowed one day to decide, and he recited from the holy book over the heads of his loved ones, and in the evening he loaded sundry supplies onto his piebald horse, took his dombra into his hands, and sang didactically to the young Kuyuk:

Clouds of dust rose unabated,
So through that dust they waded,
Till Yo'lli-the-old and his horse
Four fathoms of dust liquidated.

After that, Yo'lli-baxshi pressed his apprentice to his breast. "Kuyuk, my boy," he said. "Now your feathers are free, and perhaps you will fly like a stallion or a hawk, or perhaps you will find a red flower, or embrace it as a nightingale's nest! And if I myself should reach my death, my ashes shall ride with me." This was his blessing. All the small hairs on Kuyuk the Apprentice's body bristled, his heart was crushed, and he saw his teacher off to the Turkmen desert; and then he walked, a small bundle in his hand as the dawn broke, in the direction his head led him.

◆

After his master departed, Kuyuk the Apprentice became simply Kuyuk, and he who had once learned the ancient craft of full recitation of the holy texts now toiled as a tractor operator or digging machine driver in the desert, a janitor in the valley, a fisherman on the Amu, and he kept his own desires locked inside him, and lived in this manner for five or six years. One day he was working as part of a brigade reclaiming virgin lands, and when he lay down in the workers' deserted wagon, exhausted from erecting concrete buildings, Yo'lli-baxshi's sod hut encroached into his dreams. "I will tear down the yurt of religion," said the policeman Qoyip, who grew up in the steppe and therefore had a mouth accustomed to expansive phrases, and he brought in a bulldozer, saying he would wreck his home. A bird flew out from inside the hut and alit onto Tyson's, which is to say the policeman Qoyip's, red cap. "Excuses make excuses, but mud makes a building," the bird mocked him. Kuyuk, startled awake in the lightless, lampless desert darkness, seemed to hear his master's clear, pure voice:

My hut made of mud is my blood,
The bird flown from my hut is my soul.
The ruins of the toppled building is my body,
Damn your dream, if this is the meaning!

However he had come to be lying in his torn work clothes on this iron bed, Kuyuk wept and cried, pleading and appealing to Allah to not cut short his master's days, but from somewhere, the moon was cutting through this darkness and looking through the window in the wagon, as if speaking to him and blinking at him, staring, telling him, "No matter who has died, you remain with me."

In the very early morning, Kuyuk again took his bundle in his hand and set off where his head led him. On the road, there were times when he ate bread and times he lived on dread. He reached the end of the road and moved on into the grassy wastelands, and one day he emerged at the foot of an ancient fortress. In the distance a stand of poplars stood waving, and our Kuyuk said, "My wandering is over! My path has reached a settlement," and he thought he might take a rest on the high spot where the fortress stood; and he saw at the foot of it a graveyard, where, under some banners fluttering on poles, an insane person was lying on his back. This big fellow seemed somehow familiar to his eyes. When he slowly descended, he saw it was the one-time false disciple to his master Yo'lli, the yellowish boaster Qimbat-guppi. There were beads on a string around his neck and azure prayer beads in his hand. Qimbat-guppi recognized our Kuyuk, too, and he rose to embrace him and led him toward his aul.

In the aul he slaughtered a well-fed ram, summoned everyone around, all the bald and blind, and held a feast in honor of Kuyuk. "This is my younger baxshi brother," he said, and hosted Kuyuk for three days. Our Kuyuk learned that Qimbat-guppi was still talking big and had become a goat-provocateur, the kind always looking to lead the lamb to the slaughterhouse of the national union of the bald and the blind. Then one day, what should happen but a learned Kyrgyz or Kazakh called Bo'riboy arrived, and meeting Qimbat-guppi at the foot of the fortress, he said, "You are the pure dervish I have been searching for. I wish to make you a spiritual master, a healer, for the bald and blind of all the union." And he began sending Qimbat-guppi to one capital city after another.

It seems that the people of the capitals were quite gullible, and apparently never in their lives had they seen a poor fool, and they went along easily with whatever the genteel-seeming Bo'riboy-marqa told them. "This one," he used to say, his eyes wide, poking Qimbat with a finger, "will make a real spiritual master for you lot. He will move rocks with his eye and eat food with his mouth. You've forgotten the mystical things," he said, "but he will bring your lives back to you!" The lost Qimbat uttered not a word, but stood there dumb and speechless. Mysticism! So be it.

Now that sort lined up like geese and made pilgrimages to Qimbat's aul. In the aul, now, there was no need for anyone's cauldron to boil, and the aul's bald and blind, though they were not mystics at all, were all blessed, as was the boaster Qimbat-guppi's big iron cauldron.

"As you share with us your destiny, coapprentice, so you shall also eat and drink!" Qimbat-guppi articulated his thoughts to Kuyuk, while winking cunningly at his nearest Russian or Tatar follower.

When I am angry, I put on my red cap so fine,
When I am bitter, I slaughter the bald and the blind,
I destroy the capital cities in all their phony glory,
And make myself the master of all that I find . . .

And so our boy Kuyuk was again renamed. Now he was Kuyuk-baxshi, and he found himself the teller of epic tales at the ceremonies of Qimbat-guppi, who knew not a single epic tale himself. Now there was a dombra in his hand, and he recited to the riffraff that came and went advice and examples matching the clever sayings of all the old Uzbek epic tales, now of Gugo'gli, now of Misqol-pari, now of Avazxon, now of Cheeky Malika. Bo'riboy-marqa, who had come from distant Moscow, pounded Kuyuk on the back, fastened a colored stone bead around his neck, and pronounced, "Now you are one of us." Bo'riboy-marqa turned out to be a very learned and refined man, and Kuyuk learned many words from Bo'riboy-marqa which he had never heard from Yo'lli-baxshi. *Selfness*, he said, and he said *identity*, and *intuition*, and much more besides; and then he took the two coapprentices by his sides, and leaving the bald and blind pilgrims in the aul, they went off to the nearest capital city.

What a wonder! Everything that happened there was even more amazing to the simplehearted, mighty Kuyuk than Qimbat-guppi had told him. In the evening, men and women gathered, downing bottle after bottle of vodka, and then Qimbat-guppi emerged right into the middle of the crowd, tearing apart his ceremonial robe hem to collar; and stripping bare naked, a pouty cap on his head, his belly round as a cauldron hanging down to his knees, he sat down cross-legged in the traditional manner.

Those men and women, one after another, crept and crawled, approaching the idol of Qimbat-guppi, weeping and crying, kissing now his arm, now his leg, now his navel, while Qimbat-guppi himself, like poking at a horse to test its strength, poked at them with his fist, in their ribs and rear ends.

Then Bo'riboy-marqa gestured to Kuyuk, and Kuyuk strummed his dombra, and sang these words:

Come, dear ladies, we'll defeat you,
Hero brothers wait to meet you,
You from one side, we from one side,
Open up and let us treat you!

After that, under the guidance of Bo'riboy-marqa, the circle all rent their garments from collar to hem, and every man threw himself at a woman, and every woman at a man. Bo'riboy-marqa, the only one still dressed among them, passed before our Kuyuk, who still held the dombra in his hand, and whose tongue was frozen in his mouth. He pulled the dombra from his hand and brought him away to another, private room. In that room, through a hole in the door, a beautiful, naked young lady stood peeping at those delights and amusements.

"She is one of us, still a little green," whispered Bo'riboy into Kuyuk's ear. "Fry her up something good!"

Then he turned to the young lady. "You, Goia! This brave young man will fill your insides with an epic tale," he said.

And then, to Kuyuk, "Goia's husband is a big cheese, who neglects passion in favor of work. Now you, as a young soldier full of passion, have your own work to do!"

And with that, this enchanting woman, queen of cunning, that very instant, undid the laces of Kuyuk's long robe . . .

Long as it had been since he had seen a female specimen in the deserts and wastelands, his faded, rusted manhood suddenly rose up, and in a flash, the boy Kuyuk was climbing astride Goia. Goia was fairly parched herself, and like the desert, like virgin land, her thirst could never be satisfied, and her red, curly hair ran wild. *"Davai, davai!"* she urged him on in Russian, clamoring against him, claiming him.

The young Kuyuk, minding whom exactly he was lying on top of, remembered Bo'riboy's guidance and delivered the following into Goia's ear:

Virgin land must be plowed,
Women and girls, let me remind you.
We are the ones to dig deep inside you,
You from one side, we from one side,
Come ye alone, or come ye in two . . .

Just as they traveled to the small capital cities, they traveled with no extra hesitation to the big capital too. There, the delights and amusements took place in the magnificent manor houses and dachas of the heroic type of people, the kind who were often shown on the television and in the newspapers. This was not a dry place, and inside the gurgling, bubbling fountains men and women of different tribes—Russians and Latvians, Jews and Tatars—all joined together in all sorts of intercourse. It was here that Qimbat-guppi was lord of all he surveyed, and he walked around majestically. He made the desirable bend over double and the undesirable squat on their heels.

Meanwhile, Kuyuk-baxshi delivered another epic poem:

They went along their way,
Giving the horse to play,
as they laughed and joked
their words grow stale and gray.

So many mountains they pass,
And valleys green with grass,
five days of weary walking,
to reach old Moscow's ass.

As if he were the epic hero Gajdumbek striding arrogantly through the villages of his red-headed enemies, so the holy-looking lamb of God, Bo'riboy-marqa, walked here the same way, making all the silly academics and so on jump into his lap when he called or flitter away when he said so, and he pampered some and tampered with others, having his way with them all.

One evening there was another feast for the devils and demons, and Bo'riboy came before the boy Kuyuk again and took the dombra carefully from his hand, and as he plucked at it, he walked toward a private room in the back. This time in the private room he was met not just by the slightly bashful Goia, but also by a Turkmen-looking young man, just as naked, by her side. As before, they were pressed shamelessly to the hole in the door, watching the lovers coupling in pleasure outside. "You are a bard and he is a sculptor," said Bo'riboy, strumming the dombra. "Stone is his medium, and yours, words and ether. Now Goia will guide your crafting together." Leaving the two drunken beasts and one bird in this corral, he disappeared from sight.

As for what was done among them, if it were a word then it would be shrouded in shame, and if it were a stone it would have flowered in flame . . .

The young Kuyuk's body, exhausted from its labors, was now at ease, but his soul, which had previously flown free through the open desert, was in anguish. It was all well and good to hang around this far-flung country's several capitals like a lamppost, it was all well and good to caress the hair of beautiful girls and massage their lovely rumps, and wandering aimlessly was also good. But when he lost his voice performing epic poems for their brothel, when he lost his breath, how his neck ached! Now his master Yo'lli had disappeared from his dreams without a trace, and there were practically no people left to confess to or ask for advice.

If he tried to talk to Qimbat about it, the boor told him to eat and drink what they gave him and not be ungrateful. "Nobody made us responsible for the troubles of this land! Let those politburros and academidgets worry about it. Carry on with your epics, maybe something good will rub off on those hermaphrodites!" That's what he said, squinting with his narrow eyes, gesturing sharply with his hand.

The young Kuyuk passed the time plagued with worry. He thought about making an appeal to the refined Bo'riboy-marqa. But it turned out that Bo'riboy had much bigger things in mind. He wanted to take this red-haired race in hand and submit them to the Turkic tribes—the Yomuds and Teke, Kyrgyz and Kazakh, Qo'ngirat and Durman—and he wanted to bring those tribes together and lead them. "Just do as I told you! Make them drunk and submissive. They are a thorn bush in the desert, and you and I are the desert itself!" he pronounced, in a very learned manner. Now and then he let drop other words Yo'lli-baxshi had not known, words like *prophetic* and *precursor*, *lyricality* and *probability*. These great words turned our Kuyuk's head, and he made them simpler for himself, in his mind:

What Kuyuk sorely needs
is clarity of word and phrase,
And what Kuyuk sorely needs
is a beauty for his nights and days.

That is what he told himself, and from city to city, capital to capital, he continued on, wrapped up with them, hunting for disciples, hardening his soul.

❖

That autumn arrived in extreme beauty. The leaves on the maple and plane trees turned yellow, while those on the apricot and peach trees turned red, and the sky stayed blue. Leaf after leaf fell to cover the transparent waters, and they flowed on, silently. Yet the young Kuyuk felt that his affairs had gone astray, and he knew he had settled his heart on the undeserving, sullied maiden, Goia. Without her he didn't want to go to the capitals, and at any feasts where she did not peep through the hole, his dombra did not sing, and he could not string together the words and sounds of the song in his throat.

In love, and my clear mind's filled with grief, what to do?
One word, and my friends are now strangers, what to do?
I came calling her name, my heart seared in flame,
She fled, all the same, what to do?

On one of these days, while they were roaming one of the smaller capitals hunting disciples, the boaster Bo'riboy-marqa came into our Kuyuk's hotel room as the sun set and told him, "Take up your dombra. You are being summoned to the garden of *you know who*. Give the master a good rhyme, show the lady a good time." He put Kuyuk-baxshi into a splendid black car and sent him off toward the forests and fields in the open country outside of town.

At the door flanked by security guards, as if she had been peeping through the hole, the sweet fruit of the young Kuyuk's heart, the lady Goia herself, came to meet him. They walked together down a sunset path of two rows of straight poplars. They left behind them the guards, with their filthy dogs. The lady Goia took his arm. The young man overflowed with desire. He was just about to meet her face to face, breast to breast, when behind them a child's voice clamored out. "Mama! Mama!" came the shout.

The young Kuyuk turned. Of all the damned things, a boy, a pencil in one hand, some paper in the other, dove in between them. Out of surprise or revenge, the bottom of his dombra struck the boy in the face. The pencil broke and fell to the ground. His mother bent over the pencil. The child cried for help. Kuyuk slapped the little face. "A wasp was stinging him!" he said. And truly, there was a bright red berry swelling up on the child's face.

And then there came the demand, "What is *this*?" And there appeared before them, in boundless rage, the hero of the land himself, his every hair bristling erect, rough and on edge.

That evening, our Kuyuk merely recited an epic poem, and nothing else happened at all. In the middle of the night, he was shown to a splendid black automobile, and one of the guards conducted him back to his hotel. In the back of the black automobile, black dustclouds of grief assailed him.

The rose blossomed, bloom after bloom
My patience expired soon as it bloomed.
My tears flowed, and then, that soon,
My tolerance was gone, woman, have pity,
My patience was done, woman, have pity.

In the morning they left to make the thousand-*chaqirim* return journey to the winter village, and young Kuyuk's love felt a thousand times heavier. Like a discarded horse, beloved yesterday, butchered today, he had been shattered into little pieces. He spent the winter in torment, as if with a toothache that never ceased. The desert snow froze his heart, and the blizzards and snowstorms reminded the young man of Kuyuk, the unneeded one, and that winter, the loveless Kuyuk suffered and tormented himself, wondering which was harder: his head, or a stone. Qimbat also kept to himself, and on the desert roads the snow fell and the ice crept through, which meant no bald and blind pilgrims came, and they hid from the cold and loneliness, warming themselves with the vodka and ale that was left; they slept like logs and snored like dogs, and other than sleep, they knew nothing.

Just as the spring came with its promise of green foods again, Bo'riboy-marqa arrived, too, returning from the big cities, and he told the two of them, "Get up! You lie here stinking away in the aul, and spring has come! It's time for sausage, time for stuffed tripe!"

And again they returned to the capital cities. They went to the Lats and went to the Litvaks, they gave the Estonians royal banquets in Estonia, and just as if God was saying "Take it, my slave!" Kuyuk-baxshi fed them the tales of the Loving Stranger and all his mishaps, and as he finished his epic poems, and his hands were touching food, the refined Bo'riboy-marqa arrived, just as he had before; he took up the dombra, stuck it under his arm, and led him to a special room. "The sculptor O'rhon was in there," Kuyuk told himself in surprise, startled, his heart thumping faster than his steps, in a rush.

The door to the private room opened, and the lady Goia, who stood pressed to the hole in the door, straightened up her body, and her face brightened. The grief Kuyuk had gathered to himself all winter long, all the pain of separation, shattered and fell apart next to this goddess who stood watching, and the surprise of their coming together swept up all the pieces like a whirlwind and struck Kuyuk's head, stunning him, leaving him speechless, but . . .

"Here, a genuine baxshi, considered a master." Bo'riboy presented him to a tall black-bearded man standing in the shadow of her beauty. "Just as you asked."

This man was an actor or maybe a writer, brought here by the lady Goia. In confusion, as if in a dream, the young Kuyuk's topsy-turvy thoughts never did understand who he was. "I'm writing a book," he said. "I'm acting in a movie," he said, and these were empty words.

Kuyuk took no liking to this well-dressed man, who was distracting him from his goddess. Meanwhile, the lady Goia handed over this booby to Bo'riboy-marqa. "I've disappeared from a reception! My car's waiting outside," she told them, and she kissed Bo'riboy loudly under his mustache, and without even a look at the young Kuyuk, she shut the door behind her. The young Kuyuk was sad and confused. He leaned out the window and looked down. That face, lovely as the moon itself, got into a black car, and the black car sunk away into the darkness of the street and his heart, like the moon sinking behind the clouds.

> I was burning for your beauty, your face so round,
> My heart bows not to Mecca, to you it is bound,
> And bends to the tracks you left on the ground.
> Now what am I to do, when you've left me behind you?

As for the bearded man, showing off his talents incessantly to Bo'riboy-marqa, his words were gold, his deeds were good. "I've spurned some, learned some, burned some, and turned some, but when it came to the wife of the lord of the manor, I fell asleep at the most critical moment . . ." Qimbat and Bo'riboy, and their two Latvian servants, gathered there together, all howled with laughter. Still hindered by his worries, the young Kuyuk just shuddered, while his ears perked up and his nose wrinkled. He thought about leaping on that bearded man and strangling him to death, but then it occurred to him that the Beard had not actually touched his beloved, had he? Maybe, on the contrary, he ought to lean closer in and have a good talk with him? I'm a writer, he had said, hadn't he? Maybe Kuyuk should show him his own path, tell about his troubles, and write his own thrown-out heart out?

The bearded man's beardedness turned out to be deceptive. "I'm acting in a movie," he'd have you believe. "Want to know what role I'm playing? A folk singer, a baxshi." And who did the faithless woman recommend to him as a model but Qimbat-guppi. Like a rider knows horses, so too could

Bo'riboy-marqa distinguish a true baxshi from a fake. Therefore it was Kuyuk he took by the arm to draw forward.

But the boaster Qimbat-guppi grew a little stouter and said, "I was the one who reeled in this boy!" And he began to say things about baxshis that were vast and amazing. So indifferent was the young Kuyuk that even water wouldn't stick to him. He just stood there silently.

"I myself," said Qimbat, puffing out his chest, "have my insides a-tremble, my heart a-rumble, my eyes shining, my mouth wide open, and as I was a disciple to my master Yo'lli, then you too will prostrate yourself before me! The first condition is to rein in your lust! Even if your master touches your wife, you submit—it is just! The second condition is to overcome yourself! Even if your master pulls your heart out, let him put it on a shelf! And last, you must give thanks for what you have, you see? Now I am your master—you bow down before me!"

That is how polished Qimbat-guppi's words were. The young Kuyuk was truly surprised. Had Yo'lli-baxshi drooled some words into the mouth of Qimbat, secrets that he had never told Kuyuk? The bearded man nearly fainted, and the saliva drooled from his mouth as he flopped down in a bow before Qimbat. At that Bo'riboy-marqa, all friendliness, slyly whispered something into Qimbat-guppi's ear, and the young Kuyuk comprehended where these words of his had their roots.

Your sly friend dreamed up lots of tricks
And he always tossed shame in the mix:
After this they'll be ours, he'll remind you—
he needs no strings to bind you.

"My disciple will teach you the rest," said Qimbat-guppi, taking Bo'riboy-marqa's arm and returning to their festivities, while the bearded man confusedly knelt down and kissed Kuyuk's hand. Kuyuk's embarrassment doubled in depth. First he had learned abruptly that he was an apprentice of Qimbat-guppi, then on top of that, he had been transformed just as suddenly into this counterfeit beard's master.

"I'm going to play you!" the fake beard declared. Kuyuk lost his mind. Who was he? And whoever he was, to have this swine try to imitate him now . . . What was his role? A lover full of sins? Or if there was no sin, or if you wanted to put it simply, would it just be perfect love itself? Would he act out everything he had lost? Yo'lli the master had cut his heart into slices and thrust something deep inside him, and now had the wild grass covered this abandoned heart?

"Help!" shouted the young Kuyuk, out of the blue. "Help!" he shouted, "don't touch me!"

◆

There was a reason for his shouting. The summer passed, the autumn passed. When winter came, the young Kuyuk's elderly mother died. Kuyuk arrived from one of the capital cities back to his aul not in time for his mother's funeral or burial, but just in time to mourn her. His eyes darkened, and weighed down by misfortune, Kuyuk's grief hit him anew. "I did not lay earth on my esteemed teacher, I did not wrap my poor mother in her shroud. What kind of man have I been in this world?" he asked himself, weeping.

> Nor have I strayed, nor sinned,
> Nor have I now path, nor home,
> Nor have I any nest on this earth,
> O Mother dear, where have you gone?

In grief for his mother, the young Kuyuk grew a real beard, and when his beard reached a certain length, he froze from the desert cold, he used up his grief, and he prepared to return to the capital city.

In one of the smaller capitals, when he arrived back at the boaster Qimbat-guppi's apartment, there, all covered in sweat, sat only the sculptor O'rhon, his head in his hands. His strength was completely drained, and the saliva drooled out of his mouth, and this is what he said: "The sky has shattered above us, and the roof has fallen down to crush us. The roof has fallen!" Rumor had it that in another of the capital cities Bo'riboy-marqa and Qimbat-guppi, and all their bald and blind attendants, had beaten that false-bearded idiot and killed him. Here, the young Kuyuk's heart skipped a beat. He scratched at his beard, and as his beard itched, he wished it were not real and could be removed as easily as a lie.

Kuyuk-baxshi never saw such beauty again in all his life, and from that time on, he only ever heard about it from the sculptor O'rhon, the only source of memory from that time that remained with him.

We lay embracing sin and did not sleep, alas,
We did not caress all the beauties we found, alas,
We left not a sign in this mortal world, alas,
Such were the only regrets of a green young lad . . .

Water

Emer must have sensed something. She wrote to him—"I'm coming"—
then quickly stepped outside. Without a single plan ready. Does water look
around when it decides it's going to flow? Emer was like water too. Once
she was flowing, she couldn't be stopped. Just ask her long-suffering mother
Bryher. When they moved from Sarajevo to London, her mother neither
ate nor drank, but she hired a tutor for her daughter. Yet once the girl finished school, she resolved not to go to university. Her mother was vexed, but
patient. Emer remained unemployed for two years. Anytime she wanted
to, she came home to eat, drink, and sleep. When she didn't want to, off
she went! Where the food is coming from, who is paying for the electricity,
who is taking care of the rent—she didn't care. Emer was like a butterfly.

True, on Sundays she used to go with her mother to the Corpus
Christi Catholic church near Brixton Hill, sometimes to cry, sometimes
to laugh. But even that was a temporary thing. On one or two Sundays, she
pretended to be sick. On others, she said she was busy. Finally, she told the
truth. "I've gone over to an evangelical church," she said.

Emer's mother froze. "Everything we are comes from our religion,"
she told the girl.

"And all our troubles!" her daughter answered.

Bryher kicked her out of the house. For a week she remembered how
her husband had given his life for his convictions and held to her stance.
Ultimately she couldn't bear it anymore. Then she searched, and she
found her daughter in a homeless shelter. She prayed, begged, and wept.
With great difficulty, she convinced her to return home.

Bryher comforted herself with the thought that if Emer ever found a
young man who was more of an Irish nationalist, he would convince her

to come back to the church. But in a far remove from a good Irish lad, a short, powerfully built, narrow-eyed Filipino boy began coming round the house instead. When Bryher had just barely gotten used to his forty kilos of awkward Asian build and pigeon-like pronunciation, Emer latched onto a Jamaican dancer as tall as a basketball player. That young man apparently had no home, and they turned the house into something like a twenty-four-hour stage or club. Bryher heard the insinuating stories. First Emer was staying with her sister Boudicca, then in a cheap hotel, taking a break there from work and home. After one or two more adventures, her daughter seemed to have calmed down a bit, and just six months ago she seemed to have found someone more like her: a widely traveled, placeless Turk.

Bryher had come to understand one thing in her life. Unfortunately, she understood too late, so late there was no going back. She should never have moved her child from one place to another while she was still growing. It was like transplanting a sapling from the garden to the stones of the mountain. It would have neither the beauty of a garden-grown plant nor the hardiness of a plant grown on the mountain slopes. Just confusion.

But all that was from Bryher's point of view. If you were to ask Domrul, he would paint a completely different picture. But he was also worried about Emer's sudden arrival. He felt like the shore waiting for a tsunami to hit . . .

◈

Emer had sensed Domrul's bewilderment. First he brought up the doctor, then how busy he was. Finally, he told her he wanted to see that specialist she had mentioned. And when he said, "If you come, maybe we'll see each other in London!" Emer thought she could hear the fright in his voice. Was he embarrassed by what had happened in Paris, or rather by what had not happened there? What was he running from? Should she give him a little time? Didn't time heal all things? Was Emer too much in a rush? Why was she asking these questions now that she was already here?

While she was getting on the train at St. Pancras, Domrul called again. "I'm on my way to London," he said. "Maybe we can meet at your place?"

"I haven't told my mother I'm coming," Emer answered. "I also haven't brought any presents."

"I'll bring one," he said. "I have one more bottle of Saint-Émilion left."
They agreed.

Emer was irritated. She did not let it show. She kept it inside. If she
brought her mother into their relationship, the bickering would start again.
In fact, she had gone to Paris fleeing just that. And Domrul was well aware
of it! So why did he need her to come and meet him at her mother's house
now? Emer placed a call to a girlfriend in Streatham. She was at home.
Where else would she be, nursing an eight-month-old baby? "We want to
come and see you," she said. Her friend agreed readily. Emer called Domrul back. He didn't answer. She dialed Domrul's number over and over
again. No answer. She sent him a text. As she got off the train, she kept
looking at her phone again and again. He didn't answer her text either.
She was perplexed. His phone must have died. That would mean he was
already on the way to her mother's place. Or hadn't he read it? Maybe he
was in a tunnel or something? She went into a Starbucks and had a coffee.
She waited for an answer. It never came. For half an hour, she sat watching people walk by. Then, reluctantly, she set off toward Brixton and her
mother's house.

◆

There is still one thing we have not told you about Emer. That is the fact
that lately she had turned into a proselytizer, or what she would call, in her
words, a *missionary*. There were five or six people in their evangelical group
in Paris who used to ride out to the remote metro stations, going into each
train car and sitting down as if they were just ordinary passengers, and
then one of them, usually Emer, a Bible in her hand, would start to preach
to all the people around her, and then all of a sudden start singing some
of the better-known hymns to Jesus Christ. At the sound of her melodious
voice, her partners, seated all around the car, would join in, and sing out
loud praise of Jesus in front of all the unwitting passengers. Then Emer
would walk the length of the car, handing out leaflets with these hymns to
the passengers, and when a new song started, it would never be the whole
car, but usually just three or four people—mostly new immigrants—who
would sing along with them. Then Emer's partners would walk around
the car, too, and pass out information about their evangelical churches in
Paris, and then move on to the next car.

Now, as she rode from King's Cross to the Brixton stop, Emer could barely keep herself from singing to and rousing up these busy Londoners. She laughed to herself. It was still almost half a month till Christmas, and if she were to sing a hymn now, the sarcastic people of London would wonder if she wasn't just celebrating too early. She must be Irish, they'd say!

That is what she was thinking as she exited the tube station and rushed for the bus at the far end of the line. Emer climbed onto the bus and went to show her ticket, but the ticket she had just used for the tube wasn't there. She dug through the pockets of her backpack, while the people waiting to get on the bus started to lose patience. She moved farther into the bus, examining more pockets. Nothing! Had someone stolen it? Or had she just dropped it? What if she went back to look? The bus inched forward. The driver, seeing her confusion, waved a hand at her. Still holding her backpack, Emer moved deeper into the bus. Suddenly her strength was gone, and her mood was ruined. Why on earth had she come here?

In that foul mood, she was nearing her mother's house. Should she go in or wait for Domrul? She felt hesitant. It was November weather in London. The rain poured down, but it wasn't rain, just the damp continuously puffing out its pollen. It was invisible to the eye, but it covered your face. She hadn't even told her mother she was coming. Lately her mother had been calling her more, and Emer had never asked why. Get a mobile! she had insisted so many times, but maybe because her mother remembered the old conspiracies, she never agreed to do it. Should I call the house or just go in empty-handed? And tell her Domrul was just about to turn up with something nice? That infuriating constant drizzle forced her hand. She pushed the doorbell. She heard no ringing. That was also a remnant of her mother's conspiracy days. She pulled the lid of the mail slot in the door out toward her, then let it bang shut. She heard footsteps. Dragging footsteps. The lock clicked and the door cracked open, chained from the inside. A fragment of her mother's yellowed face appeared.

"It's me," Emer said. Her mother was not even surprised. She opened the door and walked inside still dragging her feet. Just as if she had been waiting for her daughter to come home from school. This ordinary air hurt Emer's pride. As she followed her mother inside, she tossed her backpack down in the corner and said, "Sorry, didn't bring you anything," by means of clearing the air. Her mother offered no response to that either.

They went into the living room. "Are you hungry?" she asked, and not waiting for an answer, passed through to the kitchen.

Emer, not knowing what to do, stood still in the middle of the room. Then, in a slightly angry voice, she shouted toward the kitchen, "I don't need your food! I had a sandwich on the train." Her mother returned to the living room, her hands empty. "Don't you have anything else to say?" asked Emer, really vexed. Her mother let out a sigh, but said nothing. She went to wipe her wet hands on her skirt. "Can't you look after yourself any better? Look at that apron! It's filthy!" Emer tried to change the subject. Her mother shook her head and pushed a button on the radio in the corner. The same old sound of comfortable old Classic FM.

"I'm talking to you, you know!" Emer warned her, impatiently, "Not to the walls and the ceiling. Have you ever listened to me, even once in your life?" The girl was screaming now. "Who am I to you? Who *am* I?"

◆

Domrul both rang the doorbell and banged the lid on the mail slot. There was a clamor coming from inside, but nobody came to open the door. Then he opened the flap over the mail slot again and shouted "Emer!" once or twice through the opening. Inside, the clamor died down at once. Taking advantage of the silence, he called out once more. "Emer!" The door opened, and when Domrul stepped inside, he could only see Emer's back. Emer was already walking into another room. Domrul stood in the entryway at a loss and heard Emer's voice bellowing from the living room.

"I know exactly what you did behind my back! All of it! So there's no point in you showing me any kindness!" Domrul's flesh trembled and his blood froze. So she knew everything! There was a moment of quiet. Domrul was still standing stiff in the entryway, his arms and legs feeling paralyzed. Again, Emer's shouting broke the silence. "Why don't you say something? Are you listening to me? How many years did I cover it all up? Now I've had enough!"

Domrul's throat felt parched, and he swallowed.

Then he heard Bryher's voice. "You've got the wrong genes! Bloody genes! All you care about is appearances, nothing else." So she had told her mother everything, too! What was Domrul doing here, then? Shouldn't he turn and run away before any more misfortune fell down on his head?

"Nothing but trouble! Everything you have done is trouble, everything you have done is a threat! What did I ever do to you to make you abuse me this way?"

"You? I'm abusing *you?*"

Here Domrul, stiff as kindling, suddenly realized there was a quarrel going on between the two women. It was as if a boulder had been lifted off his shoulders, but only for an instant, because the next instant Bryher's dejected voice rose even higher above Emer's: "Stop it. Don't come here again, and don't call me either. Enough! One day you'll have a child too, and this will all come back on you! Then you'll understand!"

"Aha! So now you're using my unborn children against me, are you? I hate you!" said Emer, and turned furiously toward the doorway. She grabbed her backpack from the corner and told Domrul, "We've leaving. Move!" And she opened the door. Domrul hesitated for a moment. Not knowing what to do with the Saint-Émilion in his hand, he put it down among the shoes in the entryway and passed through the door after Emer.

"My job is to be a social carer, but Emer is a missionary who goes about and tells people to be good! Saying if someone slaps you on one cheek, offer them the other cheek! But in day to day life, what impact does your work have, and what is the effect of your convictions?" Domrul wondered to himself. Taking advantage of the crowds in the tube, he moved off a bit from the overwhelmed Emer, wrapped up in what had happened at her house. Their eyes did not meet, and they barely exchanged two words. Emer was leading him. Apparently to Eastbourne. To Domrul's place. There was nowhere else to go. Remembering Eastbourne, Domrul's heart skipped a beat.

At the Vauxhall Station, everyone got out of their car at once. Emer moved closer to Domrul. "She must be sick. Something incurable," she said.

"Who?" asked Domrul anxiously, thinking that very instant of his old woman.

"My mother," answered Emer, as if exonerating herself. "But she'd never tell me," she added, and sank into her own thoughts again. If there was any bitter irony or commiseration in those words, Domrul did not notice them.

Emer was still tormenting herself. Why wasn't it different? If you started a conversation with that phrase, it was as if it wasn't you, but the conversation itself that was trapping you. You are left not knowing yourself what kind of path you have taken. Well, fine, her mother had not said hello, and she had looked so uninterested. And Emer had just come over uninvited, and empty-handed too. Was that any reason to rub her face in it? Domrul had said he'd bring something, but had he?

"You were going to bring some Saint-Émilion," she said in Domrul's direction.

"Yes, I left it there," he said in a timid way.

"Where?"

"Where the shoes were lined up."

"Where's that?"

"At your place."

Emer said nothing.

"So the gift was delivered after all! Well then, what went wrong?" Ever since their quarrel, Emer had been looking, perplexed, for a way to untangle this ball of yarn, but no matter how hard she looked, she could not find one actual reason or excuse for things with her mother to have gotten so out of hand. Where had that feud come from? Her thoughts were even more confused, and from that her resolve went awry, and at Victoria Station she followed Domrul to exit the choking train car.

◈

All night long, Emer cried. "Should I kill myself and get it over with?" she said. Domrul tried to comfort her. He took her outside a couple of times and walked along the sea. Made calmer by the constant din of the wind and waves, Emer would return to the apartment, and then she would remember her mother again and pick apart some aspect of that conversation one more time, now blaming her mother, now reproaching herself. Again she cried, again he comforted her. They never did lie down to sleep. And Domrul was never put to the test. Secretly pleased with that, his heart ran up against other troubles. Now Emer was in Eastbourne. It seemed she was in no rush to go back, either to London or to Paris. Soon as her attention lifted from her mother, she would naturally start asking about Domrul's old woman. Don't make me sit here useless, she would say. Let me help you, she would say. Then what would Domrul do? Could he call in sick to work again? In fact he was already practically a cripple and not going to work. When he came back from Paris he didn't go in, and today he used London for an excuse to stay away. The bosses had started to look at him more closely. What should he do?

The sun was just coming up when Emer, wiping the tears out of her swollen eyes, stood up and said, "Come on, let's walk to Beachy Head." Domrul wanted to make some excuse about work, but he had already told them he would be in late today. So he agreed. The rain, which had fallen on and off again all night long, had disappeared with the dawn. The sky was immaculate and the sun, like a swaddled infant, was just peeking, spic and span, over the edge of the sea.

After a sleepless night, there is a special pleasure in meeting the dawn. Even the wind seemed gentler, and the sea calmer, and the city cleaner. For some reason, though, it makes a person hunch down a little quicker too. Domrul had his arm over his girlfriend's shoulders, and they walked together along the empty path toward the hills that lined the deserted shore. At the top, beyond the rows of tamarisks, the smooth noise of the occasional car could still be heard, and other times there was the wind, the sea, the rustling of the bushes, and their own steps, rolling on and on.

In about half an hour they reached the hills. They thought that the paths through the hills would be deserted as well, but no. Somebody already had passed pulling three hound dogs, all panting, and someone had stuck tiny headphones into his ears, putting out a tempo for rock or jazz, and started jogging. But there weren't too many of them. Today there were just one or two people here, rare specimens.

Within another half hour they had gone through three passes and come out where the cliff rose over the lighthouse. Domrul knew this place was called Suicide Point. He said so, then bit his tongue. What had he said that for? What an idiot!

"Right here?" asked Emer, her flashing eyes stabbing into Domrul.

"No, I was just saying . . ." Domrul said, trying to escape. "Come on, if we go over another two hills, there's a village pub, and by the time we get there it'll be open and we can have some coffee." Emer was listening, but seemed not to have heard a thing. Her eyes were sparkling, moving in a sort of excitement, as if she were just about to take a few steps and fling herself toward the cliff.

Domrul took a step toward the cliff himself in alarm, took hold of Emer's arm, and repeated, again, the words he had just said. This time Emer seemed to pay attention, but as they were moving away from Suicide Point, she turned her head back, not one time, but several, sighing, and looked and looked at the edge of the cliff towering over the lighthouse.

It was just past eight o'clock when they reached the village of Belle Tout, on the seventh or eighth hill, and walked into a pub next door to the local lighthouse. In they went hoping for some coffee or tea, and what a surprise—Domrul saw that in possession of a table in the middle of the room there sat two elderly women. The first was Antonina Ivanovna, and the second was Gaia Mangitkhanovna. The next instant, as if remembering something, Domrul looked as if he were about to turn around, but it was too late. The excited Antonina Ivanovna was already calling them over with a shout and a wave of her hand. Emer looked alarmed that maybe something was wrong with that elderly woman, and she was the first to draw near to their table. Behind her crept Domrul, unenthusiastically.

"Domrul! Domrul!" Antonina Ivanovna was shouting in her usual state of agitation, as if she were seeing the young man for the first time in a hundred years. Emer turned to him. The look of alarm had not yet left her face, but now this look was transferred to Domrul.

Domrul moved forward, thinking that what would be, would be, and in a resolute voice, he declared in Russian, "Hello! This is my girlfriend, Emer." Antonina Ivanovna's agitation turned to excitement and pleasure, but Gaia Mangitkhanovna's hard gaze passed judgment, weighing Emer's small frame from head to toe, and she said nothing, but lifted a tiny espresso cup to her lips, now drawn thin.

Antonina Ivanovna stood up from her seat and started fussing about how she would go and bring another chair. Domrul picked up two chairs from the next table and dragged them over to their table himself. They sat. Domrul asked Emer what she wanted to drink, and he left them to themselves, hurrying to the bar. When he returned, carrying one cappuccino and one double espresso, Antonina Ivanovna, still excited, was using one hand to point out Gaia Mangitkhanovna to Emer, and the other to gesture toward Domrul, telling her, in her broken English, "He . . . him . . . woman . . ." mumbling about something or other. Under his cap, Domrul's thinning scalp was sweating. He took the cap off his head and rubbed at his hair. What was that crazy Russian woman saying? Out of nowhere, Domrul thought of Dostoyevsky. Anywhere there were Russians, there were scandals and shame, wasn't that so? His heart felt as if it had been shattered at the bottom of the cliff at Suicide Point. And his body, just an empty sack now, would soon topple over onto the table.

◆

No, maybe there weren't enough Russians, because no scandals or shame occurred just then. Not even one secret was exposed.

Emer had one impressive quality that Domrul adored. If, say, they went together to a dance club and were caught sitting squeezed into a corner amid the dancers, Emer would start giving a long, detailed description of everyone caught up in the dance. "Look at that poor plump girl. Take a look, sometimes she's got her arms hugging herself, and sometimes she holds them in front of her like a pitchfork. Poor thing wouldn't give it up to anyone but herself." Domrul would cackle with laughter at such a sharp assessment, while Emer would already be sizing up someone else. "That one must be the town flirt. Not even looking at her young man. Just dancing with herself. And look at her eyes, they're hunting! Her fellow's getting left dry tonight!" Her gift was being able to use a person's motions and movements to uncover their hidden thoughts and feelings.

"Your old woman," said she, once the two old folks caught a taxi back to town, "never relaxed her jaw. She pouted as she looked at you. She was jealous of you. Made it clear as day she had no time for me. Really, what was she talking about?"

"When?" asked Domrul, rubbing his eyes as if from the wind.

"Well, you didn't translate anything apart from the fact that she was happy to meet me."

"I think that's just what she was saying."

"Is Russian really that wishy-washy?" asked Emer wryly. "She talked for at least three minutes without stopping. I'm so happy that my face twitches, my eyes are sparkling, I can't fit my own happiness inside me, you know, my arms are just trembling with joy . . ."

"Stop it!" Domrul interrupted her. How could he possibly have translated the old witch's cold mutterings?

"Just look at this birdie you've chosen for yourself! She's a whore, not even a birdie! Just look, her head is like a gearbox! Is it so difficult to find someone better? Look, the street is full of girls. If you walk into any café or canteen you can find a good solid Polish girl. Look how she's sitting, she'll have her legs apart and her crotch wide open like a cow waiting for a bull! Does this girl even have parents? Or is she a leech raised in an orphanage? Uneducated and uncivilized! Look at how she stares! You dump that whore! She'll never be the one for you!" By the time she had finished up the blackness of her words, the old lady was using the disrespectful "you" again.

"No," said Domrul, rubbing his eyes again as if tired and faking a stretch. "You know, it's from their Stalinist culture; they pronounce even nice words with lots of venom."

"And her girlfriend, sitting next to her, was hiding her eyes all the time to escape those nice words, is that it?" Emer concluded.

Domrul, without a word, sank down into the hill's autumn grass.

They say that every disaster contains a blessing, and it's true. Emer never did insist on joining Domrul to help him with his work. As they rode the bus home, she told him, "I'm handing you over to your old woman!" and she crashed into bed and fell into the sleep she had been owed since the previous evening.

Domrul, for his part, changed his clothes and headed out to work. As they had agreed, he pressed the bell, once short, twice long, and one more time short. As he waited for the door to open, he realized for the first time how the signal fit the sound of Gaia-MANGIT-KHANOV-na. He smiled to himself. The door did not open. Again he pressed the doorbell, one short, two long, and another short. He looked at his watch. He was a little late. But his client had just seen him that morning.

Finally, there was a weary voice. "Come in." And then he heard, "Please come in," a little politer. "Both the doors are open," the voice added.

The door inside was in fact open. Domrul entered, shut the door, took off his coat, changed into his house slippers, and walked toward the living room. Gaia Mangitkhanovna was there, on the couch where Domrul had recently lain, covered in a thick quilt. She looked at the hesitant young man out of the corner of her eye. "Don't be afraid. My health has taken a small turn for the worse," she said, gesturing to a stool. Domrul came and sat down beside her.

An interesting sensation suddenly descended over him. He had gotten used to the old woman. He realized he had nothing left to hide from her. He suddenly felt an unfamiliar warmth. Gaia Mangitkhanovna seemed to sense it too. "I was a little hot-tempered this morning, but I only told you the truth," she said. Then she looked at the ceiling for a moment, and in a somehow colorless voice, she said, "My own daughter was brazen like that too." This was the first time Domrul had ever heard mention of Gaia Mangitkhanovna's children from the woman herself. He remembered what Kuyuk-baxshi had said, but he still wasn't sure whether those words had been about his begum.

"I have a favor to ask of you this morning," Gaia Mangitkhanovna appealed to him in a tired voice. "There are a few pages on the table. Read them to me." Domrul picked up a yellowing bundle of paper from the table. A document in Russian, typed on an old typewriter. Written at an angle in one corner were the words, "To the lovely Gaia, from a passionate dervish." The writing seemed familiar to Domrul's eyes. He looked at the title. *The Dervish and the Mermaid.* He placed himself comfortably in the chair. Then he lifted his voice and began to read.

◈

The Dervish and the Mermaid

A dervish weary of walking in circles over the hot sands of the desert used to bring his vagrant body to the first hardy *Haloxylon* shrub or moist tamarisk that invited him into its slim and fragile shade, and from inside that shelter he used to shut his bright red eyes, and then the heat of his body, beating like the taut skin of a kettledrum, would cool from a sheer lack of strength, and also as the only possible response to the weak wind wafting in from under the distant wing of a late-morning, wandering wasp.

Then he would try to nudge himself gently along behind that lady wayfarer of a wasp, and only the first step into the air felt like falling; the empty place under his heart used to shift soundlessly, or more precisely it would slacken, loosen like a saddlebag with its ties undone, pouring out sand onto the desert—but he would need to keep his balance, navigate the elastic currents of air at his belly and between the soles of his feet, he would need to then either cross his legs under him to coax out of the surface currents and spirals a stubborn, sparse coolness, or straighten out to his full length, his flexible feet paddling toward the small, far-off point where that temptress the wasp, in free flight, as if born on the fine whiskers of the force of gravity, had already disappeared . . .

One day, as he pitched through the flexible strands of the afternoon air, sensing the rhythms the air made as it struck his feet, the dervish heard not the warm, familiar whistling of a butterfly's pollinated wings flapping as it frolicked in the springtime, but rather a long, throaty scream let out into the air in a rhythm just suited to his abrupt, high leaps. His whole being yearned to turn in that direction, and his body, obedient, worked to follow it. The sound was swelling louder, and at first the thing took the form of a swan; but it was a seagull, like a rainbow arching through the pure air, its calls penetrating like a lance through the secluded places. The wildness of that loneliness startled him and drew him closer in. In his lifetime, the dervish had never seen a bird as free as he was himself, and just like the dervish, the bird was soaring free on the long, narrow strands of air, and at that the dervish, enchanted, also wanted to float through the springtime heavens, but he lost count of the strata of air underneath him as he hesitated over the bottomless blue depths. And he saw that under him was not the blue of the sky, but of the ocean.

The dervish suddenly knew that to be true, once the bird perched on the sandy shore; and the dervish was amazed to see that the desert, in its vastness, housed another, unexpected element: here the waters of the sea gathered in heaps, just like the waves of the sand. He walked behind the bird along the sandy shore, and he read the inscriptions printed by the gull's narrow feet in the moist sand and gazed upon the designs in the pearly shells and beheld the calligraphy of the seaweed. Now the soles of his feet, accustomed to the weightlessness of the air, felt burdened by the water seeping up from under the heavy, dense sand. The waves rumbled in the distance.

Just before the sun set, the sand brought him to an inlet. There, fig and persimmon trees were growing. Tall, stately cypresses stood guarding them, and to let his face catch the friendly, wayward sun, the dervish sat down beneath a fig tree. But the sun slid across his joyful face, then chose its own habitual refuge, though it was true that it became entangled in the tattered rags of the clouds that had long ago gone limp; but just then, its evil twin the moon started out on just the same journey, and as it crested the peak of its path, brushing right past the very tallest cypress, the dervish heard a folk song emanating from inside the frothy waves of the sea. Alert as ever, he turned toward that sound, which was a voice like a bell around the neck of a lost goat wandering the desert, but the voice disappeared, leaving behind only fragile, heart-shaking threads. Yet the air seemed too thin to set them jangling.

The sweet ache of that missing voice lasted for a short while, and then the sound of that song, like a fine jewel, began again. The full moon was reflected twice over, in the sky and on the water, and there, up to her waist in water, stood an astonishingly beautiful maiden combing her hair, while the waves moved as if to pull that wide-spreading hair out to sea. A black cat walked, humming, in circles. Small golden fish, startled by the black cat's shadow, scattered in commotion and confusion along the black face of the water. The dervish was spellbound, and as he leaned back against the fig tree, he wished this miracle could go on forever, just like the black sea, emerging from the pitch-black sky and returning to it.

The dervish cast his gaze one step toward the water, and the little golden fish swam across his moist eyes, and they set his ears ringing; and then a clamoring began as of dozens of ringing bells, and then, with a splash of—oh, Allah, long, fishy tails!—forty mermaid sisters materialized on the surface of the waves, and they moved in an ancient circle dance around the one, lone mermaid, who sent her gentle waves in their direction.

On this two-mooned night (and this night was their Night of Destiny), when the mermaids enraptured men to come to their side and captured their souls, either transforming themselves into women or remaining fish in the sea, sly and slippery as ever—on this double-mooned and destiny-filled night, the mermaids took into their arms the dervish dozing under the fig tree, thanks to the sharp smell of the steppe which radiated off him and clashed strangely with the salty scent of the ocean. The mermaids brought him before their queen.

"Who are you, and what do you seek?" she asked, her hair rippling like the waves themselves around her. The dervish did not know what to say. After all, as he had always followed the fate written on his brow by God and traveled the paths suitable to the currents of the world, he had never known, before now, what a question was. Even now his heart, free of doubts, like a shawl with no knots, had led him to this place, and he was following his heart along the currents of his path. And then, how to make sense of the past impetus that had led him here? How to unravel the push to the future that lay hidden before him in the mermaid's question? What was passed had passed, the future was unknown, or more precisely, if someone knew it, it was not him; and for that reason, the dervish chose to remain mute. In that moment of silence, his eyes took in the mermaid's free-flowing hair, her cold arms and neck, her two breasts round as bubbles, dripping with water, her navel, deep as a passage back to ancient times—or in a word, he beheld things that could occupy and fill the silence that reigned as he stood mystified at how to emerge out of that last question.

But this evening, the dervish did not choose her. This night was indeed the mermaids' Night of Destiny, and on the ground and over the water of that two-mooned night, the mermaids drew in and intoxicated two-legged men, and hoped to perhaps, in melding with them, bring forth some muscular roe of their hips and peel the scales away from their skin or, on the contrary, transform again into hideous, bug-eyed fish, slipping off to the black muteness of the bottom of the sea. The dervish looked to another.

He chose one who was sitting and burying herself in the sand to be his own confidant and companion for this night of love and fornication.

She was unmoved by this night, and she looked upon these lovelorn mermaids not so much as competitors, but as sisters. Their conversation started at a very far-off point, and neither of them intended to be the first to show their interest. And this conversation, surrounded by the single mermaids swimming in an envious circle around them, was wondrous. First the genteel politesse of this mermaid provoked the dervish's anger. It never violated the boundaries of the innocent patterns she had learned, though the dervish was trying to cleave through these slippery bubbles; the very attempt revealed more about him than about her, and the mermaid remained firmly within the boundaries of her clever eloquence; she spoke word after word, and she described how she had not kept her very first human soul for herself, but rather presented it to her own infant, who now lived among human beings. As they conversed, the mermaid dined upon some seaweed, and the dervish, in the meantime, was preparing a new question. He knew where they were going, but every new question he attached to his hook could, at any minute, backfire on him; he could have drowned in the obliterating depths of that clever conversation. But that evening the dervish, not hiding his eyes, learned the price of love: a wandering man's legs. At that, he looked at his own sturdy limbs, relaxing under the water, and then he realized it was not he himself, but rather his legs, that were the part of his body that preserved the sense of the sand and air, the plants and the bottom of the sea, the rocks and the mud, and he knew then that walking and wayfaring were dearer to him than passion.

For another hour, without revealing their hidden intentions, they sat in conversation, and then, using the evening prayers as an excuse, he told the mermaid he would pray for her child, too, and he returned to his old fig tree.

He gave praise to Allah, but his runaway thoughts fled back to the mermaid. However much he strove to take shelter in the good and merciful bosom of the Almighty, it seemed the same amount of force was impelling his furious red eyes to return to the bosom of the mermaid and the scaly armor descending downward from it.

He wavered between God and the mermaid, and hastily, he finished up his prayer, which had now transformed into a curse; and suddenly he saw that the mermaid had come to join him under the fig tree, praying awkwardly for her son. The disgust already born in him from her artificial answers again infuriated the dervish, but in the moonshade under the fig tree, the scent of her body, so near, overcame that disgust. He touched the mermaid's body with his hand and caressed her smooth skin and asked, "So, you have come?"

"Yes, and what of it?" she answered him.

"Will you stay with me?"

Now he was asking the questions, now he was the one who found himself constrained by doubt, and for that reason, the mermaid seemed to understand his questioning mood; and what was to happen next, between them, in the sea and there under the nighttime shelter of the fig leaves, took on a completely different aspect, because as he was buried in doubt, the mermaid doubted, too, and that must have been why she cautiously touched the dervish's legs and asked, "Do you mean it?"

It was not the dervish's heart but his legs, so accustomed to their own dimensions, that unexpectedly ached at the crossing of this boundary, and with the caution of a clerk drawing up the accounts, he asked, "What if, instead of my legs, I give you my two arms?"

"No. That is unacceptable."

"Both my arms and an eye?"

"No, only the legs."

"Both eyes."

"Only the legs!"

"All right, just this one leg, for half the love . . ."

Such a laughable, meaningless offer. Swatting that very leg with her strong tail, the mermaid moved swiftly to the sea, and there her sisters were busy loving each other, the choppy surface of the black water glowing with their golden scales.

The dervish was at ease with his own shame. The shame was now irrevocably mixed up in the pit of doubt. Now he returned one more time to pray again to the Loving Spirit who, in his everlasting exile, had always been free of shame; and the dervish paused, for ten cool minutes, behind a sand dune, and then at once, as he emerged, he walked back to the sea.

All around him the mermaids were swimming, some alone, some in pairs, and others already in the form of ugly fish, before their return to the uninhabited depths. He was looking, among them, for the beloved witness to his own wavering disgrace.

The full moon sank down beneath the horizon of the sea, and the night seemed to be entering a night of its own. Or perhaps it was the morning twilight by the time the mermaid appeared in her usual way, with shellfish and seaweed visible between her lips. He waved to her like an old friend, and the mermaid returned his greeting with a smile. The dervish did not move to meet her, but instead approached their leader. She was still dispatching waves of vexation all around her, and she was charming, but in that charm there was some sort of barenaked shamelessness, as much as any body shamelessly stripped bare.

"And now what do you wish?" she asked. "For you to send her to join with me!" said the dervish boldly, and these empty words only proved his previous feelings. He spun about and strode away from the sea. Again he moved through a circle of shame, and all of them saw it and understood it, especially those eyes which thrust their gaze, like hooks on a line, into the dervish's back . . . The dervish could smell the meat hooked on the line he had cast, and he strode off over the drying sand toward the cypress standing guard in the distance.

As the dervish was praying in bewilderment, she came. The dervish met her with open arms, but she slipped from his hands and sat down on the sand. "Are you still unable to overcome your lust?" Could this be an unanswerable question? Because a confirmation would be too little, but a denial would very much resemble a confirmation. In response, he attempted a kiss in the mermaid's tangle of hair, and soon enough, everything the dervish had amassed, in all his years and all his travels, disappeared, and all of a sudden he said—"I love you." All the meaning of this phrase was evident in the stress he placed on each word. He started it all with his own self, of course, and the "you" was much quieter, just an afterthought, attached haphazardly to the verb, the love. Realizing that in an instant, he hurried to add the words the mermaid was waiting to hear.

"And I am prepared to give you both my legs. That is what you asked, I believe?" His hands held the mermaid's cold waist, then moved lower, sliding over her thighs, but when he moved to pull his hands in toward himself, he felt scales pushing back against his movements.

"Yes. But now I don't want to," said she, simply and unexpectedly.

"How is that?" asked the dervish, confused. "Why? How is that?"

"Because," said the mermaid, in a manner just as stupid and self-assured, as if taking refuge again in the clever eloquence of their prior conversations.

"What does that mean?" he asked, trying to penetrate through his own confusion, while at the same time pressing his lips to her belly.

The mermaid resisted neither the question nor the kiss, instead leaving him with his torment and yearning. "You know, I . . . I need to go. They are waiting for me . . ."

"Who? The purple seaweed and the shellfish?" He fired those bitter words sarcastically in the mermaid's direction.

"Maybe."

"Listen, sit a while with me anyway."

"No, I need to go," she answered, and she blew him a quick kiss good-bye, and with a flick of the tail she landed in the water, leaving just a breath of salty vapor and a grit of sand between the dervish's teeth. That was all that remained of her.

He sat for a long time under the fig tree, not understanding what had happened. His sore head was spinning, and he let his tousled hair hang down over his legs, which seemed to have had no use and no value for some time now in that predawn desert; what passed through the dervish's heart at that hour is something known only to himself and to Allah, and maybe to the mermaid, too, who had vanished at that hour when the black and white threads dividing the sea from the sky could not possibly be distinguished; but at that hour in the desert when the sun sinks its teeth into the plum of the sky, the dervish started to tear and claw at his own legs, until, whether from the pain passing out through him, or the shame of it, or out of love, he wailed out loud. It was this great wailing, from the very center of his heart, that finally jolted him awake.

The sun was setting over the sand, and the first early-evening serpent to emerge scrambled away from the dervish's feet and buried itself under a heap of sand at his side; as it darted away it shed its rattling silver scales, and the *Haloxylon* shrub, crooked and blind, shuddered as it passed.

◆

When the story was over, Gaia Mangitkhanovna opened her closed eyes, and she looked at the ceiling again. "That's all for today. You may go," she said, and sent Domrul away.

The tale had made quite an impression on Domrul. Something was stirring up a kind of rebellion in his heart and filling it with commotion. It was as if he had heard that story before, somewhere, but could never remember it, no matter how hard he tried. Struggling with those thoughts, Domrul arrived home and found that Emer was not there. Just a slip of paper on the table that read, "I've gone to the lighthouse."

Domrul's heart leapt in fright. The lighthouse! At the bottom of Suicide Point. Emer's mood was foul. If she tried something . . . He remembered how her eyes had looked, seeking something out at the precipice that morning. He grabbed for his phone. He called her. The phone beeped and went to voice mail. "Hello, this is Emer, please leave a message and I'll return your call as soon as possible . . ." And then another long beep. Domrul hung up. He went out in the same clothes he had just arrived home in. He walked to the bus stop and waited for the bus. The bus wasn't coming, so he spat in disgust, scrambled down to the road along the sea, and started to jog. Sleepy as he was, his head nodded a little, and if he were to close his eyes, he sensed that he would run in his sleep like that dervish. Or would he start to fly? When the idea of flying thrust itself into his brain, he shuddered. God forbid! He needed to go faster! His heart, whether from lack of sleep or from his rushing, or from those evil thoughts, was pounding, thumping and thumping, racing forward faster even than his legs.

Ten or fifteen minutes later he reached the gates of the Italian garden. He wondered whether he should take the path off into the hills. But the sea was now pulling away from the shore, and for that reason, at the base of the white slopes that fell straight to the sea, the big boulders, and the sand mixed with gravel and lime, were laid out in a long pathway. At this hour, with the waters of the sea having receded, he could reach the lighthouse itself. Domrul did not go toward the hill. He rushed along the shoreline toward the foot of the hills instead.

He reached the last of the vacationers' wooden cottages. He left the fishermen's nets behind. The untamed, rocky seashore opened up before him. As he jumped from rock to rock, Domrul's feet were getting smashed to bits. His shoes were slipping off his feet and filling with the water and sand beneath the rocks. He spent ten minutes hopping through that rocky place, then half an hour, but the lighthouse behind the steep chalk walls of the cliffs had still not come into sight.

"What if the tide starts coming back in!" Domrul worried suddenly. "Is there a path that escapes up the hill? Or would the only way out be to climb the lighthouse?" He was ashamed by his thoughts. Even rushing after Emer, he was thinking about his own safety! He increased his speed again. Emer . . . Emer . . . Maybe she was a mermaid! Until now, that had never entered his thoughts . . . Or was Domrul just distracting himself? Yes, luckily, here there was a little ladder going up the hill. That meant that if anything happened, he would need to come here. What had he told himself just now? Was it his own bad thoughts he was trying to escape from?

On the shore, beneath the lighthouse, would he see her body lying there, like a mermaid, her legs wrecked, where the sea splashed the grass, in the space the water left empty? Or would the seawater eventually, in its heaving, heaving waves, carry her off far, far away? Where on earth was that lighthouse? Couldn't she have left him some sort of sign?

Here the corner of the great white chalk walls and, finally, the mottled red of the lighthouse came into view. It would take another half an hour, jumping from rock to rock, to reach it. Around the lighthouse, he could see some dubious-looking people. His heart sank. "Emer . . . E-mer!" he yelled, full volume. His voice flew off into the air, collided with the steep white cliff, and returned to him with a softer sound. "E-merrrrr!" he called, again and again.

Suddenly, from the top, as if all that noise had been piled up to fill the space, another sound came tumbling down. "Do-o-o-m-rullllll!" came a distant, tender voice. At first, Domrul did not understand what had happened. He thought his sleepless head had gone dizzy. Then the voice came again, sounding clearer and nearer. On one of the hills, at the edge of the precipice, leaning over the wire barricade, two arms of a familiar body were stretched out and waving.

"E-mer!" he shouted, alarmed, waving back. For a moment, this senseless yelling delivered him from his worry and anxiety, and they began walking toward one another. Emer's shadow now disappeared behind the rises, now materialized again. Domrul himself, in just the same way, despaired over not being able to put these pieces together. Now that he could see Emer, he was worried again; was she running too near the edge of the cliff? Would she stumble and fall?

She came to the wire that blocked the path to the cliff's edge, at the overhang, and Emer hung over it herself, and looked down again. "Domrul!" Now the sound was not an echo at all, but her own voice.

Domrul's foot twisted painfully, but he clung to a pile of slippery boulders and emerged on top again. The next time he saw Emer's head, he shouted to her. "Emer, near the rugby field there's a ladder down to the sea, let's meet there."

"All right!" Emer agreed, and she vanished from the top of the hill. Domrul, cursing, conquered the pain in his twisted foot, and dragging the injured, luckless appendage behind him, he turned to go back.

He couldn't make it up the hill. His foot was all swollen. Emer came down. Seeing Domrul in that state, she hugged him. She cried. Domrul melted, too, and he kissed her and called her a mermaid and stroked her hair. Emer laid her jacket down on a patch of ground covered in sand and limey chalk dust, made her backpack into a cushion on top of a flattish rock, and made Domrul lie down. Carefully, she removed the shoe and sock from his swollen foot. She squeezed and squeezed the water out of the cuffs of his wet trousers and started to roll them up. The blood rushed to Domrul's head, full of air, and his head spun. Emer's smooth hands gently massaged the sole of his foot, his exhausted muscles relaxed, the tenseness disappeared. Then she took her scarf and wrapped it firmly over his heel and shin and started massaging from his calf upward. As he lay staring at the sky, Domrul's manhood suddenly rose up.

◆

Had Domrul ever told Emer she was a mermaid? Domrul was lying there, delivered from all the troubles in the world, looking into the autumn sky that was now turning dark blue, when Emer returned from the direction of the retreating sea, bringing with her a pail of water in one hand and a whole pile of mussels. "Before the tide comes back in, we'll cook here and bring your strength back!" she said, and before darkness fell, she emerged at the top of the ladder and dropped down a bundle of branches and twigs for firewood. She built a fire pit out of rocks. She put a copper pail, left behind by some fishermen and filled with seawater, into the pit, then stacked the firewood underneath it. When that was ready, she lit a match and set some paper burning. In the sea breeze, it blazed up in an instant, and maybe because the fire had taken off, the day itself seemed suddenly to darken. Far off, the sea roared, and among the clouds at its edge the moon suddenly flashed into view, not yet letting the waves travel their way.

The fire's hot smoke and steam made Domrul's face go red. Emer, though, was still bustling about, using a whetstone to clean the mussels. When the water was bubbling and boiling, she dumped the prepared mussels by the handful into the pail. How lovely was this early darkness of the late autumn, with the wind stirring the fire rather than the waves of the sea! The busy Emer turned her face, with its moonlit beauty, and Domrul could not help remembering the story he had so recently read. He thought he would be willing to give up his other leg for this beauty. What if he told Emer the story? If he did, he'd have to tell her about Gaia too. After the tense meeting that morning, there was no need for that. The totally empty place, the totally black sky, the sea, gradually nearing from far away, Emer and him, and between them, the blazing bonfire.

"It's started to boil," said Emer, and leaned over the pail. Her eyes flashed in her lit-up face, and in her eyes, the flames danced. It all made her look like a sorceress from the ancient Irish tales. "Good, they've all opened. They're done!" she said, and with a long stick, she began dragging the red-hot embers and half-burnt kindling out of their fire pit. As water splashed from the pail, it bubbled noisily against the coals and hot stones. Then she started piling wet sand and lime on top of the embers. Domrul was able to use his good foot to drag over a little more sand. The embers hissed and started to go out. Gradually, the water stopped boiling too. Emer pulled the coat Domrul had been sitting on a little further away, put a glove on her hand, and carefully pulled the pail hanging over the stove toward her. The water splashed onto the coals and started to hiss. A couple of mussels fell into the coals along with the water. While she continued her efforts, the sound of the sea suddenly drew nearer. Just as if the waves were also hurrying to the feast, gathering at the foot of the hills, they were hurrying relentlessly toward them.

"You know," said Emer, "let's eat up on top of the hill. I'll take the pail over first, then you . . ." Then she thought again. "No, first you, then the pail," she concluded. Domrul spent the next fifteen minutes half hung over Emer's shoulder. He found a way to climb up the rungs of the ladder and emerged on the grassy slopes at the top of a low hill. Emer laid out her jacket on the grass and set down her backpack as a cushion again, and despite Domrul's weak objections, headed down once more. In the absolute darkness, Domrul looked around him. The city could not be seen from this hill, but there were lamps from the ships in the ocean alongside it, now visible, now blinking out again.

The noise from the sea was now coming from his feet, from the place where Emer had descended. Domrul's heart was wrapped up in worry. Should he call out? But you shouldn't startle someone on a ladder, he thought, and restrained himself. "Emer is a mermaid. Emer is a mermaid," he repeated to himself, trying to overcome the worry that plagued him. The sighing waves had now clearly reached the cliff face. Their collisions came with a rumbling that was both a sound and a tremble. Domrul suddenly sensed that he was left in this world all on his own, a one-legged man. His insides felt broken. "Emer . . ." he whispered. Just then, as if she had actually heard him, Emer emerged at the top, the copper pail sloshing in her hand.

The sea had eaten up most of the mussels itself, but it had left a few for Domrul and Emer. The mussels cooked in seawater were truly divine. Emer's jeans had gotten soaked, and in the sudden moonlight, she took off her pants and stripped down to her silvery legs, really just like a mermaid.

She and Domrul wrung as much of the water out of her pants as they could and draped them over a wild cherry bush. Then she took the jacket out from under Domrul and wrapped herself up in it.

They ate some more mussels, which were still warm. They huddled up against one another and sat looking at the nighttime sea. From their right, from behind the cliff face, the beam from the lighthouse glimmered over the sea, and that made the fear and fright of the night's darkness take one step toward disappearing.

In the sea breeze, Emer's jeans dried a bit. After she put her damp pants back on again, Emer propped herself under Domrul's arm and led the limping Domrul down the long trail through the hills to the bottom. As they walked all alone through the night, Domrul told Emer the story of the dervish and the mermaid. The story ended just as they reached the bottom of the hill, and Emer spoke. "Who told you that story? Kuyuk-baxshi?" she asked.

"No!" Domrul hurried to answer. "I heard it when I was just a kid," he said, and suddenly shuddered at what he had just said. Yes! That really was a story he had heard when he was a child. Even though he hadn't known then what a dervish was or what a mermaid was, when he was three or four years old, his father had told him that story. Domrul even suddenly remembered where that had happened. One time, his father had taken him fishing on the Qordaryo. Yes, it was coming back to him now: there he was, on the bank of the river, a green twig in his hand, sitting between his father's knees. Talking about mermaids also reminded him, now, of how his father had reeled in a catfish.

"Didn't you hear me?" asked Emer, bringing him back to reality from his dreams. "Did you hear what I said?"

"What did you say?" Domrul asked slowly.

"I said I want to go see Kuyuk-baxshi. Actually, I'm planning for the spring," she said, and paying no attention to Domrul's sudden sputtering, she went on. "I'd like to bring him to London. What do you say, would you come too?"

Now what sort of heartfelt worries should Domrul heed, and what on earth should he say? Should he speak out of surprise, or remembrance, or jealousy, or hope? He was at a loss.

Meanwhile Emer took out her telephone and dictated Domrul's address in Eastbourne. She was calling a taxi.

By the time they got home, Emer had a fever. Whether from her wet jeans or from the effect of the chilly seawater before that, she seemed to have caught cold, and though she lay down in a hot bath and drank a hot toddy made of whiskey, honey, hot water, and lemon juice, nothing helped. She shimmered with sweat and she shivered with cold. His foot still pulsing in pain, Domrul first hopped to the kitchen, then draped his girlfriend's head with a damp towel, and when it was nearly three o'clock, Emer fell asleep on his bed. In the chair where he sat, Domrul's eyes drooped too.

In his dream, Domrul was walking through an outdoor market. The market was a bazaar from his childhood. Someone was selling pistachios, someone had balloons, and someone had candy. Domrul was happy. He was the age he was now, but in his dream he was carefree as a child. But then it was as if the wind gusted in from somewhere in the clear blue sky, and worries began to play on his heart. He wondered why that was, and wondered who seemed to be following him. Who? thought Domrul, as he scanned the shops and stalls. His eye caught on an old woman, and his soul hardened. Yes, that very same old woman, the witch! Domrul turned to flee. At the edge of the bazaar, he leaped over the barricades set up for the cattle. And he knew that the witch was pursuing him. The path was clear ahead . . . Domrul ran across the street. But his legs felt buried in sand. If only he could move! The old woman was right behind him.

Here there was what people called a "living wall," a haven of green flowering shrubs as tall as he was, and Domrul ran right into it. Thankfully, there among the bushes, tight as it was, was a little path, and letting the boughs and branches scrape against his arms and legs, he followed that path to flee. From behind him, two eyes stabbed into his back like drill bits, like spotlights. When he emerged from the path, he saw a hill like a fortress, and eagerly, he clambered up the dirt wall of the hill. How he reached the crest of the hill, he did not know. In his heart, just one wish was beating, one fear. All he needed to do was escape from the witch coming up behind him like the scorching breath of a killing heat wave. He emerged at the crest of the hill and realized that this hill was no hill at all, but the steep shore of a great lake or boundless sea, and if he could not stop, he would fall right off, all the way down.

When he awoke, his heart, legs, and arms all trembling, it was ten o'clock. Emer was not where she had been lying. On the table there was a note: "I couldn't wake you. I'm going to see my mum and go back to Paris. XXX."

◈ ◈ ◈

Fire

We keep talking about Domrul, but we still don't know many things about his life, other than the tragic events of his early childhood. What we have already said about him may have led the reader into confusion. For instance, we mentioned that Domrul had met Emer at an evangelical church event. That may have made you think that Domrul was an evangelical, as well. But inside that assembly there were others, too, Arabs, Persians, Turks, and otherwise. It's no secret that Turks join all the religions they can possibly find out there in the world. If you were to ask Domrul himself, it might be enough to remind him of what happened one day as he walked into the museum attached to London's central Masonic lodge. He saw there a Turkish fez inscribed with the word *sirat*, for "way," written in Arabic calligraphy, and he couldn't help thinking, "They've got some of us among them too!" But Domrul, by birth and by conviction, was a Muslim. A modern-day Muslim, we ought to add. And here, it is also proper that we provide a little commentary.

The beginning of this commentary is how Domrul and his aunt fled the valley together, first to Kazakhstan, then to Stavropol province in Russia, and then, before finally coming to this country, to Cyprus for a short time, where they were delayed after a stay in an international settlement camp there. They reached that camp just in time for the hottest part of summer, and no matter what medicines and potions the camp doctors tried, nothing helped Domrul's mangy scalp, covered in scabies. His aunt, afraid of having to bury the poor emaciated boy in foreign lands, asked around and learned that a holy man lived in a little village called Lefke. They told her his address and his name. The respected Shaykh Nozim al-Haqqani. "Go and see that teacher of ours," the local Turks told her.

Domrul's aunt had grown up in the valley, of course, so she baked some somsa in the *tandir* oven, put it into a basket, and as if she were taking the child from the settlement camp to the doctor's office, she hired a car to take them from Lefkosha to Lefke, and that evening the two of them walked into our teacher's residence.

Shaykh Nozim had just sat down to an evening meal with his disciples in his expansive courtyard, and the still-hot somsas were just the thing. Domrul's aunt was taken inside to join the other women. As for Domrul, Shaykh Nozim pointed to the place across from him, and he cut a piece of meat from his plate and put it on the boy's dish. He asked him a few questions in Turkish. After dinner, when the prayers had been said, he invited the boy to come to his side, and he placed his hands on Domrul's head and recited a blessing.

After all of that, he stood up from the table, and Domrul followed the shaykh to a mosque in the corner of the courtyard; the evening prayers were recited, and the Sufi chanting began. Once he got older, Domrul realized it had been a Sufi *zikr*. But at the time, as he remembered, he just repeated what the shaykh said as he stood by his side and did what they did in the candlelit darkness. The shaykh pronounced beautiful words in a beautiful voice, and the company assembled behind him repeated those words along with him, and then the shaykh recited the *fatihah* and they recited the *alhamdulillah* that Domrul knew by heart. An hour or maybe an hour and a half must have passed in this way. But how would a little child who had fallen asleep in the midst of this beauty know for sure? Only later, after he was grown and had attended many similar ceremonies, did he come to that conclusion.

He remembered that Shaykh Nozim himself had lifted him up in his arms and carried him out. In the summer night, under the densely packed trees, Domrul slept in our shaykh's arms, and when he came down from our master's embrace, he rushed toward his aunt, who stood beside the door. And you know, the shaykh had set him down, held his head in both his hands, and kissed his forehead, and Domrul could just barely remember how he spat onto his own thumb and spread some saliva onto Domrul's lips.

Starting the very next day, the scabies and scabs began to disappear from Domrul's scalp. Though his reddish hair did remain rather thin.

◈

Many years later, Domrul was a student at SOAS at the University of London, and he caught sight of a familiar, noble-looking face on a poster on a university wall. Yes, the master of the Naqshbandi Sufi school, Shaykh Nozim al-Haqqani-Qibrisi, would be speaking about the Naqshbandi way of Sufism at the university theater.

That day, the lecture hall was crowded full with people. All the seats were occupied, and there was no room to move even on the stairs or in the area in front of the stage. Domrul, as if he had known this from the beginning, had settled into a seat in the first row just before the lectern, and he compared the darkness in the auditorium to the darkness of that mosque in his distant childhood.

All at once, following the rector onto the stage, there came a group of long-bearded men wearing green turbans, handsome and regal, and leading them, Domrul saw with excitement, was Shaykh Nozim. He was overcome with some kind of pride. Looking at the throngs of people around him, he wanted to boast, "I know that man! I've sat on his lap!"

After a short introduction, Shaykh Nozim approached the lectern, and for the next forty minutes, in surprisingly good English, he spoke—about the founder of the Naqshbandi order, Bahouddin Balogardon, be His secrets holy!, the golden line descended from him, and the Thirty-nine Pillars of the Epoch who passed before him.

Domrul wrote down every single word the shaykh uttered. Then the time came for the question and answer part of the event. Somebody asked a question to show off his own wisdom, somebody else tried to get a first-hand quotation for his own research paper, and the third was more modest, simply educating himself. Then there was a red-haired Scottish-looking young man with flashing eyes.

"Will you be performing the zikr in London? May we join you?" he asked.

Shaykh Nozim gestured to one of his younger disciples, seated on the stage. "Shaykh Ibrohim will remain here and will answer all the organizational questions," he said, and then he closed the event with the fatihah.

As soon as the event was over and the crowd was dispersing, Domrul pushed and shoved his way up onto the stage and walked up to Shaykh Ibrohim. The man called Shaykh Ibrohim turned out to be a local and a thoroughbred Englishman. His aristocratic pronunciation made that clear. "The public are invited to a service to take place at the Seven Sisters Mosque, tomorrow evening, commencing promptly at seven o'clock," he announced solemnly, over and over again, in a voice like a court herald reading the edict for an execution. Later, with just this same pronunciation, he launched into a discussion with the SOAS sound engineers about the recording of that day's discussion.

Quite regrettably, due to the crowds, somebody's foot had yanked the wire out of the microphone, and the discussion had not, in fact, been recorded. In his aristocratic English, Shaykh Ibrohim let them know that he was "profoundly disappointed," and his worry about what they were to do next drew taut his clear young face.

Then Domrul spoke. "I took notes on everything, word for word. Maybe that would help?" he asked.

That was how Domrul became acquainted with Shaykh Nozim's London press secretary, Shaykh Ibrohim.

The next evening, Domrul went to the Seven Sisters Mosque, performed his evening prayers with the people there, and joined in Shaykh Nozim's zikr as well. Memories from his childhood bubbled up and burst in his heart and his mind. The wandering life he had lived from the beginning, with his aunt, the dirt of the refugee camp on the outskirts of Lefkosha, the cool shade of Shaykh Nozim's courtyard, and the flickering candles of the mosque there all took shape before his eyes. And then, as the zikr went on, Domrul wept, without letting anyone know. All the trials Allah had given him, and his boundless mercy, squeezed his heart like a pomegranate. Behind Shaykh Nozim, he repeated the glorious names of Allah, and then along with everybody else, he also recited the proclamation to our prophet: "Allah, bestow Your mercy upon our Master Muhammad the messenger!"

When the zikr was finished, as Domrul walked out into the vestibule of the mosque feeling he had been scrubbed clean in a spiritual bathhouse, he met Shaykh Ibrohim, who had been waiting for him.

"Have you brought with you your excellent notes of yesterday's encounter?" he asked.

Domrul took out the notes he had copied. "No, please, you must deliver them to our teacher yourself," Shaykh Ibrohim told him, and as the public left the mosque he led Domrul toward Finsbury Park. They walked till they reached a house clearly belonging to some Turkish guy. Inside it was full to the brim with people. The house was an average one for the neighborhood: not too much room, and no excess of splendor. In the middle of the circle, moving that circle first to laughter, then to sighs with his stories and tales, sat the resplendent Shaykh Nozim.

Food was being served just as they entered. In an instant, everything sank into silence. Then Shaykh Nozim looked at Ibrohim and asked, "Ibrohim, my son, have you arrived safe and sound?" Ibrohim also made use of the opportunity and moved to the right side of the shaykh, bowed before him, and kissed his hand. Then he looked to Domrul, still standing at the door. "This is the young fellow who took down everything you uttered last night, word for word."

Shaykh Nozim gestured for Domrul to approach. Under the gaze of everyone there, Domrul walked to the center of the room and knelt down before Shaykh Nozim, bending over the teacher's hand, but the teacher, unexpectedly, placed that hand on Domrul's head and bent over him, as well, and kissed him on the forehead. "Your teachers must be quite strict if you write down everything that everyone says!" he joked. Everyone burst out in laughter. Domrul wanted to say something just then, but the woman of the house was already passing plates full of food to him and Shaykh Ibrohim. Then Shaykh Nozim took a piece of tender meat from his plate, placed it into Domrul's dish, and winked a friendly eye.

Whether Shaykh Nozim recognized him after so many years was not what Domrul was wondering at that moment. Being in the presence of the Pillar of the Epoch for the second time, and knowing well his generosity and reverence, Domrul was simply struck dumb, both in tongue and in spirit.

◆

"Belief," Shaykh Nozim said that evening, looking out over the people gathered there, "must be like a person's clothing, fitted to the size of his heart. The right garments fit you comfortably and in good proportion. What would happen if, say, a person were to put on clothing twice as big as his size? He may become tangled in those clothes, annoying himself and making other people laugh. He will eventually strip those garments from his back where he stands, or hurl them away, or tear them to shreds. Belief works just the same way."

With that guidance, Domrul found himself attaching easily to his religion. He covered his heart with the kind of devotion befitting an urban, western Muslim. One summer he went to Cyprus and served Shaykh Nozim in Lefke, and one evening during supper he asked our teacher, "In the hustle and bustle of city life, could someone be busy with something else during the prayers or zikr?"

The master answered him simply. "No!" he said. Then he added, laughing, "You did not phrase your question correctly. In my opinion, what you wanted to ask was this: While you are busy with other things, could you also pray or perform the zikr? The answer to that question is yes," he said. "Our teacher Bahouddin used to say, 'Heart to the Beloved, hands to work!'"

When we said before that Domrul was a modern-day Muslim, we had in mind how he sometimes recites his prayers while walking down the street and repeats the holy names of Allah in the zikr as he jogs down the stairs to the tube. Crippled as he was at the moment, even the last time he had limped along the seashore toward Gaia Mangitkhanovna's fortress-like building, he had repeated to himself, thirty-three times, every name of Allah mentioned in the last verses of the Hashr surah. Just that past year, his merciful teacher had been consigned to the earth. May his secrets be blessed! When he heard that dreadful news, Domrul had gone promptly to London, to a side street off Oxford Street, to Shaykh Ibrohim's aristocratic home. "Ibrohim is at home," a servant said, and led Domrul inside.

Passing from room to room, one after another, the servant led him to a bedroom. In that room lay Shaykh Ibrohim, wrapped in a quilt of goose feathers, and Domrul threw himself down before him. They embraced there where he lay, and both men wept openly, letting their emotions overflow. Domrul said a prayer. The servant brought some tea. Domrul hesitated to ask, "Why are you in bed? Has our teacher's death laid you flat?" What he did ask was, "Won't you go to Cyprus?"

At that, Shaykh Ibrohim pronounced in his aristocratic English, from under that thick quilt, "I cannot stretch my loins. I've just been circumcised."

Our teacher had one thing in common with the otherwise unmatched, astounding Khodja Nasreddin. It seemed that right there in Domrul's mourning mind, our shaykh, with a lighthearted slyness, had just winked at him.

◈

Now that we've told you all this, we are afraid of leaving the impression that Domrul was some sort of Sufi disciple and mystic. From his outward appearance, we could ascribe to him certain traits, perhaps a striving for perfection and maturity. In any case, what does youth not strive for? But when you got to know Domrul better, when you looked further into the depths of his heart, you could see that what this young man was striving for was calm and quiet. In reality, this means the absence of petty complaints, ambitions, and boastful struggles.

Domrul first discovered that in Emer. Later, he observed that he himself, just like Emer, was empty inside. On the one hand, this could be construed as something cultivated among the English, with their modern disinvolvement and indifference, their infection with consumer philosophies. But it also had another side. As anyone who has gone through tragedies in their childhood must know, a child who has lost his mother and father and everything else goes through life like a traveler pressed up against the back window of a tram car. His lifelong gaze is focused on the past—not on the tragedy, but on the peace and quiet that preceded the tragedy, the paradise that was lost. Therefore his present state is pain, pulling him away and distancing him from the past, while his future is darkness and emptiness. What, then, ought that kind of person to strive for?

Domrul was living to watch Emer, and the discoveries he made in her moods and nature, her doings and dealings, he could adapt easily to himself, and they fit him perfectly well. We wouldn't say that Emer was fleeing from the future. After all, the tram carries everyone off to the future, whether they like it or not! But your gaze is not forward-looking, but rather on the passing, vanishing tracks. So therefore the future always seems to be stabbing you in the back like a bloodthirsty traitor. Emer was always startled by unexpected events, but every event, for her, was unexpected. In truth, Domrul could also see that in himself. As if his aunt Sakina's skirts there in the cellar, where they hid during those devastating days, had promised to always keep him safe in their dark, conservative embrace, then and now.

◆

Today, too, Gaia Mangitkhanovna pulled a thick quilt over herself and lay on the couch in the living room like yesterday. She had gone white again. She took one look at Domrul's limping and asked if his wound had gotten infected.

"No, I twisted my ankle," said Domrul.

"Show me!" ordered Gaia Mangitkhanovna from where she lay. Domrul rolled up his pants and pulled down his sock. His foot was swollen and turning green. "On the top shelf in the freezer there's a jar of black Mumiyo ointment. Go get it and rub some onto that swelling," she commanded. Domrul did what Gaia Mangitkhanovna said. He brought the Mumiyo from the freezer and sat down on a chair facing the sofa. He rolled the lower cuff of his pant leg up again, took off his sock, took some oil in his hand, and started to rub at his swollen flesh. "Rub it in clockwise!" said the begum, showing him how to do it, watching him from the place where she lay. Bent over as he was, Domrul could not guess which direction a clock would turn on his leg, and he got a little dizzy, but then it must have made sense to him, and he began moving his fingers in the right direction. The swollen flesh went red. "Rub up higher too!" Gaia Mangitkhanovna told him. Domrul pulled up his pant leg, already rolled up to his calf, so it stopped above his knee, and he began massaging the Mumiyo oil into his thigh, as well.

The same feelings as last time began toying with him. Gaia Mangitkhanovna was still watching his movements, her eyes unwavering, and Domrul remained caught between the impudence of the other day and the bashfulness of today, and eagerly, he rubbed the oil onto his reddened flesh.

"It's interesting," he thought, "how love and trust are such different things, how you can love someone but be unable to trust her. Yet being able to trust someone does not, in fact, mean that you should love her. Is this one of the native attributes of this imperfect, incomplete world?" He was still rubbing the oil in, and his skin, whether from the oil or the quiet surrounding him, or maybe from the begum's insatiable gaze, grew progressively redder, and now his young man's lust and passion was rising, not for no reason, but of his own free will.

This time, nothing happened. Gaia Mangitkhanovna didn't make him read a single manuscript or book. All she said was this: "This week rest your foot, and Antonina will look in on me. Take care of yourself a bit, and next week, you'll go with me to a place called Brookwood. For now, you may go."

One week later, with the foot much better, Domrul steered out of the garage a Mini Cooper that he had rented at Gaia Mangitkhanovna's orders and in her name. The begum was waiting at the building's front door at the agreed time, and when she emerged, he directed the car toward Brookwood. Gaia Mangitkhanovna was dressed more colorfully than usual, with a blue-green overcoat and a scarf ranging from violet to a pale shade of jasmine, and she wore a fancy cap on her head in just the same color as her coat. If you saw her from behind, you'd think she was a lovely girl.

And how excited do you think Domrul was to drive that spanking new car? It had been a long time since he had driven such a fine automobile. As they wound along the highways that wrapped around Sussex's sweeping green fields and meadows, he was reminded again of Cyprus. It so happened that when he was still at the university, he used to make a few pounds working evenings as a waiter at a strange Turkish restaurant at Covent Garden, not far from SOAS. The steady salary and tips he made compensated for his sleeplessness and exhaustion.

The owner of the restaurant was a hilarious Turkish man named Rashad Niyozy. Everyone called him Amja, or Uncle, and in his lifetime he had gone completely broke three times, and three times had become a millionaire all over again. Amja used up all the money he made betting on boxing matches or buying rare vintage cars. Out of his hundreds of rare cars, the oldest was a 1912 Studebaker, and the newest was the very latest model of Bentley, custom made especially for him. Amja kept his cars in a village outside Girne in Cyprus, where three full-blooded, full-spirited hired mechanics (and when we say full-spirited, we mean their wages really satisfied their spirits) kept the cars in tip-top shape, coddling them day and night.

Who knows why Amja's love landed on Domrul. Maybe it was because he was reminded of his own needy, poverty-stricken youth, or perhaps because he had always dreamed of becoming an opera singer but never got an education. In any case, while the other waiters, the Poles and Italians, were frightened of him, he didn't growl like a dog or behave that way to Domrul. And best of all, when summer came, as a bonus for being the most valuable employee, he gave him a ticket for a flight to Cyprus, and attached to that ticket was a map of his own, empty village, with written orders to pick out any car he liked.

That summer, Domrul had some serious fun. He was on his own in the village on the mountain facing the sea. One day, he took out a Safari and rumbled through the rocks and hills, and the second day he picked a silver 1970s Mercedes, and he passed over to the Greek side of the island, leaving the locals to stare after him with their eyes wide and mouths agape. Then on the third day, he drove a plain Mini to Lefkosha to pay a visit to Shaykh Nozim.

Remembering those times, and the late Amja, Domrul now filled his lungs with air, and he steered this new Mini Cooper along the hills and fields of Sussex, driving the begum to Brookwood.

◆

Amja had behaved like nobody else in the world. Another summer, he came to Cyprus himself, and one day he brought Domrul out to his house on the coast. The villa was full of dogs. There were over twenty or so, most of them no breed at all.

"Where did this collection come from?" asked Domrul, trying to hide his fear with a joke.

"I pick them up on the streets," said Amja. "This one here is Lady. She was lame. This one is Duke. Some kids had tried stoning him to death. This is Fiona. She had been hit by a car . . ."

Those dogs were as loyal to him as, well, dogs. When Amja went out for a swim in the sea, all of them, big and small, swam in a swarm around him. "I'm sinking! I'm sinking!" he would jest, and then the biggest of the dogs, Lady, would take Amja's trunks between her teeth and drag him back to the shore. All the others would eagerly cheer her on, some howling, some diving down under Amja, nudging up against him from under his waist.

Near sunset, Amja pointed Domrul to his newest red Mercedes convertible, and taking with them whichever of the dogs managed to jump into the car on time, they set off to watch the sunset from a cliff over the sea. They stopped at the edge of one cliff that fell at a slant toward the seashore, got out of the car, and sat down on a boulder together, daydreaming in silence. Far off, the bright red sun was sinking toward the top of the sea, and closer in, sitting quietly, Domrul cast a glance at Amja's bright-red bare shoulders. As if they too sensed the grandeur of the moment, the dogs also kept quiet and settled down behind Amja. The sun gradually sank, and Amja let out a heavy sigh, one of the dogs yawned, and then all of them went together to a roadside restaurant and returned home, content, later that evening.

That night, Amja tossed down some blankets and pillows to make them beds on the villa's roof. "We'll fall asleep looking at the stars!" he said. Since his long-ago childhood, Domrul had not slept under the stars all that often, and in his pleasant memories he went flying back to those times, to that far-off valley, while the dogs lapped and lapped with their tongues over his forehead and the soles of his feet where they stuck out from under the blankets. He put up with it. He had already surrendered.

"A dog!" Gaia Mangitkhanovna suddenly shouted. Domrul slammed on the brakes. The car squealed and skidded sideways. Fortunately, there were no other cars anywhere around. The stray dog who had just missed landing under a tire limped off, continuing across the street.

"A suicide attempt!" said Domrul, shaking as he started to relax. The dog looked neither at him nor at the car parked slantwise across the street.

Domrul started the car moving again. "God has saved another soul!" he said.

The dog's, or yours?" asked the begum sarcastically. "You ought to come down out of those daydreams. Keep your eyes on the road! Don't get carried away!" She went on needling him.

What had Domrul been remembering? Oh yes, Amja and his dogs. If Amja were here with him now, would he have tossed that dog into the back seat and taken him home? He remembered one more incident too. The next evening, after sunset, happy after a bottle of raki in a nearby restaurant, the two of them were walking back to Amja's house, when at his neighbor's house an enormous dog, tied to a chain, saw them, started barking like mad, and growled with the saliva spraying out of his mouth, then began to howl. Could Amja have left him alone? He walked right up to that dog and knelt down, and becoming the beast's mirror image, he started to bark, drool, and howl just like him. The mottled dog would have liked to jump at him, but Amja did not retreat, just crept toward the howling animal, coming right at him. The dog was the first to quiet down. Then, whining, he tucked his tail between his legs, and tottering a little, rattling his chain, the dog slunk back into his box.

That was just the kind of wonder the late Amja used to produce.

If you were to ask Domrul about Sufi life, and whether that kind of life was possible in today's space and time, he might have thought back to both Shaykh Nozim and Amja as a pair. "Yes," he would tell you. If you were to go on to ask him to describe what that life consisted of, what it was really like, in just a word or two, he would have thought for a minute, then answered, "It is a life free of pretensions and empty ambitions." In any case, that's what we have heard.

As they were coming along a road through the woods now, he would look at the centuries-old trees all around them. "Do those trees have any pretensions?" he would challenge you. Then he would point out the lake that opened up at the end of the road. "What does that lake ever complain about?" he would ask you. "There's a novel by Robert Musil called *The Man without Qualities*," he would go on, continuing his train of thought. "Maybe that quality-free man is like a Sufi for our times."

This belief of Domrul's—whether he knew it or not—was the harvest he had reaped from his own life. Ever since his time sitting in that basement, suffocating under his aunt's skirts and waiting for his death, he had considered his life a borrowed thing. The butchers who raped his mother should have caught him on the tips of their sharpened bayonets too. But he was left to live. His wishes and intentions were left there, in the place where his parents were still alive, and after that hell, what pretensions could possibly remain to him? Should he have taken revenge? On whom? Should he have wreaked vengeance? On what?

Emer's love for him was because of that very thing. He was both an innocent child and a possible husband free of pretensions.

◈

In her own time, Gaia had tried to get on her mother's nerves. "I would never lose control over my husband like you did!" she used to say, but then she took revenge on her own husband: "I've had enough of my children being like you—self-indulgent and self-content!" she would say, and she brought up her son and her daughter in continuous fear and constant discipline. She was informed of every step they took and notified of everything they did. Like two little soldiers, from the moment the two of them woke up, they had their every minute scheduled and their every activity supervised. Could it be they resembled not so much soldiers as ants? Those who had seen them then remembered how they were always lugging around a heavy bag or juggling a huge cello or accordion, and throughout their childhood she hustled them first to school, then to music lessons, then to clubs, then to the stadium, and in the evening, like insects returning to the nest, they returned, exhausted, home.

With that kind of mother, contradicting her or setting yourself against her was out of the question; if there's one task you have not done or one activity you have not completed, the punishment is bound to be severe and merciless. She will scatter unrefined salt in the corner and make you kneel there bare-legged, and slap you with the rod when the time came, or when the time didn't come, she would slap your head with a hand so firm the soup would start boiling in your ears.

You may be wondering where the father was. Why didn't he get involved? The father was busy with work and with ascending the ranks there. It was a real treat when he came home, on a holiday or when he was sick, and asked, "What grade are you in?"

But the children grew up and got to know their own thoughts and feelings, and their immature minds and unripe hearts began to absorb what the people around them were saying: that they were the offspring of the Father of the Country. Then both of them, at the same moment, suddenly went bad, like rancid bread dough, so bad they sent out shoots; and now their commander found it impossible not just to keep them in line, but even to keep them acting like human beings. People like to say that seeing things unseen leaves a person unseeingly cursed, and now Gaia's children zeroed in on a hundredfold pleasures not usually experienced in youth or adulthood, and their mouths, eyes, assholes—whatever hole they could find, they stuffed it like gluttons.

As if the foulest of infections had been brought into the tidy anthill.

While her daughter was at university she apparently hooked up not just with one man, but with two, and then split up with both of them. The things she did when free and single did not overly offend Gaia Mangitkhanovna. She interpreted all of it as a result of their father's bad seed. But Gaia's beloved son going astray, imitating that rotten cow, ripped out his mother's heart. No, her son was not as much of a wreck as her daughter. While her daughter spread her legs like a cow for every dick on the hill, Gaia's son, on the contrary, gave his heart only and especially to one person, but that person was a whore with three children, someone who had passed through the hands of a hundred men. How did that bitch win over her son, that stupid, clumsy nincompoop? With treachery and cunning, that's how! She had made a tame sheep out of him. He lay down when she said to lie down, and he took what she said to take.

While Gaia Mangitkhanovna seethed at her daughter, her daughter said only this: "You're so busy guarding my cunt, but look to your son! He's like the fourth piglet in that sow's litter!" After that, Gaia Mangitkhanovna put a spy on her son's tail, and you know, he really was playing with those three little pigs like a fourth dirty swine, her own son, big as a boar.

One day, she locked him in her house, and Gaia Mangitkhanovna threw down before her son the photographs her spy had taken surreptitiously. "What is the meaning of this?" she began, nagging him as only a mother can. But her son paid no attention. "Where did you find that filthy whore? Do you know who you are and who she is? Does that head of yours work at all?" demanded Gaia Mangitkhanovna.

And her son replied quite coolly. "She is not any different from you," he said.

"What are you saying? Do you hear me?" Gaia Mangitkhanovna was shouting now.

But her son answered, "What if I go and take your picture too?"

Gaia Mangitkhanovna's breath caught in her throat.

◈

In this manner, each given over to their own thoughts, listening to the GPS telling them where to go, they eventually reached Brookwood. True, the first place the GPS led them, instead of the Brookwood monastery, was a road in the middle of the forest. From there, they wandered this way and that for ten more minutes, then finally found a wooden signpost to their intended destination and drove toward the monastery. "Is the begum thinking of shaving her head and joining a nunnery in her old age?" Domrul wondered, but then he looked at how she was dressed. "Maybe Antonina Ivanovna told the begum about the wonders of this place. The begum has come for some sightseeing," he thought, that suspicion over-riding his earlier idea.

They drove along a little footpath and came out on monastery grounds. Under some huge old trees, gravestones and tombstones came into sight.

Suddenly Gaia Mangitkhanovna said to herself, "Correct!"

What was correct?

They traveled another four or five hundred meters and came in view of a church-like building, encircled by tall brick and stone towers. Domrul pulled the car up behind another car standing there and stopped. They got out. The triangular-framed church and the buildings behind it were surrounded by bindweed. Having seen Gaia Mangitkhanovna and Domrul approaching from a distance, a thin young man dressed in black came outside.

He greeted them in English. "How can I help you?" he asked.

Before making his inquiries for Gaia Mangitkhanovna, Domrul asked, with a touch of fervor, "Are you a monk?"

"Yes. This is an Orthodox monastery," answered the young man, in a rather bashful and somehow familiar aristocratic accent, and he adjusted the little black cap that covered his hair and looked a lot like an Uzbek *do'ppi*.

"Orthodox? But you're English!"

"Yes, well, as it happens, Englishmen can be Orthodox too." Here Domrul realized who it was this young man reminded him of: Shaykh Ibrohim. Could he be his brother, or an uncle, or a cousin? But Domrul suddenly couldn't stand the way the young monk talked.

"Yes, I know," said he. "I myself belong to the Sufi *tariqat*, what you would call an order. Two years ago I was at the Saint Michel monastery in Devon, and when I looked at the monastery's daily schedule, it was just like the one the Sufis have. From the sunrise prayers to the evening service." The young monk shrugged his shoulders, as if asking how he could know.

"Do you have the internet?" Domrul asked him abruptly.

"No, we don't."

"Computers?"

"No."

"Do you read books?"

"Yes, the guidance God has sent down to us."

"Do you ever get out into the outside world?"

"Yes, to do the shopping."

If Gaia Mangitkhanovna had not butted in to their English-language conversation just then, Domrul would certainly have pestered the poor monk with questions for another hour. "Ask that long-hair where the Orthodox cemetery is," she discourteously interrupted them. "And how much does a burial lot cost?" she added. Another command.

Domrul jumped, startled. Who knows whether it was because of the abruptness of the interruption or the content of her question? But he got himself in hand. "The lady would like to know where the Orthodox cemetery is here. And also, what is the price of a burial plot?"

The young man, unfazed, waved a hand around him. "Everything here is an Orthodox cemetery. For the Orthodox, a plot here costs fifteen hundred pounds. For a two-person site"—and here he cast a doubtful glance at Gaia Mangitkhanovna and Domrul both—"two thousand pounds."

Domrul's muscles twitched again.

"Can we look around?" Gaia Mangitkhanovna asked him.

Domrul translated.

"Yes, certainly!" the monk agreed, and shook Domrul's hand like an old acquaintance and went back into the magnificent church.

"Come on!" commanded the begum, to get Domrul moving, but Domrul was feeling sorry for himself.

"I meant to ask about Shaykh Ibrohim!" he thought sadly.

So they had come to the graveyard to look for a grave!

"From what Antonina said, there's a section here for Muslims too. Let's take a look," Gaia Mangitkhanovna said, summoning him. She walked in front, and anybody watching them would have thought they were husband and wife. Though of course, the husband in that sort of family usually walks in front.

"Who is it she's looking for a place in the Muslim section for?" Domrul wondered. "For herself, since she's a half-baked Muslim? Or is she trying to be polite to me?" Domrul followed behind the begum on the gravel path, his dragging feet making the gravel rattle. He started picking his feet up off the ground. Under the majestic trees, a bit ugly, there stood stones arranged in soldierly ranks, pointed up like fingers. On the other side, sculptures of angels with their wings spread wide adorned the tombs of more notable people.

Gaia Mangitkhanovna stepped off the path and started walking through the pines and oak trees to examine the sculptures more closely. Domrul followed along behind her. Today was neither a Sunday, nor a holiday, nor a day of commemoration, and the cemetery was empty all around them, which meant the silence that reigned here filled his sorrowful thoughts. Statue stood after statue, and they moved deeper into the forest, where even the pathways disappeared. Here there were no more sculptures or even gravestones. The forest itself seemed to be coming to an end, and it seemed more neglected here, the trees more crowded, their bottom branches growing thicker together.

He stared at the begum's deep blue overcoat and jasmine-colored scarf, and along with the sense that they were the only two living souls in a world of dead bodies, came Domrul's arousal. He came up behind the begum and gently embraced her. The begum, as if she had been expecting it, offered no resistance. Domrul lifted the begum's scarf and kissed her white neck. His hand undid the buttons on her coat and moved to cup her breasts under her slippery silk blouse. The begum stood tall, unmoving. Then she began to lean slightly and settled her shoulders against a birch tree nearby. Domrul moved aside her coat and tore open the buttons on her silk shirt, down to her waist . . .

The funny thing is that afterward, the begum's dignity still remained intact. Without letting him know, she wiped herself off with her small handkerchief, and brushing off the clothes she was wearing along the way, she walked to the nearest statue and calmly sat down. The one whose dignity was vilely destroyed was Domrul. Not knowing how to wipe away the juices still seeping from inside him, he picked up some damp leaves of a stinging nettle plant, and he found a stump in the thicket and sat down upon it, which made the seat of his pants all wet, which meant even more trouble for what remained of his honor, just shame upon shame.

◆

Domrul was thinking about how attached he was to the begum. At first, like a mosquito stuck to flypaper, he had fallen into her trap. He struggled, he ached, he beat his wings hard, fighting to get free. If only he were a bug, so that he could fly away! Maybe he shouldn't have come back from Paris, shouldn't have left Emer's side. No, he had returned of his own free will. Not just returned, but gotten himself stuck in that very same flypaper again. He was caught up once more with all the other mosquitoes taken prisoner there. What was it that was so sweet about this sticky trap? Or did the fine lines on her face look like a spiderweb to him? A spiderweb riddled with holes?

Whatever the case, he was drowning in that treasonous sweetness, in that deceitful pleasure. Why?

Domrul was no saint. He had a procession of five or six girlfriends before Emer. He could remember the pleasure he took in those girls his own age, one after the next, but what he found in the begum, in Gaia Mangitkhanovna, in that old woman, was something different. Sometimes, when we come across the barely detectable bitterness in the taste of the dry, withered apple or plum or peach, the fruit invites and inveighs us even more keenly to take a bite of its pleasures. Domrul had never in his life imagined that such delightful juices could still flow through the arid body of this old woman, still so finely preserved, and he had never imagined this bitter taste and scent. Until that sudden first encounter.

The emergence of that pleasurable nectar, in drips and drops, reminded Domrul in a flash of when he was a child, and how before eating a peach he would separate the two halves and watch the juice dripping over the pit. He had forgotten that memory, but it remained secure in his heart and his flesh.

In a different life, in Cyprus, he and his aunt had baked bread for the whole camp. In the evenings, Domrul would knead the dough in a large dish, and knead it so well the sweat would be pouring off him; in the morning, even though they would place a baking pan over the dough in its dish, even though they would wrap it up in a tablecloth or quilt, the dough would always have puffed up and overflowed its bowl. The begum's soft, puffed-up, overflowing belly, all of her flesh, had a certain resemblance to that risen dough.

And now Domrul had identified the root of his vexation. A souvenir. Now to bring it back to life . . . Yes, by all appearances, in this unnatural love of his, a certain miracle was involved: the revitalization of a body which had already escaped the realm of love. Domrul remembered the dervish who had watered a tree going yellow in the desert and brought it back to life. Yes, just like that. The strength of love, locked in conflict with the embrace of death.

Wasn't this souvenir made of the very same stuff?

◈

Gaia had grown up a strict materialist since childhood, and she had never believed in God. But she did still harbor some childish superstitions. The old traditions she got from her mother, and some she picked up herself, helped her pass her exams and smooth out her troubles, and sometimes protected her from the mischief of others. She never stepped on the thin cracks in the concrete when she walked, or onto her own shadow, and she always used her right foot to step first into important places. We saw how she used the cards to tell her own fortune, but after she got together with Bo'riboy, those bits and pieces of old customs and superstitions came to rshadowed by something bigger and closer to her zoological mind: extrasensory abilities.

According to Bo'riboy, when he had been born back in his native aul, all the wolves of the desert had gathered together in front of their yurt. That was when his father named the infant Bo'riboy, because *bo'ri*, of course, means "wolf," with the *boy* part added in to ensure the child would grow to be wealthy. Bo'riboy would pick up the guitar and sing some song or other, and in the tender sound of those songs there could sometimes be heard, just barely, the whining tone of wolves' voices, and because of that, if among those sitting around him, anyone had a headache, that headache would disappear, and if anyone had a cough, the cough would disappear. Gaia had even run that experiment on herself, more than once.

That reminded Gaia of one of her late mother's stories, which seemed now to teach a completely different lesson.

"When you were born, everything was teeming with ants," her mother Rohila used to say, as Gaia's neck stiffened in fear.

"That's because you never cleaned the house!" Gaia had snapped at her. Now, when she thought about it, it seemed apparent to her that there was something miraculous there, just as in Bo'riboy's tale. Didn't she think that she was the queen of the ants?

Bo'riboy dredged up that filthy Qimbat-baxshi somewhere, and while he paraded him around like a bear in front of other people, Gaia dressed up like an ant queen for one of their parties. O'rhon the sculptor had made that costume for her. Then, from their private room, they stared ravenously at the bare, slim-waisted, shapely young women in the next room, and they truly were like ants, and the men throwing themselves upon them in passion and aggression looked just like crazed insects too. In her suit of copper or bronze, Gaia entered a state of excitement and allure previously unknown to her. She was protected from every direction that way, and if anyone tried to reach her, as soon as they did she would move flirtatiously to crack through the enemy's neck with her two steel jaws.

No, nobody approached her or got anywhere close to her that evening, and even that grimy Qimbat, whose lust never got a rest, rolled into a ball and fell asleep. But starting that night, when Gaia was alone, all by herself, shut in her room, she would put on that suit of armor and go back to indulge, over and over, in that same old fantasy.

As they drove the car back to Eastbourne, Domrul gagged at the odor emanating from his body, and as if forewarned, Gaia Mangitkhanovna, maybe to avoid meeting his eyes, was sitting in the back seat. So Domrul could not look in the rearview mirror, because it felt almost as if the begum seated back there would saddle him up and ride off on him, as if she were monitoring his every move. For over an hour, as they traveled, barely a word was shared between them.

In Eastbourne, stopping the car outside the begum's fortress, Domrul did not get out and did not wave goodbye. Gaia Mangitkhanovna got out of the car in silence herself.

Domrul was steering the car onto the main road, wondering if he had done the right thing, when a sudden clamor—shar-rrrrak!—jolted him awake. He had banged into a car coming from his right and ripped off its bumper. Domrul immediately slammed on his brakes and froze there inside his car. All he wished was to become a mouse and flee into a hole in the corner. But a stout bellowing Englishman was approaching him imperiously, and Domrul raised both his hands in surrender. "Sorry! Sorry!" he said, stepping outside.

The filth of sin covered him.

❖ ❖ ❖

Water and Air

Autumn passed and winter passed, and at the beginning of spring, Emer called Domrul, because they had previously agreed they would go to see Kuyuk-baxshi and bring him to London. Domrul had told her it might take some time for him to get a visa, but then in all the hustle and bustle when he went to London, he had forgotten to submit his documents to the embassy. Just a week later, Emer, ready for the trip, called again, and Domrul, without mentioning his own forgetfulness, blamed everything on the bureaucrats at the embassy. He could sense Emer's impatience. "Maybe you can go yourself, and after you go I can follow you?" he proposed. Emer agreed.

Domrul may not be able to go with Emer, but we wouldn't want to miss our chance to take the trip. While Domrul puts Gaia Mangitkha-novna on the case, using her connections at the embassy to speed up the visa process, we will go with Emer, and depart with her for a journey to our own native land.

Every time she flew, Emer always felt filled to overflowing with new ideas. She always picked up her diary and began plotting out plans for the next weeks and months, or basically for her life in general. Now, too, instead of sitting here in her seat watching the little television, she was opening up her diary, intending to plan her trip. Her central task was to get Kuyuk-baxshi a visa at the British embassy. She had the required letters in hand. On Monday, the day after tomorrow, she would start the job. As part of that job she would meet Kuyuk-baxshi and draw up a schedule for his performances and for how to entertain him in London. She drew two thick lines under that assignment. The third job would be to meet some local evangelicals. They had already made some arrangements for

that over email. Emer wrote "sharing experiences," and unc
drew not just one, but three thick lines. Naturally, there wor
interesting sights to see too. She wrote that down as well, but though tɔ
herself, "I'll do that if they're on my way." Then she remembered another
thing. "Gifts for Domrul, etc.!!" She put two exclamation points after that
sentence.

The plans whirling in her heart seemed to be much more natural
than this flight. What was it her heart was seething for? What had her so
excited that she opened up her diary breathless, as if her life, from this
point forward, would suddenly and fundamentally change? Maybe she
could take dombra lessons from Kuyuk-baxshi? Or learn about the lives
of local women together with the evangelicals there? Those weren't plans,
exactly, but she put them down on paper with just as much enthusiasm.
She thought some more. Her heart was not yet full. When a human being
rises ten kilometers above the earth, his or her horizons are broadened by
multiples of ten, are they not? And therefore her heart desired vast and
grandiose things off on those distant, broad horizons.

Perhaps experiences and adventures she had never known before were
awaiting her! It was with this abstract but inspiring thought that Emer shut
her diary.

In fact, she would encounter one of those unexpected things just as
soon as she reached her hotel. It had been arranged locally that a handsome-faced Tatar named Ildar would be assigned to her as an interpreter.

Because it was close to dawn when the plane landed, Emer did not pay
too much attention to the fact that an interpreter had been attached to
her. But when she came down to the hotel bar at noon for some breakfast,
her interpreter was sitting there waiting for her loyally. Emer did not like
anyone observing her while she ate. Especially when her eyes were red
from her short and jetlagged sleep, and her cheeks had gone all puffy. She
grimaced inside. But she showed nothing. The interpreter, on the other
hand, as if ready to display his good nature to go along with his handsome
face, jabbered on and on, describing this country's produce from dairy to
grains, and saying he would have to take Emer to the biggest market in the
city and treat her to some bread called *non* from the tandir. Every word he

said put out a hundred new branches, and he told her what non was, and what kind of market it was, and he described to her what the tandir was made of as if taking pride in his perfect English, showing it off.

Emer somehow finished drinking her tasteless coffee, after adding twice as much sugar to it as usual. The interpreter asked about her schedule for the day. While Emer wiped her mouth, he fit in questions about their plans for Monday too.

"I need to go to a certain person's house," said Emer, and stood up from her chair.

"Shall I call a taxi, or shall we take public transport?" asked the interpreter, ready to go.

"Public transport," Emer answered, and headed back to her room. Looks like I'm not going to get free of that idiot, she despaired as she walked away.

In her room, as she was putting on her makeup, her thoughts again returned to the interpreter. "What if I *can* get rid of him? Would that be possible?" If she did, would she be able to find her way through the city with her English and French? She still remembered a little Serbian, but was Serbian anything like Russian? But she would still need an interpreter to speak with Kuyuk-baxshi. She'd cooperate with the chap for the day— he really had the look of a spy about him, didn't he?—and then she'd see what happened.

With that thought, Emer went downstairs again and stepped outside with her interpreter. The weather was foul. It was a good thing Emer's backpack still held the umbrella she had grown used to carrying around long ago, in London. True, unlike in London or Paris, here the foul weather held no real threat. On the contrary, the scent of the trees that had just recently flowered, mixed with the smell of the new life sprouting out of the ground, touched the nose gently and tenderly. Even the flow of the clouds was slow and weighty.

"Where are we going?" the interpreter inquired, tossing on his trendy jacket. Emer took the address Kuyuk-baxshi had written out of her pocket and showed it to him. "Phoo!" the young man reacted, with a whistle. "That's practically Land's End!" he declared, fitting in a characteristically English expression.

Emer spoke at the same time as he did. "He's an immensely famous person!" she said.

"He probably lives in a penthouse!" answered the interpreter, getting in another reference to the English way of life, and he steered Emer toward a tram stop. "Of course, I doubt the building at the address on that piece of paper has a penthouse at all," he added.

Enjoying the view of the city streets and people, they rode for forty minutes on the tram, then got on a bus. They spent another half hour bumping and bouncing in the crowd and finally reached a neighborhood straight out of Soviet times. These districts reminded Emer of the outskirts of Sarajevo. In truth, it had turned into a kind of run-down shantytown. The five-story concrete buildings were wearing out. Some residents had their balconies walled in with glass, and others with plywood; others had covered over their broken windows with plastic film, some had laundry hanging out, some were burning dried cow manure; in a word, the place looked deplorable.

Could it be that the famous Kuyuk-baxshi lived in one of these buildings? Emer was perplexed. Among the streams of washwater and the stinking trash heaps, they finally found Kuyuk's building. One just like all the others. They walked up to his apartment. The stairs were in a shambles, the guardrails had been removed, the light fixtures were all broken, and where the doorbell should have been, only a broken wire remained. They knocked on the door. No answer. A unibrowed woman peeked out of the door across the hall and said something. The young interpreter shook his head and knocked louder. A little while later, the door opened. And there stood Kuyuk-baxshi, who had only just woken up.

He did not recognize Emer right away. But Emer began prattling in French. "Kuyuk-baxshi! Kuyuk-baxshi!" she started, then he gathered who she was and went to hug her. Maybe because the interpreter spoke his own language, Kuyuk extended his hand to shake—politely, but with a bit less enthusiasm. They stepped inside. On the four bare walls hung only a few posters from Kuyuk-baxshi's appearances in foreign lands, and on the floor there was just a thin rug. He left his guests for a moment, went into the next room, and returned from there carrying two quilts and placed them down over the rug. Then he disappeared again and came back with a tablecloth in one hand and two hunks of non in the other. He handed the bread to the young man and spread out the tablecloth over the floor covering, then took the non, placed it on the tablecloth, and invited them to sit down.

Jamoli dastagul, qabog'i g'uncha,
Jahonda ko'rmadim suluv ul buncha,
Yuzda xoli mushki anbar tuguncha,
Xo'bliqda maqtasam, yana bor shuncha . . .

"Well, that's it!" Kuyuk said, turning with his exclamation to the young man, and added, as he left the room again, "Go ahead and translate what I said!"

The interpreter gave a hasty rendering of what he had heard. "He said you're the most beautiful girl. Your eyes are like almonds, your face is like a flower . . ."

Emer burst out laughing. "If my eyes are like almonds and my face is like a flower, God only knows what kind of mixed-up plant I must be!" This time Kuyuk-baxshi returned with a teapot and some cups. He had put some white sugar into one of the cups.

Kuyuk sat down, too, and spoke to the interpreter. "Please translate whatever my guest says!"

He poured the tea. First a bit into his own cup. Then he poured twice as much into another one and passed the teacup over to Emer. He handed another half teacup to the young man. Then he poured more for himself, too, then for some reason switched to a strangely accented Russian. "Ninety-five tea, green, from Samarqand. One thousand years will live!" he said. Emer just barely understood the Russian.

Kuyuk-baxshi switched back to his own language and said to the young interpreter: "You whisper in the pretty one's ear, younger brother, and we'll have a cup of tea, then we'll go and see a sheep slaughter. Say no words to a bald man, he'll bring himself around, as they say."

Kuyuk's mouth goes drier and drier,
Like the dry road to Paris, all I require,

She may be our guest, and my heart's desire,
Has our Emer not come here to inspire?

"That's it, you can go ahead and translate, can't you?" said Kuyuk-baxshi, elbowing the young interpreter who sat at his side and laughing out loud.

An hour and a half later, a car from the village called Qozoq-Qishloq pulled up in front of the building and honked its horn. Kuyuk-baxshi peered at the car from the window and then pronounced, as if giving a blessing over their table, "Now we shall go experience some real hospitality!" And he returned from the next room with a quilted robe over his shoulders, a cap on his head, and his dombra in his hands. And they rode in that car from the outskirts of the city to a land even farther away, Qozoq-Qishloq. The sky was still cloudy, with the rain unable to decide whether or not it cared to fall, just like people deciding whether or not to step outside, and the muddy roads the car traveled over were empty. When the car stopped, Emer learned that everyone in the village had gathered for a wedding feast. The interpreter told her as much, in a whisper, and now having this snobby urbanite at her side was purely an advantage, because otherwise Emer would never in her life have ended up in a place like this one, among people like these.

Trumpets blared at the sky as if they had been expected. The hosts emerged and warmly greeted the baxshi and his guests. With hundreds of people crowding all around them, the three of them were herded into the courtyard of a traditional house, to a raised platform draped with grape vines. They were invited to sit on this platform. Emer understood nothing, and with Ildar translating into her ear, whatever he said, she kept quiet and obeyed. They sat down. The baxshi said something and placed both his hands against his cheeks. Everyone else repeated that motion. Emer lagged behind them, copying what Ildar did.

Their teacups were filled first with tea, then with a cold beverage that only resembled tea. Everyone was looking at Emer, speaking energetically about something or other, and the interpreter worked to make her understand all their earnest utterances, until he found a chance to tell Emer the important thing. "This is brandy. Distilled using local plants," he said, raising his teacup. Everyone sitting on the platform or standing nearby also raised their cups and looked to Emer.

"They're waiting for you to take a drink," Ildar whispered.

Emer swallowed two sips from her cup, and it scorched her mouth and her gullet. True, in a moment, the burning taste somehow mixed with a stickier flavor, and the ecstasy hit Emer's head in an instant. Everyone applauded, and everyone emptied their own cups, one after the other. Kuyuk-baxshi offered Emer some sort of bright-red meat surrounded on all sides by a yellowish fat to help her chase it down.

She had chewed up and was just swallowing a strongly flavored piece when Ildar whispered in her ear. "That is the local delicacy. Horse meat!" he said. Emer gagged a little. Ildar handed her a piece of non.

"Here, this will help!" Emer swallowed the bread without chewing it.

More brandy was poured into the teacups. This time, to forget the flavor of the horse meat, Emer purposely used the brandy to rinse out her mouth before she gulped it all down. Her head was spinning. A man who had met them at the gates walked over and whispered something to Kuyuk-baxshi. Kuyuk-baxshi spoke his words to Ildar. Ildar translated, in turn, to Emer. Emer's mind perked up, and she watched them astutely. "You are invited to be our guest at a special ritual!"

Kuyuk-baxshi stood up from his seat, and Ildar rose after him. Emer bobbed up as well and got down off the platform onto her suddenly unreliable legs. They were led to a corner of the courtyard. At first, Emer understood nothing. When the man had said it was a ritual, her spinning head had thought there might be a bonfire, or the bride and groom making their appearance. But here, under a tree, stood a red-cheeked man, fat and mustachioed, wearing an apron, something clasped in his hand. When his eye landed on Emer, he shouted "Bismallah!" and leaned over a pile of something at his feet. "What is that pile? Firewood, maybe? To make the bonfire, maybe?" wondered Emer. Here at this stout man's feet, with a heart-rending bleating, a live beast lay dazed, and when Emer saw the fountain of blood gushing out from it like milk, she fainted dead away.

When she woke up from a dense, unfeeling sleep, her eyes damp, Emer tried to figure out where she was. Her head felt heavy as lead. Kuyuk-baxshi was sitting above her with that handsome-faced young man. Stars like shining grapes flickered through the grapevines overhead.

Kuyuk-baxshi said something. "You frightened us all!" the young man said, maybe translating, maybe expressing his own feelings. Where she lay, Emer made an effort to get her mind together. In the darkness of the hour, as if searching for a wall to lean on, she remembered when and how she had come here. The plane . . . the hotel . . . the tram . . . the bus . . . Kuyuk-baxshi's bare apartment . . . the car . . . the village . . . the wedding . . . yes, she knew where she was. At that feast. She remembered drinking. She attributed her unconsciousness to that drinking. "Now I've shown them how Irish I am, haven't I?" she thought bitterly. "Did I do anything crazy?"

Kuyuk-baxshi spoke again, his voice kind. The young man did not translate this time. Emer wanted to stand up. She needed to look all around, wanting to be certain about everything in that place with her. She took hold of Ildar's and Kuyuk's arms. They must have sensed what she wanted, and they gently lifted her up and sat her down. Kuyuk-baxshi immediately placed two pillows behind Emer. Emer leaned back on the cushions. Her head was spinning again . . . Her eyes went dark.

Dozens of people had gathered around. Kuyuk-baxshi seemed to be issuing them orders. In an instant, there arrived steaming dishes holding heaping heaps of noodles, in squares big as her hand, topped with strips of tender meat. "*Beshbarmoq*! Five fingers!" The interpreter pronounced the name of the dish.

Emer's stomach was empty. Aside from her morning coffee and the bit of non at Kuyuk-baxshi's place, and that brandy, she had had nothing else all day. Kuyuk-baxshi reached out a hand to the dish to show her how to eat it. The translator interpreted his movements for her with alacrity. Then everyone turned to Emer. Emer too dipped her frozen fingers into the boiling pasta and hot meat. The taste of it was amazing. Kuyuk-baxshi again demonstratively used all five of his fingers and looked at Emer invitingly. Emer again wrapped a hunk of meat in a piece of the pasta and placed it in her mouth. The three of them finished the bowl of beshbar-moq in no time. Then Kuyuk-baxshi burped loudly and sang a song.

> On a cloudy day a mallard will roost on your hand,
> Ducks and herons will come there, too, to land,
> If my Kazakhs throw a feast with beshbarmoq,
> Be their master, and they'll agree to your every demand.

Ildar translated it piece by piece. Emer smiled. Kuyuk-baxshi was happy, and he whispered something to Ildar. Ildar leaned toward Emer. "Now the main dish will come, but first, it's customary to have a drink to whet the appetite," he said. Emer, beshbarmoq still all over her hand, did not offer much resistance to that custom either. They took shot after shot of a brandy they called cognac. Now Emer's heart felt even lighter.

A bit later, someone came in with a sheep's head, which seemed to have been cooked smiling on its big platter. No, this time Emer did not pass out, but her stomach revolted. The dish was put down in front of them. The sheep's head was definitely looking at Emer. Kuyuk-baxshi took a knife out of its holster at his belt, chopped an ear off that head, sliced some meat off the ear, and held it out to Emer. "Here, tell her to listen to her elders!" he said. Ildar translated.

Emer's guts twisted inside her. She forced herself. She put the slimy slice into her mouth, tried to swallow it without chewing, then gagged a little, and the things inside her, the beshbarmoq and brandy distilled using local plants, all came back up again.

◈

Gaia Mangitkhanovna's stubborn heart had begun desiring unexpected things. Just today, without eating breakfast, before her carer had come, she had for some reason wanted to take a bath. Fine, if one doesn't take a shower in the morning, a bath is a normal kind of thing, but this heart-felt desire had not appeared with a pop inside the begum, or come up in an instant; instead it was a strange trembling that somehow overtook her whole body. Like a typhoon over the ocean, in some kind of fever, she locked herself in the bathroom, tossed her bathrobe at the laundry bas-ket standing in the corner, and stripped naked. Her body was trembling in sweet anguish, and keeping her eyes averted from her erect nipples reflected in the mirror, she used her trembling hands to turn first the hot tap, then the cold. The water roared in and began to fill the bathtub.

She had experienced them when she was young, these fits of hysterical ecstasy. At home, she would shut herself in the bathroom, make the water roar in, and join in the din, singing a song. When the tub was full, she would step into the water, turn on the shower, and without interrupting her song, she would turn the fountains flowing from the showerhead straight toward her loins. First, as the warm tickle and the song brought her to a peak, the fire would wrap around her belly, and finally, unable to bring her voice up to the climax of *that* song, she would start to wail, her whole being engulfed in the flames of an irresistible lust, melting.

Now she had fallen into the clutches of that mania again. She meant to begin singing, but her body, trembling in agony, made her voice fall into pieces, small and clumsy. At that, Gaia began to howl. She was thinking about her carer. If only he were standing here right now, he would take up this sponge and rub her ever weaker and more desperate body all over with it.

Still trembling violently, Gaia Mangitkhanovna put her feet into the water, and as usual, went to sit down on the edge of the tub, but in an unfamiliar bout of feebleness, her bottom slipped, and with a plop, she sat down hard on the floor of the bathtub. The water sloshed and splashed out into the room. Now it was not her cunt, which had just been burning so hotly, but more the pain in her tailbone that filled Gaia Mangitkhanovna's howling with anguish.

Many years ago, her husband had come home drunk from some friendly international drinking fest. "You know, a colleague of mine melted his enemies in a bathtub filled with acid! What if I did the same thing? First I'd throw you in for a test, witch! Ha-ha-ha!" he had laughed, thrusting into her.

Suddenly Gaia Mangitkhanovna felt as though she had fallen into just that sort of pool. As if her body had started to dissolve, her hand was too weak to part the water, her tongue lacked the strength to call for help, and her legs were too disobedient to stand her up from the muddy bottom of that acid bath.

◆

The day after all that shame Emer didn't want to go anywhere, and when she woke up in her hotel room, she lay there and lay there, the quilt wrapped over her head. If she had been at home, maybe she would have just hanged herself, but she was afraid of bringing even more shame upon herself in somebody else's country. In her mind, if she stepped outside, everyone would be pointing a finger at her. "There she is, the alcoholic Irishwoman!" they would say. Finally she got tired of so much lying around, and she got up and went into the bathroom, locked herself inside, and stayed there submerged under the warm water for half an hour or more. She wanted something steeped in bitterness, maybe some tea or coffee, but there was none of that in the room. Soon as she left her room, that snob from yesterday was sure to be waiting for her. She was hungry, and her appetite was teasing her empty insides. She turned on the television. It was showing sheep and cows. She switched it off straightaway. She sat there looking at her face in the mirror, at how puffy it was, from the crying or the drinking. Emer got dressed. She looked at her watch. Quarter to one. At two o'clock, she had a meeting scheduled with a consular officer at the British embassy.

That's what she would do. She would go out, and if she couldn't avoid the snob, she would tell him, "I'm going to the embassy. They won't let you in there, anyway. So I don't need you today."

It happened just as she had thought. The snobby young man was sitting there in a black leather jacket, playing with his phone. He shot a look at Emer and drifted in her direction. Emer spoke the words she had prepared.

"You won't get lost on the way?" he asked, as if concerned. Emer detected a trace of sarcasm in how he spoke.

"No!" she answered pointedly. "This time, I won't get lost!" and not waiting for an answer, she headed for the door.

She walked up to one of the taxis waiting outside the hotel, and declared, "British embassy!" "Bri-tish, Bri-tish!" repeated the driver, nodding his round head with a full mouth of golden teeth. Emer got in and he roused himself to action.

"Twanty dollar!" said the driver, turning onto a wide road.

Emer didn't waste her breath talking. "Okay!" she said.

After a bit they came out onto a wide avenue, crossed over it, then came to another. Fifteen minutes of driving without stopping, and they turned off the major road onto a smaller one. Before a building wrapped in a steel grating, with small spruce trees arranged in front, the car stopped, and the driver, barely turning his round head, showed his golden teeth again. "British, Bri-tish! Heeere!" Emer got a twenty-dollar bill out of her pocket and handed it over, then stepped outside. The taxi moved off. Emer looked up and saw a concrete building decorated with a sign, in great big letters: British-American Tobacco.

She yelled, annoyed, at the back of the taxi. Maybe the taxi driver actually heard her shouting, or maybe he was stopping for some other passengers, but not too far off in the distance, Emer saw the car stop. She rushed up behind it. Emer got into the car again, and not knowing whether the driver would understand her or not, she told him, "I said the British embassy, and you brought me to the British-American Tobacco offices. I'm not about to pay you another cent, but you'd better take me to the British EMBASSY!" Emer let that blizzard of English words storm down on the driver's head.

The driver didn't understand a thing, just pointed to the concrete building with one big finger. "Bri-tish, Bri-tish!" was all he would say.

At that Emer stood up in the car, stuck her head outside the window, and shouted out a question. "Does anyone here speak English?" she called.

A young couple approached the taxi. "I may talking English," said the young man.

"I need to go to the British embassy," Emer told him. "This man brought me from my hotel to this British-American Tobacco building. He charged me twenty dollars. Can you tell him to take me to the embassy, so that he understands?" she asked.

The young man may or may not have understood himself, and his eyebrows crept higher and higher up on his forehead as he listened, and he cast a glance once at the girl there with him, but he finally started explaining something or other to the driver. Now the girl joined the conversation, too, and Emer realized how haphazard the boy's understanding had been, and she started talking again, slowly, repeating everything for the girl. The girl may have been a little sharper, because she told the driver something, then asked Emer, "Embassy?" Emer trusted her and nodded her head. The driver, on the other hand, was shaking his head as if refusing, but the girl pronounced the word "dollar" again and looked over at Emer, and when she said "Twanty dollar," Emer and the driver, as if in agreement, both nodded their heads.

Just before the car started off, the boy shouted out behind them, "Manchester United! Rooney good!" And he shook Emer's hand. His girlfriend immediately started to pout. Emer had to smile.

Another twenty minutes later, they got off the main road and drove toward a familiar-looking area ("Isn't my hotel around here somewhere too?" wondered Emer), and then found a smaller road, and drove up in front of a bunker-like building guarded by concrete barricades. This one looked much more like an embassy. It was now ten minutes past two. She was late. Annoyed, she wanted to get out, but the door didn't open.

She looked up at the driver. He half turned his round head, and showed his golden teeth. "Twanty dollar!" he snapped.

"What the fuck for?" Emer cursed.

"Boy say. Girl say," he said, in clumsy Russian this time. That's when it hit her, with what remained of her Serbian. That young couple must have told him she'd give him another twenty dollars.

"Phoo," said Emer, and took another twenty-dollar bill out of her pocket.

After another half an hour, while the embassy people checked her documents, Emer's already dispirited mood was brought even lower. Naturally, the local consular secretary told her, "The consul was expecting you at two." In her perfect English, the remark came out spitefully. "Now you'll have to wait. Help yourself to some magazines."

Emer was annoyed, but picked up a magazine to read. The old queen smiling from the wall across the room materialized in the same shape and form on the first page of the magazine. She grimaced at the first few pictures, which all shouted out, "We are Great Britain! Great in this, Great in that . . ." Someone had naturally made some good money on that lame-brained ad. Disgusted by the magazines, she turned to look out the window, through its metal grate. The weather was as foul as ever. It looked like rain, but for some reason, the rain wasn't coming.

When the consul—a young man with athletic-looking features—came out of the next room, it was nearly half past three. If he had apologized for being late, Emer might not have seethed inside, but just like the secretary, he too reproached her. "Miss Finnegan, we expected you at two o'clock. Right, then, what can I do for you?"

Emer's mood had reached rock bottom. "They checked my paperwork for half an hour like I was a terrorist, then I waited for you for forty minutes more!" she told him directly.

"Those are all mandatory practices, you know," the consul explained, quite woodenly. "We don't follow those protocols for lack of anything better to do."

Clearly, their conversation, and their relationship, was wrecked from the start. Both sides sensed it.

After that initial lack of ceremony, Emer spoke in a gentler voice, in a more pragmatic manner. "I'm here representing an association of evangelical churches. Here's my certification," she said, holding out to him an official-looking piece of paper.

The consul was on the alert. "I must tell you from the start that the embassy does not get involved with any missionary activities," he warned her. Not waiting for a response, he examined the document, trying with little enthusiasm to figure out what it all meant. He was waiting.

Emer continued. "We'd like to invite a famous performer called Kuyuk-baxshi to come to London."

The consul settled himself more comfortably in his leather chair, and with a certain sarcasm in his voice, he asked, "So is he an evangelical too?"

"No!" Emer objected. "Is being a Christian a requirement for coming to Britain?" She could sound just as sarcastic as he did.

"No, of course not. But since it's your association issuing the invitation . . ."

"Our organization was founded under British law and we operate according to that very same set of laws!" Both times, Emer emphasized that word "law."

"Of course, of course . . ." said the consul, as if retreating, but that was just superficial. "We'll need to know the exact reason for this trip," he said, in a voice that suddenly sounded wrapped in weariness.

"He's a baxshi, like a bard. We want to set up some concerts for him in London."

"Concerts?" The officer seized on that word, and his chair squeaked. "Concerts? Miss . . . sorry, what was it?"

"Finnegan."

"Yes. Miss Finnegan, concerts are permissible for the appropriate organizations. For that they need a lawfully issued license!" Now he placed a special emphasis on the word "lawful."

"I'm sorry, I wasn't clear. He'll be appearing in churches. To bring the religions closer together. Surely you have no objection to that?" As Kuyuk-baxshi might have said, she may have fallen off her horse, but she hadn't fallen off the saddle.

"Were you aware that in order to carry out professional activities, he will need a work permit?" asked the consul, pulling another dagger out of his sheath.

Emer's mind was spinning. The collar of her shirt seemed to be strangling her. She wanted to crash through the windows and scream at the whole world. "Water . . . water . . ." she whispered, and then passed out, right where she sat.

◈

Once she returned to the hotel, Emer sobbed and sobbed. She got into the bathtub again and took a very hot bath. She lay down in bed. She could not sleep. She got up and switched on her computer. She called Domrul for a video chat, but he did not answer. She surfed the web a little. Emer's heart could not relax. After half an hour, she tried calling Domrul again. This time, he picked up. His freshly shaven face appeared. They greeted one another. Domrul asked how Emer was doing. "I'm just heading out to work. You just caught me. So let's talk fast!" he said.

Instead of talking, Emer suddenly burst out crying. She simply couldn't stop herself. "Is everything all right?" Domrul was asking, over and over again. "What happened? Tell me!" Emer was sobbing nonstop.

"What, did that baxshi of yours do something he shouldn't have?!" Emer sighed heavily, made herself stop crying, and broke off the connection.

A second later Domrul began calling her back online. Emer did not pick up. She shut her laptop. She sat in silence for a bit. Suddenly, the telephone in her room rang. Emer, dashing for it automatically, stopped halfway across the room. That would have to be Domrul. But she had never told him where she was staying or what the number was there! So who was it? While she wondered, the ringing stopped, just as she reached the phone. Then, as she was returning to her seat, the telephone rang again. Emer picked up the receiver.

"*Assalom alaykum*, Emer-khonim!" said Kuyuk-baxshi's voice. Then he said something else in his own language, and after that he handed the phone to another person. It was a young girl's voice, speaking very diligent-sounding English.

"*Salam*! My name is Guljamol. I am in the seventh grade," she said.

Emer's heart immediately melted for this girl. "Yes, hello, I can hear you!" she said.

The girl may or may not have understood, but leaving nothing unsaid, she went on in the same tone. "I have a big family. My father, my mother, two brothers, and three sisters."

"Very good!" Emer encouraged her.

When the girl was starting in on a description of the city where she lived, Kuyuk took the phone again and worked fervently to make Emer understand something, somehow, in Russian. Emer only caught the words "tomorrow" and "airport." Finally he handed the phone to the girl again. This time she was no longer telling her smoothly memorized story, but rather trying to get across Kuyuk-baxshi's urgent message in a scattered, tattered version of English.

"Uncle Kuyuk," she said, "Tomorrow . . . go on airport . . ."

"Okay!" answered Emer, trying hard. "So tomorrow Uncle Kuyuk will be going to the airport, right?"

"Right!" confirmed Guljamol.

"Carry on!" said Emer.

"Carry on," repeated the girl, as if it was a part of her lesson she hadn't learned.

Then Kuyuk-baxshi assigned the girl another difficult piece of translation work. "Aul . . ." she said, not knowing how to translate that word. "Melisa Qoyip," she said, and finally, "die."

Emer comprehended that somebody had passed away. Then Kuyuk-baxshi made another attempt to get her to understand something in his crazy Russian, and finally finding the right words, the girl took the phone again. "Uncle Kuyuk question you go?" she said.

"Will I go?" Emer repeated the question.

The girl must have thought Emer was correcting her mistake. "Will I go you?" she corrected herself.

"Yes!" said Emer, bringing the conversation to its logical conclusion.

Emer had no idea what she had agreed to. That short "Yes!" had emerged from the depths of her despair, and she had rushed to pronounce the word. The next morning a call from the front desk woke her up at dawn, before six o'clock. "There's a man here with a car for you. He says he's going to take you to the airport," they told her. When she asked, she learned it was Kuyuk-baxshi.

Emer threw some clothes on, took the clothing from her closet and laptop from her desk and shoved them into her backpack, and headed downstairs. Thank God that there was no sign of that handsome-faced young man at this hour, and only the enthusiastic Kuyuk-baxshi stood talking with the sleepy desk clerk in the lobby. Emer said hello to Kuyuk and asked the clerk to save her room for her.

"And what about your interpreter?" asked the clerk.

"Interpreter? We'll talk when I get back," she told him.

In the ancient car that was waiting for them outside, they rode off toward the airport. There, Kuyuk-baxshi worked his connections to procure two tickets, and by six thirty they were flying to Nukus on an old, compact little airplane. Must be like the flight from London to Paris, or, say, Belfast, about forty or forty-five minutes, Emer thought. But they flew on for two hours. Finally they landed in the place called Nukus, got off the plane at a rather ugly airport, and caught a cab. The weather was cloudy here, too, but some sort of relentless wind was gusting and gusting, shaking the old taxi's windows.

They rode another hour in the cab. Kuyuk-baxshi sat in front and talked in his own language with the driver, a narrow-eyed man with swollen eyelids. Emer heard her name from time to time and sometimes met the driver's slanting, flashing eyes in the mirror, but otherwise she stared at the uninhabited scene outside, not yet able to dispel her feeling of gloom. Desert, desert, and more desert.

Sometimes houses, made of the bone-dry earth and the same colorless hue of the soil, appeared, but then the desert wasteland always swallowed them up again. Finally, several hours later, they reached an aul, a tall elm tree hanging over its entrance. "My aul!" repeated Kuyuk-baxshi, gesturing all around and pounding a fist to his breast. They circled around the lifeless mud houses and stopped in front of a grandiose, cement-covered building with a roof of sheet metal. The iron gate was wide open, and five or six people were sitting in front of the gate, while the black silhouettes of a few more individuals could be seen inside. The taxi stopped before reaching the gate. Kuyuk-baxshi and the driver got out. Emer picked up her backpack and followed along after them. Here, Kuyuk walked without stopping, and in a loud voice he delivered one of his quatrains, this time adding a wailing, bellowing cry after every line. The people sitting at the door started wailing in response. Emer was bewildered. She realized she had landed in a mourning ceremony. What was she supposed to do? Should she wail too? Just then Kuyuk-baxshi's singing and wailing abruptly went silent, and he was rushing to embrace and whisper in the ears of the people sitting near the door. After that, he looked behind him, and in his ordinary voice, as if making a presentation, he told everyone, "Emer."

◈

"Their funerals are just like their weddings," Emer was thinking. They brought out meat, they sent out noodles. The men took surreptitious sips of vodka out of their teacups. Well, at least there was a woman from Riga called Irma here, who spoke English fluently, and they introduced her to Emer. When Emer asked, she learned that Irma wasn't here alone. There was a group of five or six people here on a pilgrimage to see the local master, Qimbat-baxshi, whom the Europeans called a "guru." As their conversation wandered, the two of them talked less about the reason for the funeral—Qoyip the policeman, nicknamed Tyson—and more about Qimbat-baxshi's extrasensory or mystical powers.

Emer wondered why Kuyuk-baxshi had never told her that he knew such a great guru. Could he be jealous? The way Irma told it, enchanted, their master was a modern-day bodhisattva, a contemporary manifestation of the Buddha. Irma and her friends had become his disciples long ago. Qimbat had earned the wrath of the Soviets along the way and been put in prison for ten years, but no matter how hard they tried to crush him in prison, he never broke. They only made him more perfect. "Once they're done talking here, we'll be sure to introduce you to our guru too," Irma promised her.

Close to evening, after they had joined the women of the house to help them wash all the dishes and chop vegetables for the next day's meal, Irma brought Emer back with her. Kuyuk-baxshi was evidently very concerned, and he pulled Emer to one side, whispering something to her over and over again, pointing with a finger and saying, "*Qilma! Qilma!*" Emer didn't understand, but she nodded her head. Of course she would be careful, if that's what he meant. Or was Kuyuk-baxshi just jealous of the other baxshi? In any case, making a gesture that seemed to mean "I will stay here," he thumped his fist against his breast once or twice. But repeating the same gesture, Emer recalled some of her Serbian. He had said the word *utro*, which meant "morning." "*Utra, utra,*" confirmed Kuyuk-baxshi, and Emer hurried toward Irma, who stood waiting for her at the door.

They walked through the darkness, toward some earthen mounds that soon replaced the houses. On the way, Irma started asking more personal questions. "Are you married?" she asked.

"No, but I have a boyfriend."

"I'm married. My husband is here too," Irma told her.

"Who is he?"

"My husband? A physicist."

"If he's a physicist," Emer asked, "how could he believe in the master?"

"Of course he believes! Our master Qimbat can make things move just by looking at them!"

"No way!" marveled Emer.

"It's true! You'll see it yourself!" With those words, they walked together into a simple courtyard on the outskirts of the aul and entered into a packed mud house full of the rumble of energetic conversation.

Just as in the rest of the aul where there was no electricity, in this house too, among a dozen people busy debating something or other, a kerosene lamp was burning. In its feeble light, Emer could see a poor assortment of household gear. Two iron bedframes, a wooden bench, jumbles of clothing hanging on the walls from crooked nails or pegs . . .

Irma, soon as she walked in, drew everyone's attention to herself, and she said something in Russian. Among those words, Emer recognized only "Kuyuk" and "Emer." Everyone looked at Emer, and they clapped. Somebody proclaimed, in English, "Welcome! Welcome to our circle!"

Irma and Emer moved closer toward the tablecloth spread out on the floor before them and the people sitting around it. Every one of them looked European, or particularly Russian, and as Irma had just mentioned, there were Latvians and Estonians and other Russian-type people there too. To see them in this place, in this landscape, sitting here this way, was at least very funny, if not to say incredibly odd. There was some sort of food in front of them, but what caught the eye more than that were several half-empty bottles of vodka. Emer's sharp glance bounced off the Russian brand Stolichnaya and recognized the Smirnoff bottles. Russia's world-renowned vodkas!

The people already seated moved over and made room for them. Finding herself in the midst of Europeans in this unfamiliar backwater made Emer feel calmer and safer. Her tense nerves relaxed a bit. Irma introduced Emer to the person sitting on her other side. "This is my husband Uldis!" Uldis asked her, in the same flawless English, "How do you do?" Then Irma and Emer were passed teacups full of vodka. Emer downed the shot easily, with no hesitation at all.

◈

Once Bo'riboy became Gaia's confidant and companion, he saw not just to her physical pleasure, but more, in fact, to her mental peace and tranquility. We spoke already about the size of Bo'riboy's pretensions and ambitions. He made some little part of those pretensions Gaia's responsibility.

ed to make your realm more like an anthill!" that trickster urged
en he caught sight of Gaia's metal queen-of-the-ants costume.

"Look," he said, "anyone good and fine in this world is the product of
an anthill. Who shapes and controls those people? Not big weak men like
your husband, but insect queens like you, ant queens! There's a craving
for order in you. Look at an ant colony. The young care for the babies, the
adolescents are the builders, the young men are the workers, the mature
ones are the soldiers, the older ones are the storekeepers, and the elders
keep watch. Your people are like that, aren't they? Your people are a clan
of creeping insects, always puttering about, always taking care of business!
That requires commanders and leaders like you and me, so that all of
those creeping insects think of their nest over themselves, hunt for their
nest over themselves, nurture their nest over themselves, guard their nest
over themselves, and die for their nest over themselves!

"Nietzsche's Zarathustra said he would never again speak to the people, but rather to the creators and the harvesters. We're not going to sit
here trying to change all those little ants either. We're going to change
the errand boy and the clerk. They're the ones who will spread the system
we're interested in throughout the hive."

Bo'riboy, that slanty-eyed devil, had found Gaia's most sensitive point,
and together they started in on their course of action, but by some evil
twist of fate when Bo'riboy and that filthy beast Qimbat were arrested in
Estonia or Pistonia, and when they nearly disclosed the mischiefs in which
Gaia had been involved, Gaia took the business into her own hands, and
through her own blue-eyed devil, working in the police force, she got rid
of her imprisoned confidant and companion Bo'riboy for good.

Now she was the only queen in the hive.

◆

The meager offering of food had been eaten, and much vodka had been
drunk, when a stout man walked into the room, a threadbare robe over his
shoulders, stone beads around his neck, and a plain-looking do'ppi on his
head. From how quickly the clamor and noise subsided, Emer understood
that this person was the master Qimbat. The master Qimbat, in one heavy
glance, let his weighty gaze fall on Emer. As Irma had just told her, he
could make things move by looking at them, and Emer felt the hair on her

arms and body standing on end. Irma seemed to be introducing Emer to the master. From what Irma was saying so quietly, Emer caught only her own name. The master Qimbat moved his head gravely.

The people grew impatient and set about gathering up the tablecloth. The circle opened up. The master Qimbat moved toward that opening and sat down cross-legged, facing the door. Everyone quieted down. Irma, who had left to carry out the dishes and the tablecloth, returned with an unopened bottle of vodka, and she handed that bottle to the master Qimbat. Qimbat drank the vodka in silence, drawing great gulps from the bottle. When the bottle was practically half empty, he handed it back to Irma. Irma took a swig from the bottle, and she passed the vodka around the circle. Everyone had a swallow, and they emptied the bottle together. Emer took her turn as well. Irma came back and sat down next to her. The master Qimbat began to speak. Irma whispered in Emer's ear, translating for her.

"In ancient times, Plato was appointed to serve as the healer for Alexander the Sultan. One day, when Plato was absent, his pupil Aristotle boasted to the others, 'I am a better healer than Plato!' The other pupils teased him. 'Well then,' they said, 'why don't you prove it!' What they agreed to was that Aristotle would mix a poison for Plato. On the day they had agreed upon, Plato drank that poison and then hurried home. He had already ordered that three cisterns of milk be brought to his house from a nearby farm. Plato poured that milk into a stone vat. He dove inside. The milk soaked up all of that poison.

"The next day, Plato walked back into the school in perfect health. Then Plato's pupils told him he should prepare a poison as well. 'Now we will test Plato!' they said. Plato responded in this way. 'The poison I prepare is exceedingly complex. Preparing it takes forty days.' Plato spent forty days doing nothing, free of cares, living the good life. Only from time to time, to distract them in the middle of the night, he would pound a hammer on the bottom of a cauldron. Aristotle heard that pounding every night, and it made his heart thump in fear. Finally, the forty days passed, and Plato poured some pure spring water into a pitcher and brought it to the school. He handed that pitcher to Aristotle. Aristotle drank that pure water, and in the space of a breath, he dropped dead!"

Everyone was still sitting in silence, trying to drill down to the point of that tale, when the master Qimbat added on a conclusion. "Never even think about rebelling against your teacher! The trust between us is just like that pure water. Rebellion and doubt can transform it into poison!"

Qimbat spoke those words, clapped his hands together, and suddenly began to howl like a wolf. From among those sitting there, somebody threw himself in Qimbat's direction, plucked at the cloak on his back, and started to pull and tear at it. Somebody brought in another armful of vodka bottles from outside. Somebody else joined in with Qimbat's howling and began tossing off his own clothing . . .

Now, aside from his nondescript do'ppi, the master Qimbat sat bare naked in front of them, just like a Buddha, his round belly hanging down to his knees, bringing the two bottles of vodka in his hands all at once to his lips, his two jiggling breasts rocking and shaking atop his belly. In that room, the delights and amusements had already started. Everyone had tossed away their clothing, everyone held bottles of vodka. To the stunned Emer, Irma was whispering, her voice full of lust and longing, "Don't be afraid, my darling. Get undressed."

It must have been a sort of ritual they had. Qimbat would put the two bottles on either side of his body and use his stout finger to point to somebody. That person would lay his head onto one of Qimbat's fat knees. Then Qimbat, choosing a friend for him, had somebody else kneel in front of his other knee. He placed his two palms over their two heads. Whispering something, he moved their two heads closer together, and as if joining them together, he pulled his own hands toward his face. That couple moved into a corner, and under a raggedy old quilt, the kisses and embraces and loveplay would begin. Once three or four matches had been made, the master Qimbat turned his head right around, and in one gesture, he indicated that Emer would do for Irma's husband, while Irma would be for the master himself.

Having drunk her fill, Emer was sitting there still clothed, her mind gone blank. Now what was she supposed to do? Should she obey them, or summon up her willpower and say no? The devilish thought occurred to her that she and Domrul should have come here together, and after that, as if responding to that idea, she shouted out, "No!"

Irma, caught by surprise, just asked, "Why?"

Holding his head straight up again, or more precisely, whipping it back in the other direction, the master Qimbat glared at her with such a heavy gaze that Emer truly believed, that instant, that any everyday object would move on the strength of it. Qimbat hurled a single word at Uldis, something that sounded to Emer like "Hide!" And he pulled the naked Irma over to his lap right in front of her husband.

That exceedingly polite and so far good-natured husband of Irma's leapt up from his seat and grasped Emer by the arm. He's going to rape me! Emer thought in a flash, and she started to scream. But Uldis told her, in his nice clean English, "Come on, get up!" And when Emer saw he had put on his overcoat, she managed to stop yelling. Whether from the awkward way she had been sitting, or from the vodka inside her, her legs were numb and wobbly when she stood. She might have fallen if Uldis had not had a firm grip on her elbow, steering her toward the door.

What is he going to do with me? she was just thinking, when he opened the door, stepped out into the courtyard, and hung Emer's backpack over her shoulders. "You're free to fuck off!" he said, and he sent her away.

Where am I? What is happening? Emer was staring at the pitch-black sky. A relentless wind was tossing the blue-black clouds from this side to that, and among them the moon seemed to be the eye of the devil Qimbat himself, looking her way; it was there blinking one moment and gone the next. Now where could she run? Kuyuk-baxshi had told her, hadn't he, to be careful? Why hadn't she listened to him? Where was he now? In this little village, she may as well be in a different world, she thought, leaning back against a thin tree outside the doorway. Close up, that little tree seemed very alive, and as it creaked in the wind, Emer thought she could sense all the fluids running through it. Or was the tree wiping the tears from her eye, touching her cheek?

There is some laughter to every tragedy, as they say, and Emer suddenly thought of Uldis, so unlucky with women, including with her. Going back to that room, being the lone witness to all the festivities—maybe that was worse than being left alone with the open sky and boundless earth.

She felt bad for Uldis. He had already suffered at other people's hands, and now Emer had to disappoint him too.

As those unexpected thoughts returned to Emer's mind, they awoke her willpower. She decided she would just set off in one direction first, from the house; if she couldn't find that Tyson-policeman's fancy house, she would walk in the other direction. There was not a single light on in the village, and Emer first turned right through the inky darkness, walking with the wind. She passed two or three houses, and in the darkness, all the little hillocks seemed to have grown smaller. She was afraid of wild dogs, and she had never gotten close to one of the little mounds, but she thought that toward the edge of the aul, the hillocks did start to shrink. At that her confidence increased, and she drew nearer to one of the little mounds. In a beam of moonlight, coming out from behind the clouds, the fact suddenly popped into her head and stuck there: this brick pile was a grave. "Mercy!" whined Emer, both lacking the strength to turn back and unwilling to stay in this place. Slowly, slowly, as if to avoid making things worse, she started walking back in the other direction. Her heart was racing, thumping and thumping.

Then she turned and started walking against the wind. The gale hitting her face scattered her inner fears, and while she tried to run, the gusts of wind, as if probing her, were trying to hold her back. She remembered a tip she had learned in her childhood in Sarajevo, about refraining from sharp movements in the face of danger. She slowly, slowly made it back to the familiar tree and latched on to its thin trunk.

Should she go back, go into Qimbat's house? Maybe the party was over and they were sleeping. But the moon, emerging again from behind a cloud and looking over her with its terrifying gaze, drew her out of that fantasy. Emer continued walking against the wind. Among the darkened, cowering buildings, she walked for some time, and then she heard a rustling sound. She walked toward the sound. The noise grew louder. It was an immense, majestic elm, seeming to toss the air this way and that, as if spinning the wind around itself. Yes! This was that same elm at the entrance to the village! Should she stay here underneath it, pressed up against its sturdy trunk, till morning? But just a minute. After the taxi had turned right at the elm tree, hadn't they come in view of the policeman's house, two buildings away? There, the breeze from the elm shoved the clouds away, and in the moonlight, a white metal roof was flashing. Emer had found the house. She had found it!

◈

The next day at nine o'clock in the morning a taxi came and took Emer and Kuyuk-baxshi to the airport at Nukus. Nestled in her seat in the taxi, Emer spent the whole ride in a deep slumber. After Kuyuk brought her to her hotel, she slept a bit and dreamed nonstop, without understanding where she was or what she was doing; she had managed to get into her hotel room with the interpreter's help, and still fully dressed, she collapsed into her own bed. Again she slept.

Later, she still had no idea what day it was. It was as if she had returned to that state of drunken shamelessness she remembered from Qozoq-Qishloq, something she now saw as a nightmare. She looked at her watch. The watch said that whatever day it was, it was eleven o'clock. She stood up. She washed her face and combed her hair. Her mind was in a fog. She picked up her diary, then walked down to the hotel bar. The interpreter was sitting there waiting. He must have sensed that Emer's heart felt rather dark, so he tidied up his smile and slipped the jokes he had prepared back into their sheath. Two espressos later, Emer felt a little bit like herself again. She opened her diary and ran her eyes over it. She had seen Kuyuk. She had met with the ambassador. She still wanted to meet with the evangelicals. She would not need to bring the interpreter to that meeting. But be that as it may, she could not think of any way to dismiss him.

"I want to see some friends, so if you have other things you need to do, go ahead!" she said.

"My work is serving you!" Ildar pronounced ceremoniously. All right. If that's the case, maybe we can open up his heart to Christ the Messiah too, thought Emer, and she made a call to let the evangelicals know they were coming and went out with Ildar to look for a taxi.

This time, maybe because Ildar was with her, they reached their stated destination without incident. She didn't even pay more than five dollars. They went into a five-story building that resembled the one where Kuyuk-baxshi lived and walked up to the top floor. They knocked on the door they needed. A short, narrow-eyed man opened the door. He introduced himself only as Lee and ushered them inside. Just inside the room, Ildar whispered helpfully in Emer's ear, "He's Korean."

They walked into the room and found maybe a dozen people shouting out hallelujahs, in unison, and one of them had an instrument that looked something like a banjo with two horns ("A *rubob*," Ildar explained), and started playing along to the hallelujah song they were singing in their own language.

Emer was suddenly overwhelmed by feeling, and although she understood only the word "Jesus," at the sound of that word in the unfamiliar tongue she felt tears of joy and exaltation spring to her eyes, all because of these young men. During the song, they all raised their hands and swayed from side to side like poplar trees in the wind. Emer joined them. At first, the bewildered Ildar connected himself to the chain of hands too.

After the song, they all sat down in the next room, around a table set full with the good things in life. They offered a prayer to Christ the Messiah. The feast began. Just like everywhere else, a few people here, too, spoke English. When Ildar translated "Our Lord Jesus Christ" as "Christ our Messiah," a slight girl with shining green eyes corrected him. "'Our Lord Jesus Christ' would be 'Rabbimiz Iso Khristos,'" she said.

Over the meal, they discussed the work they had done, and Emer, after filling her empty stomach, gave testimony; she told them how new members were being recruited in Paris, in particular, and about new ways to do what they called in Uzbek "capturing followers." She described her missionary work on the subway lines and trains that crisscrossed the city.

Among these people who thought like her, Emer felt all the dust that had settled over her heart these past few days lift up and disappear. The last thought to cross her mind was "Our Lord Jesus shines so brilliantly here!"—and then a knock sounded at the door.

Everyone fell silent. The man of the house, the Korean, Lee, walked up close to the door. "Who's there?" he asked. Instead of an answer, that door swung wide open, and like Satan's army straight from hell, armed demons, their faces covered with black masks, stormed in and shoved every single person seated there straight down onto the floor.

The room was turned upside down. Some of the young men were forced down flat on the floor and handcuffed. Ildar shouted out, "I'm here with a foreigner!" They took one look at his formal suit and tie and led him off on his own. Then one of the ones who was left grabbed up Emer, who was screaming nonstop in English, and rushed her downstairs and outside, where they shoved her inside not a Black Maria, but an ordinary bus. Ildar was not on the bus. That bastard! He sold us out! thought Emer, furious. Nobody paid any attention to her English. The windows on the bus were tinted dark, but she could make out seated figures, a detainee between every pair of masked men. Emer soon found herself between two of them. The bus took off.

"I'm a foreigner!" Emer shouted again, and this time the masked figure responsible for her twisted Emer's handcuffed wrists up behind her back so high that she squealed, and the words she was saying were utterly forgotten. Until the pain dissipated a little, she sat mute. Lord only knew where they were taking her! The bus came to a stop, and each masked officer shoved a prisoner down the steps and outside, where Emer beheld a seven- or eight-story concrete building on her right, with other tall concrete-block apartment buildings all around. Her turn came to be prodded off the bus, and they were all herded, heads bowed, down into the basement story of that building.

Not just a basement, actually; they descended down through three floors underground. They passed through a door made of iron bars. One of the masked men shoved them hurriedly into a room on the right. There, a woman wearing a uniform, wasting no time, first inspected the green-eyed girl who spoke English and then started digging through Emer's pockets. Every object she found she tossed to one side, where another woman in uniform collected them in a box. Then she steered Emer out of the room, with a firm grip on her elbow, and they set off.

Emer saw a long corridor with prison cells arranged on each side. She was led to the very last cell, where the woman guard unlocked the iron door with an immense key, shoved Emer into the cell, and then removed the handcuffs from her wrists, and muttering something or other, shut the door they had come in through with a bang. The key turned in the lock.

Was this actually happening, or was it a continuation of her nightmare? Why had she been arrested? Why had any of them been arrested? Where had Ildar disappeared to? Had he sold them all out?! But none of them had done a single thing that was against the law! What was going on here? A dream, or reality? Now what was she supposed to do? She'd be crazy not to demand a meeting with the British ambassador! Calmly and firmly.

Emer went to the door and started pounding on it with both fists. Nobody responded at all. No matter how much she wept and shouted, nobody even looked her way. All at once she lost hope, and Emer sat down on the bunk attached to the wall. She looked around. A small room, all concrete. Above her bunk hung another just like it, also sticking out from the wall. So they might put some other person in here to join her. Across the cell, a metal bench was bolted to the cement floor. There was a bucket in the corner. A light bulb glowed behind an iron cage on the ceiling. That was it.

She had no idea what else to do, so she stretched out on the bunk.

◆

For two days, nobody came, except the guards who brought her porridge. Nobody stopped by to ask how she was doing. For two days, Emer stewed in her own thoughts. Human life, really, was as thin and fragile as a hair. Three days ago, in a nameless village in the nameless steppe, even as she was left all alone in the great big world, she had never fallen so low. Because she had been free. She could step to the left, step to the right, whenever she wanted to. Here, though, there was no room to walk at all. If she rotted away here, nobody would ever know. And there were all the things she had read about the situation in this country: prisoners boiled in hot water, tortured with electrical shocks . . . Now the same fate had fallen on her! Why had she ever come to this terrible place? Did she think everything she had read was a bunch of fables? Had she thought those things could only happen to other people? Had she believed they would not touch her? This all looked now like the fruits of her own careless thinking.

On the third day, in the morning, they woke her up, gave her no time to wash, cuffed her wrists together, and marched her to a room at the end of the corridor. Two men in uniform sat waiting there, one across a table and one to one side. They pointed Emer to a stool to the right of the table. The guards who had brought her there removed her handcuffs and left.

The man sitting across from Emer did not raise his head from the papers he was examining, but the one seated to her right ran his eyes over her, head to toe.

The man across from her put his papers down, raised his eyes, and said something in Russian. Emer only understood the words "Emer Finnegan."

The one next to her translated. "Are you the suspect known as Emer Finnegan?"

"The suspect?" stated Emer, honestly surprised.

The interpreter translated.

The investigator (he must be the investigator, if he's asking questions!), with no change to his voice, looked through a couple of papers and said something else. This time he spoke at length, while the interpreter took notes. When the investigator stopped speaking, the translation followed.

"You are suspected of violations of criminal code article one hundred fifty-six, inciting national, racial, ethnic, or religious hatred; article two hundred sixteen point one, urging participation in illegal public associations and religious organization activities; article two hundred sixteen point two, violating the legal requirements with respect to religious organizations; article two hundred forty-four point one, preparing or distributing materials constituting a threat to public security and public order; and article two hundred forty-four point three, preparing, storing, publicizing, or disseminating illegal materials with religious content. Under these statutes, criminal charges have been—"

Emer's mind was spinning. She felt like she was going to faint. But she had one more thing to say, or sob: "I am a British citizen. I demand to see an ambassador or consul!" she said. The interpreter interpreted.

And then the investigator went spitting, raving mad. Screaming, he stood up from his chair, shrugged his shoulders out of his jacket, and started unfastening his belt. Emer was now genuinely terrified. He's going to either hit me or rape me, she thought in a flash, and she prepared to defend herself. At that very instant, an alarm rang out in the cell.

Emer shook and shook, and she had no idea what was happening. People came into the room, and people left. When she had nearly come to, one of the interpreters was putting a plastic cup of water down in front of her. She drank and drank that water, spilling it all over. She asked for more. The interpreter did not go himself, but called someone else over instead. A soldier brought her another cup of water. Emer swallowed again and again. "You seem like a good person," she started whispering to the interpreter in English. "Help me! Please! Call the British embassy and tell them I'm here! I'll pay you whatever you want!" She said those words and then bit her tongue again. What if one of them heard her, what if they were writing this down? He'd think she was trying to bribe him in the course of his official duties, and that would only make things worse.

But the interpreter just smiled gently. "Your consul is here," he said . . . and she beheld a miracle. There, indeed, was the very same officer Emer had met at the consulate the other day, walking right into that concrete room.

Emer couldn't stop herself. Sobbing, she threw herself in his direction. But the man protested loudly. "Miss Finnegan! Please!" he said. Emer stepped back again reluctantly. The interpreter sat down in the place recently occupied by the investigator, and the consular officer took the interpreter's chair.

"I am being accused of crimes," Emer complained.

"Yes, we know," replied the consul, all business. "These are very serious charges."

"I haven't done anything wrong!"

"The brochures you brought were confiscated."

"But those brochures are about Our Lord Jesus!"

"I am unable to comment about that."

When he had first come in, this man had struck Emer as the person closest to her in all the world. Now, before her very eyes, he shrank down to size, an ordinary clerk, and she knew all her hopes over the past three days would leave her with nothing but regrets. No, you can't expect any help from these types, Emer realized.

"What is going to happen to me?" she finally asked, a sense of dread weighing inside her.

"We don't know just yet, but your situation is quite serious."

"Aren't you going to help me?"

"Whatever do you mean? I've come all this way and I'm sitting right here, you know."

The interpreter was still sitting there quietly too. Maybe that was why the man from the consulate was speaking so cautiously? Had there never really been any chemistry between Emer and this guy at all?

"They meant to rape me." Emer decided to share her ultimate pain.

"We will be monitoring the propriety of the investigative process," continued the clerk in that same official tone.

At that moment, Emer finally understood she would be left on her own to face her terrible future, and out of the inconsolable depths of her despair, she asked for one favor. "Call Eastbourne, 01323-41-42-43. Find my boyfriend Domrul. Ask him to come here right away."

Fire and Air

During Domrul's first six months working for Gaia Mangitkhanovna, a lot of things in their relationship . . . changed, to put it gently. No, not in any extraordinary sense, but you might say that Gaia's arrogant neglect dropped out of the equation. True, she still kept herself rather detached, but the closer she came to the appointed hour, the more her doubts evaporated, and everything started to seem simpler.

For that reason, on the evening that Domrul heard news of Emer's incarceration, the first thing he thought to do was to have a tête-à-tête with Gaia Mangitkhanovna. There was no question of going to the office. (At that hour, who would he tell anyway?!) He hoped he could make some arrangement with Gaia, fly out at dawn, and deal with the office later. The important thing was an agreement with Gaia Mangitkhanovna.

The news of Emer's imprisonment, naturally, made him shudder all over, but the feeling that it served her right, that he had *warned* her, after all, was stubbornly and vengefully mixed in to his concern. Domrul had been aching to share that feeling, but for some reason he always felt that Kuyuk-baxshi's sly, squinty eyes were mocking him.

Without even noticing how soaked he was getting in the spring rain, he walked to Gaia Mangitkhanovna's house and rang the buzzer in their coded pattern. After a short time Gaia Mangitkhanovna's sleepy, displeased voice asked in Russian, "Who's there?"

"It's me, Domrul. It's urgent!" he answered. The door opened.

By the time he came up to the ninth floor, the apartment door was already ajar. Domrul entered with a decisive step. He shut the door quickly behind him. Not pausing to take off his sodden shoes, he strode on into the shadowy living room, and sensing Gaia Mangitkhanovna's presence there,

146

he announced into the darkness, "Emer's been jailed!" Straight to the heart of the matter. No response. Impatient, Domrul spoke into the darkness again. "Emer has been jailed! Do you hear me? That's why I'm here."

At that, from the rocking chair in the corner, Gaia Mangitkhanovna's voice, nearly sobbing, and full of pleading, trembled out. "That wasn't me. I didn't do it," came the whisper.

Gaia Mangitkhanovna was clearly stunned into some sort of paralysis. One second she was sobbing desperately, the next she was begging Domrul to forgive her, and the next she was arguing her case before some panel of judges. The old woman's lost her mind, he thought, not knowing what to do next. Should he call an ambulance? They would ask him what he was doing at Gaia's apartment at that hour of the night. If he said she had called him herself, they would take one look at the state she was in and see she couldn't even remember her own name, let alone call someone else for help. Maybe he could call Antonina Ivanovna? She would understand. He could hand her over and rush to Gatwick. Antonina could call an ambulance, too, and they wouldn't say a word to her.

So that is what Domrul did. He called up Antonina. Then he took off his coat in the entryway and switched on the light in the living room. Gaia Mangitkhanovna was huddled in her nightgown in her chair in the corner, a truly sorrowful scene. She was still trembling a little, still mumbling disconnected syllables. Domrul brought some water from the kitchen and offered it to the old woman. She spilled a little of the water down her front, then started drinking in gulps.

"Want some more?" Domrul asked. She nodded her head. Domrul brought more water.

She drank. Then, grasping her cup in both hands, she lifted her gaze to Domrul's eyes. "You're not going to kill me?" she asked, cowering before him.

"No!" Domrul answered. The old woman seemed to grow calmer. Then Antonina rang the doorbell.

So now he was on a plane to Istanbul, and from there he would fly on to Emer's aid. Domrul was finding it difficult to understand Gaia Mangitkhanovna's strange words and actions. Why had she said "That wasn't me. I didn't do it?" What a greeting! Had Domrul's fearsome appearance ed her? And then she had asked if he was going to kill her! As if Domrul had come to murder her. And truth be told, hadn't Domrul come in fast and furious, as if nothing could stop him? At that unconventional hour, too! What's more, when he had shouted into the darkness that Emer was in jail, hadn't that sounded like an accusation?

But if she wished to, could she have had Emer arrested? Easily! If she could have had Emer arrested, doesn't that mean she actually did it? But for what reason? To draw Domrul closer to herself? Did she think Domrul wouldn't find out that Emer was in prison? Hadn't she asked if he was going to kill her? There she had been, begging her appointed executioner not to kill her! But honestly, one part of it still troubled him. Hadn't Kuyuk-baxshi said that some people he knew had been arrested? Who were those people he had mentioned? Why hadn't Domrul asked her, interrogated her? It was stupid. He could have finally given some clarity to these worries and doubts. If only he could turn the clock back six hours.

◆

Tolstoy, or some other great thinker, once wrote that we spend the first half of a journey pondering the things we have left behind, and on the second half of a journey our thoughts turn to the things that await us where we are going. Domrul, certainly, was unable to pull his thoughts and memories away from Gaia Mangitkhanovna the whole two hours he spent waiting to change planes in Istanbul. He had been her caretaker for half a year now, which felt a bit like sinking into an inescapable swamp. But it seemed a particularly comfortable and even a healthy kind of swamp. There was no way out for him now. Domrul's relationship with Gaia was wrapped in a dirty secret, and if that secret were to be revealed, his own filth would be visible too. But if the secret could remain a secret, his dirt and filth could also stay a secret. Every secret has a certain power of attraction, and a dirty secret, too, draws the eye with its dirty laundry, bewitches us. After the unexpected first intimate encounter with the old woman, Domrul had been disgusted with himself. He was a scoundrel and a skunk. And the second time the unexpected happened, too, it had been as if he had plunged headfirst into a puddle of filth. The third surprise was already beckoning. After that, diving into that type of dirt became a habit.

Now that he knew it, Domrul had just one argument with which to comfort himself: Gaia Mangitkhanovna would take that dirt with her to her grave. Fine, Domrul reasoned, but then what purpose motivated Gaia Mangitkhanovna? After all, she was hardly the innocent victim of Domrul's passion. Actually, it was the opposite! *She* was the one who had played the fool, drawn Domrul to her side, and tied him up there. *She* was the one who had trained Domrul to respond to her every whim. She herself had often described other situations with a Russian proverb—"If the hen won't cluck, the cock's out of luck!" But what need did she have of that filth? Or was it not actually filth to her? If it wasn't filth, then what? Lust converted into habit? The eternal power of old age over youth? The last curtain on the last stage before death came for her? What *was* it?

And if you put it that way, had any man ever been capable of understanding what did or did not reside in the heart of any woman?

As he thought about that, Domrul made a discovery about himself. We started this passage with a reference to the greats, and we will end it with the greats as well. Jung would have said that Domrul considered Gaia to be his Shadow, but she was no Shadow; she was turning out instead to be his Anima. A genuine Anima, sticking to him like a Shadow.

◆

Domrul's interest in Emer had started with her name. It was written "Emer" in English, but that word in Irish was pronounced more like "Avair." Emer's mother had in fact called her Avair. But for Domrul, and for all the rest of us, Emer kept her Emer-ness. On top of that, she was more used to that non-Irish pronunciation, and she had stopped telling everyone, as she had done in her early childhood, "I'm not Emer, I'm Avair."

The name Emer (or Avair) is one of the oldest, most storied names in Irish history. The original Avair was first the betrothed, and later the wife, of the hero Cú Chulainn. Domrul couldn't help but spell out that name in his head as Kuchalan, in a way that made the Turkic roots in the hero's name quite clear to him, so naturally he tried to find some comparison between the old story of Avair and Cú Chulainn and the ancient Turkic sagas; and while he labored over that task, he never noticed how strongly tied he was becoming to the young woman who had transformed out of the mythical Avair into his own Emer.

The mythical Avair had attracted Cú Chulainn with six admirable traits: her beauty, her sweet singing voice, her skillful speech, her fine embroidery, her wisdom, and her chastity. Domrul started to search for those same traits in his own Emer. "Can you sew a flower vase out of postcards?" he asked her once, out of the blue, remembering his own closest brush with embroidery in school. Or he would quiz her flirtatiously, "Didn't you ever want to marry other guys before me?" A surprised Emer would change the subject, at which Domrul had to concede she *did* have a quick, sweet way with words and would keep quiet for a time.

Now, though, Domrul remembered one story out of that ancient myth most of all. The part about Avair's only jealousy. Because Cú Chulainn was such a well-built and handsome young man, he had many lovers aside from his wife Avair. But only one time did Avair's jealousy rise to the surface. One day, Cú Chulainn was sailing the sea, when up above him he heard a cry, and he saw a seagull flying overhead. The hero felt mischievous, and he took up a stone in his sure hand and threw it. The rock broke the seagull's wing, and the wounded gull suddenly disappeared from view. It was no ordinary seagull, but Pand, a beautiful maiden from the other world. Discerning a woman's form off in the distance, Cú Chulainn drew nearer, and she lashed him with the whip in her hand. The hero grew weak and collapsed onto the sand. For one year, Pand fed Cú Chulainn and brought him back to health, and she enchanted him. "Now we are in love forever, and we will go back to the other world together!" she said; but just when Pand was about to return to her own world with Cú Chulainn, Avair came to her with a group of women bearing knives, intending to stab and kill her. But at that, Pand turned into a bird once more and flew off to the other world.

Why was Domrul remembering this part of the story? And how was this tale so appropriate for him right now?

For the second half of his trip, Domrul was thinking about his abandoned country along with Emer. He planned out what to do. Once he had a plan, he made an effort to feel something about the fact that he was returning to his native land, where he had not shown his face for twenty years now. Beneath all the fuss, that feeling, like smoldering old embers, suddenly blazed up in flames again. He was coming back to the country that had threatened him with death, the country he had fled, the place where his sweetest memories lay side by side with his bitterest regrets. Which of those would prevail this time? The succor of his childhood memories, or the bitterness of the massacre, the destruction and destitution that had ended his childhood?

No. He had to get free of these empty, idle thoughts! He was going to rescue Emer! That was all he ought to be thinking about! Resolved, he walked off the plane. But the light of the early spring dawn, and the breeze from the mountains, came and sent his mind spinning. It was the feeling he experienced at the end of a zikr suddenly overtaking him, and in surprise, he sighed, "Oh, Allah!"

Domrul walked through the airport with a certain amount of worry. Whatever the case, sitting in that basement for three days, awaiting his own death, had left a wide scar on his heart. How would *they* receive him now? In which language would he speak with them? But he passed through the border guard checkpoint and customs and stepped outside, where cab drivers surrounded him, jabbering in this language or that, but all saying "Wherever you're going, I'm the cheapest!" And their chatter brought Domrul's mind back down to earth. He saw that twenty years had gone by, and nothing seemed to have changed here.

Had that horrible tragedy even happened?

Here, as he traveled the slowly waking streets of the city in a taxi, a sad tune from the old days playing on the radio, the driver asked him with a burst of interest, "Where did you come from? What's it like over there? You think I could go there?" The same questions as always. True, in the past, the person answering those questions had always been Domrul's father, returning from the resorts in Crimea or Sochi, and this time it was Domrul himself responding to them. As if nothing more important had happened in the interim.

Domrul answered just as craftily. "I've come from Istanbul, life's not bad, lots of people from around here over there," he said, keeping the conversation in hand.

Given that he had arrived from Istanbul, the driver was surprised to hear he wanted to go to the British embassy so early in the morning. "Want to get a visa? Is that hard to do?"

Domrul didn't really think about it and just answered "Yes." He paid the driver his fare in dollars and got out. He was struck just as suddenly as before, in the nose and in his very brain, by the scent of apricot blossoms, by the odor of the dust drying in the street. Domrul stood still for a moment and looked up at the sky. Somewhere under this sky, in some corner of this earth, his mother lay. Maybe also his father.

He looked at his watch. It was now past eight. The embassy should open at ten. Maybe he'd sign in with the policeman guarding the doors, walk over to some market or other, and get some hot non and cream for breakfast? Yes, that's what he would do. Hello, fatherland.

The consul received Domrul at twelve o'clock. His first question, after the introductions, was, "Are you an evangelical too?"

"No!" answered Domrul. "I'm a Naqshbandi Sufi."

"And have you come here with a pile of brochures as well?"

"No, why, should I have?" Domrul asked with surprise.

The consul heaved out a sigh. "Certainly not! Your girlfriend was snatched up for her missionary activities. They found recruitment brochures on her," he explained.

There was nothing about the consul's appearance, body language, or tone that Domrul liked one bit. As if all of it were his response to mosquitoes that wouldn't stop pestering him.

"I wanted to ask you. What can you do to help Ms. Finnegan, a British citizen, obtain her freedom?"

"We have made every effort within our ability. We've sent a letter to the foreign minister. I've met with Ms. Finnegan in prison." The consul recited his list.

"Has she been given a defense attorney?" Domrul pressed on.

"In this country, the lawyers are appointed by the state. A woman named Rustakhezova was assigned to her yesterday. You can find her at the city bar office. Do you have any more questions? One thing I must emphasize to you. You yourself are a British citizen, are you not? In any effort you undertake, you must refrain from blemishing the reputation of the United Kingdom. As you become engrossed in the local ways and local customs, do not forget, under any circumstances, that you are British!" The consul laid out that rule and stopped. "That is all I have to say."

He stood up from his chair. Not offering to shake hands, he opened the door and told the secretary, "Show him out!"

Domrul stepped outside, his soul black as ink. But there was no way he could give up now! He needed to gather up all his willpower and find the defense attorney's office. He wanted to speak with that Rustakhezova woman right away. He crossed the wide street and hailed a cab. He asked to be taken to the city bar association building. The driver turned out to be a decent fellow. "On Azimova Street?" he asked.

Domrul shrugged his shoulders.

"What are you doing taking a taxi, brother? It's a five minute walk from here!" the driver told him, and eagerly showed him the way. Domrul's spirits rose. Not everyone in this world was like that arrogant consul!

Five minutes later, sure enough, he reached the city bar association office. Ms. Rustakhezova was out to lunch, so Domrul sat down in a chair in the waiting room and dozed a bit. By two o'clock, the lawyer had returned. She was the same woman-of-steel type as Gaia Mangit-khanovna, but different from his begum, the same way that a horse that pulls a carriage is different from the one that prances about unburdened. Domrul knocked gently on the door behind her and stepped inside. He introduced himself. When he said he had come from London, the lawyer's indifferent eyes suddenly flashed to life.

"Where did you learn to speak our language so well?" she asked him kindly.

Domrul responded carefully, "At university."

She continued in a bossier tone. "My children grew up here, but they only speak Russian. Should I send them to London?" she joked. They laughed. Once she heard what Domrul had come to ask her, she went on in the same tone of voice. "I've started looking into the matter. It's quite a difficult one. But we'll try!" she said. Then she lowered her voice noticeably. "And you won't stand to one side either, will you? Can we count on you offering your help?" And she placed a finger to her lips.

Domrul came out of his visit to the lawyer with mixed feelings. On the one hand, Ms. Rustakhezova had promised to arrange a meeting between Domrul and Emer one of these days. On the other hand, her hints about his help worried Domrul. No, it wasn't quite what the consul had warned him against; he had given Ms. Rustakhezova "a little gift just for you," some tea in a pretty metal box from Harrods, after which the promise of the meeting had surfaced. No, it was the lawyer's appetite, the gaping pit all around her, that worried Domrul. We forgot to tell you the last thing the woman had said. "Here, we all know each other. We're all in the same grave!" she had told him.

Well, as the English say, one step at a time. First he'd see Emer, then figure it out. Now, though, he needed a place to stay. If he went to a hotel it would cost money, and he had a reason to save his cash now. He had Kuyuk-baxshi's invitation with him. Could he overcome his aversion and go to his house?

Domrul took the paperwork out of his side pocket and dialed the number printed on the page. Kuyuk-baxshi answered the phone himself. He was delighted to hear Domrul's voice. "Where are you, my friend? You didn't say you were coming! I could have met you myself!" he said. "Where's your Emer? I haven't heard from her for three or four days now!" he said.

At that question, Domrul's jealousy snapped. He told Kuyuk that Emer was in jail. Kuyuk-baxshi didn't believe him at first, but then he began to moan and groan. "Where are you? My disciple and I will come pick you up and bring you here, right now," he said. Domrul told him he was right across the street from the big toy store. "Stay right there. I'll be there in half an hour," Kuyuk ordered him.

It was more like forty-five minutes before Kuyuk pulled up in an ancient automobile, and when he caught sight of a policeman at the intersection, he frantically beckoned Domrul over to the car. But the policeman whistled and began walking their way. Kuyuk-baxshi left Domrul with the young man driving the car. "Master, help me now!" he sighed, and walked off to meet the policeman. He stood talking with him for ten minutes, then dug around in his pocket, pulled something out, and handed it to the policeman, then drew out a blessing with his hand and walked back to the car.

"It's the end of days!" he proclaimed, climbing in. "Not one of them recognizes or has any regard for his fellow man!"

> Left to myself, he'd never upstage me,
> With my manly power, he'd never engage me!
> Now I've paid the fine, which does sorely outrage me.
> Caught by the police . . . what are we to do?

And he told the driver, "Home, and quickly!"

Despite those instructions, once they were on the way, Kuyuk unexpectedly spoke again. "Come on, next to the river here we'll have some *lagmon*, we won't find a crumb at my house," he said, and started off for an attractive, shady restaurant overlooking the river. The poplars lining the riverbank had just put out their deep green blossoms, and new green shoots were emerging, poking out from the soft ground. They walked out onto a platform suspended above the swollen river. They ate some bread, they drank some tea, and dishes loaded with fried meat and dough were brought out, one after the other. Domrul stretched out his legs and sat back, leaning on a cushion. The meal had made him feel much better, and the view had put him at ease. He felt that, from far away, he had missed this sky, this springtime, this life. Kuyuk-baxshi seemed to sense Domrul's mood, too, and sat drinking his tea and eating his meal quietly, listening to the singing of the birds and the rushing of the river.

When the tea had been drunk and the food had been eaten, Kuyuk-baxshi broke the restful silence. "Now, younger brother, we'd better confer. Two heads are better than one, as they say. What are we going to do about our girl Emer?" Domrul turned to look at him, irritated.

Kuyuk-baxshi continued. "What is there for us to do? In this day and age, as you've just seen, people don't seem to recognize each other anymore. All they recognize is money. But I have one old friend. He's a sculptor. Once upon a time, he made a couple of sculptures for the big men in this city, and word of him spread far and wide. There was a time he got my friend Qimbat out of jail. That Qimbat was sentenced to ten years, but he got out in five and a half. Let's call him!"

What could Domrul say to that? When Kuyuk-baxshi had said "sculptor," it had reminded him of his father, and he gave a start, and with his ear caught on that word, he sat saying nothing. Kuyuk-baxshi was dialing his friend's phone number. He waited a bit. Then, "Friend! Is that you? You've become rare as old money!" Kuyuk started with a joke. "Won't you come and join us? My guest from London and I are sitting here by the side of the river, eating lagmon, and your name came up. There's room for you here! Oh, you're busy? Yes, burdened up with work, sure! Good thing God gave you that burden, isn't it? If he had set you free we'd never get to see you! Friend, we've got one problem. My guest's fiancée came here to visit me and Qimbat, and they've put her straight in jail. They say she's a rabble-rousing missionary! No, she came to take me to London. Her name is Emer . . . Not Emar, Emer . . . Her last name? What's her last name?" Kuyuk-baxshi asked Domrul, covering up the phone with one hand.

"Finnegan!" Domrul answered.

"Pinnigan, it's Pinnigan," Kuyuk repeated. "Take a look, friend. She's just an innocent girl . . . It would be wonderful if you could come, friend! I've got this young man here as my guest. I'll introduce you. He looks a lot like you."

> My eye deceives me, your face blurs before me,
> Alas, alas, are all the words that reach me,
> Where have you gone to, my dear one, my light?
> I see you in the guest I have before me . . .

They talked a little while longer and laughed and laughed, and then he hung up.

After that last lovely landscape, the neighborhood where Kuyuk-baxshi lived, his bare apartment, looked slightly unnatural to Domrul's eye. But be that as it may, his heart had warmed again toward Kuyuk, and he had begun to look at the bard with his other eye, one that bore him no malice. He had no computer, no television, and no radio, and other than the room of his apartment where the walls were plastered with posters, one atop the other, where they talked and drank some tea, there was no room for anything else. It was mostly Kuyuk, leaning on his cushions, who led the conversation, and as Domrul had not slept the day before, and had no rest as he ran around today either, in time his eyes began to droop, and their conversation grew haphazard. And that was fine, because Kuyuk-baxshi asked him a question or two at the beginning, but for the most part he himself was telling the story.

"How is England? And how is that old woman of yours, friend?" he began.

Domrul lazily summoned up some words. His answer was something along the lines of how everything was fine.

"Have you brought a picture of your old lady?" the baxshi asked, drawing Domrul a little closer as he switched to a less formal form of address, calling him *sen* instead of *siz*. Or is that just what Domrul sensed now? Whatever the case, he paid it not the slightest bit of attention.

"No," was all he said.

Kuyuk-baxshi took two handfuls of dried apricots, the kind called *turshak*, out of a sack on a shelf and put them in a dish. He told Domrul to put the bowl of withered fruit onto the cloth spread on the floor, and Kuyuk-baxshi filled the bowl with boiling water and slipped a saucer on top of it. He started talking again.

After a bit Kuyuk-baxshi took the dish off the shelf, lifted up the saucer, and revealed the turshak, now transformed into shiny round marbles of apricots. They burned in your mouth. For some reason, at that instant, Domrul remembered Gaia Mangitkhanovna with an acute longing. God only knows why she was on his mind.

"So! There was a Goia we used to know!"

Domrul's eye was the first to close. The next thing he saw was a young Gaia Mangitkhanovna, the beauty of the land, but with everyone there keeping their distance, not daring to approach her. Every one of their hearts held a certain dread, as if she emanated not the delicate scent of perfume and rosewater, but the stink of sedition. Kuyuk-baxshi was one of them, too, his dombra in his hand, acting out what they told him to do. Piece by piece, every word she said, he caught it in his hand, and like an apple or a flower he held it up to the light, and you could see its colors shining like jewels; but the lady Gaia was not distracted by any of that, but pressed on over the road she knew, smashing every apple and flower under her feet.

Here, Domrul shuddered a bit. Whatever the reason, he then heard Emer's name. Kuyuk told him, "Your Emer, younger brother—she's some girl!" His knee brushed up against Domrul's foot. "Just you wait, one of these days I'll be singing an epic just like the one about Vomiq and Uzro, but called Emer and Domrul, and it will render everyone who hears it speechless!"

"Sure," said Domrul, less than enthusiastically, and he was about to say something else, but another wave of drowsiness must have hit him, and the words he was saying seemed to scatter like sand around him, and his own legs were sinking in that sand.

The full moon landed on Domrul's face. That full moon had just bobbed up to float above the sea and the city. Gaia Mangitkhanovna had risen up above the mountains and boulders and was moving away. Domrul wanted to catch up with her, but he was surrounded by water on his left and a swamp to his right. Gaia Mangitkhanovna, meanwhile, was swiftly advancing. On the far boundary of the night, where the moon had risen, stood Emer. Could it be that they would meet without Domrul?

He understood how despicable that would be. What would happen then? He must not allow it. Whatever it took, he would have to stop her! All he had in his hand was a tiny mirror and a plastic comb. What if he were to throw them? What good could that do?? He would hurtle them with all his might and force himself to climb up out of this dream.

"There it was the middle of the night, and she tramping around the aul all alone, your girl Emer, till she walked into Qoyip the Policeman's house!" Kuyuk-baxshi was finishing up his story.

"So she escaped!" thought Domrul, much relieved, and he sank down into a pitch-black slumber.

◈

Gaia Mangitkhanovna was lonely without Domrul. At her age and in her condition, it was a shame to run into such a misfortune! Though it was possible to hide that from other people, she could not hide it from herself.

Life can be so strange, she thought. Your decisions on one side, and what you actually accomplish on the other side. When you spend your whole life with someone, you might say, "I need you!" And it turns out that he is actually the most needless and useless thing to keep around. And the person you hire for five days turns out to be, in the twilight of your life, the rock that you lean on!

Trying to escape those thoughts, Gaia Mangitkhanovna called up Antonina Ivanovna. As if she realized how unhappy Gaia was, she told her, "This evening Elizaveta Petrovna and I are going to a gym outside Eastbourne to see a dancing competition. There's a dance ensemble coming from Bulgaria. Would you like to join us?" she asked. It just so happened that in Communist times, Gaia Mangitkhanovna and her husband used to go to Bulgaria, to the vacation spots in Varna and Sunny Beach. She had watched the Bulgarians dance the *horo* and danced along with them in their circles. So she agreed at once.

Before dark fell, Antonina rang the bell from downstairs. Gaia Mangitkhanovna went down to join the two other old women in the waiting taxi. She came down and was instantly full of regrets. The thing was that Elizaveta Petrovna was in the last stages of multiple sclerosis. The former university professor could no longer remember who Gaia Mangitkhanovna was, where she was going, or what language she was speaking. All that would have been fine, except she had also forgotten what all the different parts of her body had been created for; when saliva drooled from her mouth, the hand that was meant to wipe up the spit would start digging a finger into her ear instead . . . Gaia Mangitkhanovna's flesh crawled, and she shuddered suddenly. As we might have mentioned, she had been diagnosed with just the same thing.

Taking the road that led from their city to London, they traveled to the gym in the countryside at the city limits. The taxi driver paid no attention to Elizaveta Petrovna's Russian chitchat, just helped lower her wheelchair to the ground. Antonina paid the driver his money and they walked into the gymnasium. The dance competition was about what Gaia Mangitkhanovna had expected. It started out not with the Bulgarian ensemble, but with some local old women from a belly-dancing club. There it was again: her thoughts on one side, and real life on the other side. The back of Gaia

Mangitkhanovna's neck went completely stiff. These faded old mamas, baring their wrinkled, flabby, flaccid midriffs, quivered from this side to that side and shared their intoxication with each other.

Suddenly Gaia Mangitkhanovna asked herself which was better: to share in the shame like they do, or wipe the tears from her eyes like snot on her sleeve, like Elizaveta Petrovna? And she thought maybe the old woman stuck in the wheelchair was better off, after all. But alas, alas, she herself had reached that age, too, and what she saw in her dreams is the young man's clawed fingers and pointy knees!

Fine. She would go on hating such childlike old women. And never ever would she succumb to the indignity of being a dull elderly woman with her mind gone for good. Everything Gaia Mangitkhanovna had built in her lifetime had been destroyed, bit by bit, and now her last stronghold was to prevent her mind and memory, her body and beauty, from wearing away to nothing! She was terrified of the alternative, and it made her whole body shake.

It was then that the Bulgarians came out on stage, Turkish-looking ones, with that Turkish fire in them . . .

Yes, she was going to have to speed up her last journey with that son of the Turks!

◆

The next morning, after some non and tea, Kuyuk-baxshi and Domrul both left the house, Kuyuk to see his friend the sculptor and Domrul to meet with the attorney. Domrul hailed a cab and after half an hour walked into the bar association office. Rustakhezova's loud voice, audible from the reception area, was giving someone advice about some business matter. Domrul walked right into her office. As she spoke on the phone, Rustakhezova pointed to a chair in front of her, telling him to have a seat. The matter was sufficiently complex that Domrul sat listening to the discussion for another thirty minutes. Finally the telephone chat was over, and Rustakhezova put her hands to her head.

"They're all as empty-headed as pumpkins. Can't understand a single thing. Really, won't you take me to London with you?" she suggested wistfully. Then, as if turning her mind to Domrul's problem, she said, "Yesterday I spoke with a very influential person. It's a serious matter. Over at the big office—you know, we call them our 'in-laws'"—and Rustakhezova rolled her eyes toward the ceiling—"they've taken an interest in this case. Now it's going to be very difficult to get this matter out of their grip. For us, it's just a job, but for them, it's big business," she added.

Then she went on again. "But I have good news for you too. The investigator on the case is one of our own young guys, and it could be possible to reach an arrangement with his supervisor. Come back here in two hours and we'll go together. I've got a few other things to work on, as you can see!" she said, and gestured back toward the telephone.

Domrul left the building. By habit, we think everyone ought to be concerned by the same things that concern us. If we're busy with a particular thing, we're always surprised to learn that other people have their own things to do, and that is annoying. Domrul was in this state right now. Besides, he had just traveled over eight thousand kilometers to rescue the person closest to him in all the world, and when you come ready to move mountains, but arrive to find your important matter dismissed with small talk, waiting around for other people, sitting around hour after hour, and that's it . . .

He had some lunch in a filthy cafeteria, and by two o'clock, Domrul was back at Rustakhezova's office. The lawyer was again rushing to wrap up some other matter, and for that reason, she kept him sitting silently for yet another half an hour. All Domrul could do was watch a fly buzz from the table to the wall and back again.

Finally, Rustakhezova finished what she was doing, and the two of them walked outside. "Where's your car? Do you have one?" the lawyer asked.

"No," answered Domrul. Why should he have a car if he didn't even live here?

"You should have rented a car! It's too far to walk," she explained.

"Fine, let's grab a taxi." They crossed the wide street and hailed a cab. Rustakhezova recited the address. They rode for ten minutes. Rustakhezova got out and stood waiting for Domrul. Domrul paid for the ride and got out himself.

"That's the one!" Rustakhezova was calling someone over in her direction. Domrul looked in the direction that Rustakhezova was pointing. A young man, dressed in a black shirt in the afternoon sunshine, was gesturing at his watch and running inside. "That's the investigator!" Rustakhezova told him. "Seems he has no time to speak with us now. Anyway, let's go try to meet with his boss!"

Fortunately, the chief inspector was there where he belonged. But in order to get in to see him, they had some red tape to conquer. The police officer stationed at the door took a look at Domrul's foreign passport. "They only get in through the Secretariat or the Pass Office," he kept saying. Rustakhezova countered that the director himself was waiting for them, but that didn't work either. They had to go chase down a permit, afraid all the while the director would disappear in the meantime, and that was exhausting work. Finally, forty minutes later, they walked into the boss's office.

The head investigator was a plump, blue-eyed, rather bald man. When he found out Domrul was from London, and spoke both his mother tongues so well, he showered praise on him. Then he looked first at Rustakhezova, then at Domrul. His gentle smile seemed to ask, "How can I help you?"

Perhaps he was playing the fool, or pretending that their problem was indeed among the hundreds of matters he had to attend to, but in any case the determined Ms. Rustakhezova told him, her voice loud as ever, "This young man here is Miss Finnegan's fiancé. He flew in yesterday," she said, introducing him again.

"Yes, yes, from London, you said!" agreed the director, putting his thoughts in order.

Domrul had never in his life been in such a situation, and so he did not know what to say at the start, and he had put all his trust in Rustakhezova. He only sat there nodding his head.

"Mr. Domrul would like to know if he may meet with his fiancée." Domrul bobbed his head up and down when his lawyer said those words too.

"A meeting, you say?" The director shook his reddish head heavily. "Right now we're in the initial stages of interrogation. Right now this could be difficult, but if our young friend can be patient for just a day or so, then perhaps arranging a meeting might be possible."

Domrul remembered his anthropology courses at SOAS. They had taught him that there are some cultures in which nobody ever says no. But without saying no, they make it quite clear that they do not mean yes, either, not at all. In such a culture, patience is the alpha and omega of all virtues.

"Is there anything else at all that you wish?" This time, the question was very clearly directed at Domrul.

Maybe Domrul had read about torture in the prisons there, because for some reason, he immediately asked, "Is she suffering?"

The boss pretended not to understand this bit of awkwardness. "Suffering, you say? Prison is not exactly a resort destination, so of course, she must be suffering a bit," he said, hiding a smile.

"No, that's not what I meant."

"Yes, I understand, I understand. You must mean all the lies and falsehoods they write where you live, don't you?" Now his blue eyes flashed, and he smiled outright. "The investigator is still interrogating her. Miss Finnegan is a foreign citizen. She is nothing more than a suspect." As he spoke those words, the boss cast Ms. Rustakhezova a meaningful look. "We operate according to the law. Miss Finnegan's official attorney, Ms. Rustakhezova, must have told you that," he said.

Another thing Rustakhezova had said—"For us, it's just a job, but for them, it's big business"—flashed through Domrul's brain, and for some reason, he placed a sort of trust in those fearsome words.

Gaia Mangitkhanovna may have won her campaign to transform a whole country into an ant colony, but she never did manage to do the same to her own little family. We mentioned her children. She must have been distracted by them, and she was also just one step away from divorcing her sanitary pad of a husband. Among everything else she had to worry about, her husband had found himself another young woman, and according to the information Gaia Mangitkhanovna's blue-eyed spy brought her, he had even managed to get her pregnant! One night, Gaia Mangitkhanovna let loose and called him a scoundrel and a devil and everything in between. Embarrassed, the bodyguards and policemen shut themselves up in their rooms, pretending not to see or hear a thing. That night started with the shattering of the official state china and ended with the splintering of brightly colored windows financed by the state budget. The leader of the nation, the people's heroic eagle, had all his feathers torn from his wings. "Are you preparing a successor for yourself now?" she cursed him, and threatened his unborn child with a hundred humiliations. "You will kill it with your own hand!" she shrieked, yanking her husband's hair out of his head. "But first, tomorrow, you will put your own son in a position of official power!" she shouted, now grabbing him by the throat.

Gaia Mangitkhanovna had something else to wail about that night. The thing was that just a short while earlier, at the state clinic where she had been examined, she had learned that she suffered from "multiple sclerosis," as they wrote it in Russian, but she had not yet told a single person. The doctors tried to encourage her, telling her that being at the seaside would help along her treatment, which sounded laughable to her. Then she had read something online about the disease, and that put her completely on edge. In her mind, her bones had already started to disintegrate inside her, and she, who at age seventy could still expect that all the cars would honk flirtatiously at her any time she walked outside on her own, felt she had been abruptly transformed into a handful of snot, and that was a time of fear for her.

But her husband's strength also seemed to have drained completely, and from that night on, he took to his bed. He never quite died, but after that, though alive, he never interfered in anyone else's business. That was a boon to everyone. It meant Gaia Mangitkhanovna could take the entire ant colony under her own control.

◆

That evening, as he sat filling in Kuyuk-baxshi on the day's events, Domrul's telephone suddenly buzzed. He saw that Gaia Mangitkhanovna had sent him an email. "Call me immediately!" it said. Domrul apologized to Kuyuk-baxshi and dialed Gaia Mangitkhanovna's number, worried about whether she had recovered well from her episode of shock.

For some reason, Antonina Ivanovna answered the phone. After she heard that it was Domrul, they just had time to say hello before all at once she passed the phone to Gaia Mangitkhanovna.

Gaia Mangitkhanovna did not bother with a greeting, but told him, in a very serious voice, "Emer's aunt, a woman called Boudicca, just called your office. They couldn't reach you, so they called me. In short, Emer's mother has passed away. You tell her—" But a beeping sound interrupted her.

Domrul's mouth was hanging open, and he couldn't catch his breath, and he kept looking first at Kuyuk-baxshi, then at his telephone. Kuyuk-baxshi handed him his already-cool tea. "Drink up, little brother! I heard everything!" And his hands made the gesture for the blessing. "May God show her mercy!" Then, with some sort of new life in his voice, he added, "And I think that Goia is the very same one. At least her voice is just the same . . ."

Domrul paid no attention to his last comment. He had no strength left with which to pay attention. Choking, he drank down a cup of cold tea. Then he looked at Kuyuk-baxshi. "Now what are we going to do?" he asked.

Kuyuk-baxshi had no direct answer to give him. To calm Domrul's tattered heart, he started from far away.

"In the Manas, the Kyrgyz epic," he began, "there is one particular story. Ko'katoy, the khan of Tashkent, had eleven daughters, but not a single son. In his old age, he took in a child called Bo'kmurun and raised him as his son. Bo'kmurun grew up to be a fearless young man. One day, Bo'kmurun was searching for a wife, and he had come to the home of his father's friend Manas the Warrior. The elderly Ko'katoy summoned his *vazir* Boymirza, and this is what he said: 'I am old now, and my death is near. When I die, tell my son to make my funeral brief. Material things are for the living, not the dead. May he waste nothing! Have him call four old women, and let them pray for me, and that is all! Tell my friend Manas nothing about my death. If he knows, he will be grievously distressed. He too would butcher his cattle and be swept away in mourning.' He said these words, and two days later, Khan Ko'katoy closed his eyes to this world.

"When his son Bo'kmurun returned, the vazir Boymirza passed on to him what his father had said, but the young man resisted. 'My father has just died, and I am expected to just sit here at loose ends?' he retorted, and he called upon the whole world to make tribute in the name of the deceased. From all over the earth they came. Qo'nurboy from China, wearing his red cap on his head; Ushan the Kalmyk; O'ro'ngu, Khan of Qanqay; the wicked Jo'mo'y; the negro Budanchan; the loathsome Kaykubod; the Tibetan khan Demil; the braggart Cho'yunali; his banished kinsman Qashay; the Kazakh Ko'kcha-botir; Amir Temur of Bukhara; and thousands more all gathered together. Manas came, too, with his army of one hundred thousand soldiers.

"And the funeral feast began. Whole flocks were slaughtered, whole vats of ale were drunk, and there were contests, races, and wrestling matches. And the whole thing ended with a war between nations.

"Now ask me, brother Domrul, whether what Bo'kmurun said was necessary, bringing the news of Ko'katoy's death to the whole world? Or was it not?"

> I shall weep and weep, for myself I shall weep;
> I shall speak on and on, my wounds for to keep,
> Though I know not the way, nor when I might sleep.
> Is there anyone who can show me the way?

◈

Two days later, the chief investigator called Rustakhezova. "Come in after lunch," he told her. So this was the second day that Domrul spent pacing around the bar association lobby or wandering around outside it.

After lunch they went back to the same building as before. This time, Kuyuk-baxshi had set up Domrul with one of his followers and a car, so in his own car, the follower who had lazed around for the past two days with nothing to do got them to where they needed to go in ten minutes flat. Once they got through all the protocol there, a staffer directed them to the first room on the right on the first floor. In that room, there was a metal table attached to the floor, with two chairs on either side of it, and a small bench along the wall near the entrance. They sat down on that bench. The windows looking out on the street in that room were covered with heavy shades, and if it had not been for one hardworking forty-watt lightbulb, in that room the broad daylight would have succumbed to the darkness.

They had waited about ten minutes when the door opened, and the same employee led Emer in. Domrul wanted to rush to her, but the employee immediately stopped him short. "Sit down!" he said, showing Domrul to one side of the table and Emer to the other. From how pale Emer's face was, and how thin and tattered she looked, it was quite plain to see that she was in terrible torment.

"How are you?" asked Domrul, making his voice as soft as possible. Emer did not answer. "How are you feeling?" Domrul felt vexed at his own formal questions, but in front of two strangers here, he did not know what to say beyond that. "Please know, we're all on your side, we're behind you!" Domrul hurried to say something encouraging. "The embassy, Kuyuk-baxshi, his friends . . ."

At that Emer tossed a glance at the staffer sitting in the corner, and without lifting her gaze back to Domrul, she spoke in his direction. "I'm guilty! I've admitted my guilt. I was here trying to divert peaceful people from the right path, while I myself am on the incorrect path, a criminal path! I ask forgiveness from the president of this country, and perhaps his excellency the president will forgive me." She said it all in one breath, as if reciting from memory. Then, as if saying that was all, she looked again to the staffer sitting behind them.

Domrul was terribly frightened—frightened of those words and frightened of the tone she had used to speak them. It was as if Emer had been turned into a zombie, a puppet, a doll on which you turned the dial and watched the show. You turned the crank, she spoke her words, and then she was quiet again.

Domrul found himself enraged. He wanted to shout, "Emer, it's me! Your Domrul! Can you hear me?? I've come to rescue you!" He wanted to wake her up. And Domrul wanted to confess his own guilt, not as a fabrication, but as the truth, and even if it could not get through to Emer's imprisoned mind, he wanted to tell her about her mother's death.

As if he had been listening to all of that, the staffer in the corner asked, "Do you have anything else to say to one another?" And Emer rushed to answer, "No, I've said it all!" She stood up. Despite the wail of despair welling up inside of Domrul, the man was leading Emer out of the room.

◆

Domrul thought he was losing his mind. If not for Kuyuk-baxshi's friendliness and support, wouldn't he truly go mad? What in the world had he come here for, and what had he achieved? He couldn't turn in his open-ended ticket and go home; it would be wrong to leave Emer in this state. But Emer was in that state anyway! There was no benefit to Domrul being here at all.

"You know," said Kuyuk-baxshi early in the morning, after telling Domrul stories that we already know, all night long, to distract him, "today, let's go to my sculptor friend's studio. We'll get some advice and look over his work, and maybe you can get a little bit of a break, brother!" After Domrul's anguished, sleepless night, he had no desire left for anything, and so he followed along blindly where Kuyuk-baxshi led.

They took a bus, a trolley, the subway, and a tram to the other side of the sunbaked city, and when they got there, they were met at the studio door not by the sculptor, but by a cleaning woman, who told them the owner of the place had made a quick trip out of town, and opened the door. "Look at what you want to see, then toss the key in the mailbox," she told them, handing over the key to the place, and then she went on with her work. They were left to themselves in the studio. It had something in common with an aircraft hangar. Tall shelves and metal scaffolding, soulless rocks and the smell of alabaster, and sculptures, sculptures, sculptures everywhere.

Kuyuk-baxshi seemed to have been here often, and to cheer Domrul's sullen heart he brought him quickly over to one corner, and after he pulled the black fabric covering it off the thing which stood looming there, he sat himself down determinedly next to the newly unveiled sculpture, and pretended to pick up his dombra. The sculpture was Kuyuk-baxshi's bronze twin. The seated baxshi looked as if he had just taken off, soaring on the wings of his song. You could look at his simple, shining face, and there it was, beneath the grandeur of that sculpted face enveloped in song, except that here the baxshi was clearly much younger.

"Do I look like a match?" Kuyuk-baxshi joked, imitating the sculpture's pose.

> In came the bald, crazy young man,
> Patched his ancient robe by hand,
> Gathered the shit, wandered the room,
> And became the statue for his own tomb . . .

Kuyuk laughed.

Then he stood up, winked an eye, and led Domrul in a conspiratorial way to another corner of the studio. This sculpture was draped in red velvet. While the bronze sculpture had been in a seated position, it was just as clear that this one was standing upright under its soft red covering. Like a magician showing off his tricks, Kuyuk-baxshi moved his hand swiftly to just touch the velvet, then froze; and then, with a ceremonial flourish, he swept the cloth away. From under the velvet there emerged the body of a carved, white, marble, naked . . . well, not exactly a woman, but more of an ant, and not just any ant, but an ant queen, shaped like a human woman. Domrul did not look the sculpture in the face. Its slim womanly waist and perfect body held his gaze. That body looked as if it had just spread its wings to take off. He was completely enraptured by the figure, and he began walking all around it, and his gaze lit on a spot on its neck, between the gesturing wings, and slid downward, seeing the mole, like a bead, on its right side, then looking from the ant's waist toward the gap between its legs; then he looked at last, in agony, to the sculpture's face.

"And this is our Goia!" announced Kuyuk-baxshi with pride.

◈

If what Kuyuk-baxshi had said was true, then there was one thing that was difficult to comprehend. If Gaia had been able to satisfy her lust and desire just as much as she desired, wouldn't she have had to transform, then, into a satisfied, calm woman? Why wouldn't her steely exterior melt away in that case? Why wouldn't that arrogant hatred of the world and all humankind be converted into love? After all, everyone knows that ordinarily, a woman who finds no satisfaction in her private life becomes a mere carcass; but Gaia had her husband, and children, and lovers, so why did she remain sunk in such coldness? You must be wondering about these things.

But, if you look more closely, like Domrul, into this woman, this *old* woman, nothing will seem quite so black and white. We mentioned her coldness, but while Gaia Mangitkhanovna was one part ice, compared to other people, she had nevertheless melted before Domrul. We do not know everything about her relationship with her husband, just whispered rumors. We mentioned her lovers, but one of them, Kuyuk-baxshi, even now was deeply in love with her.

On the other hand, it's impossible to know whether any of them had ever satisfied Gaia Mangitkhanovna. Her husband, as we have learned, was husband to another before he met her. We've also heard about all the women he had his way with while he lived with Gaia. And the lovers? What kind of real pleasure, what kind of satisfaction, can lovers provide? The kind that's here today and gone tomorrow. And now Domrul had found a symbol for that: insect royalty, the ant queen. A type of Cleopatra! The kind who loves who she loves, and who destroys, the very next day, anyone she doesn't.

It seems the sculptor had known that too.

❖

Domrul had apparently let one thing escape his attention. This thing seemed to be moving alongside him, never touching him. Actually, his old boss Rashad, the one he called Amja, used to tell him one story over and over again. "One day a man was bringing his sheep to market, walking along and thinking idle thoughts, when suddenly he looked and saw he held the rope in his hand—but the sheep was gone! He shouted in alarm. At his shouting, the thief who had stolen his sheep approached him. 'Oh, woe is me!' said the thief. 'It seems I've dropped my wallet in the well. It had a hundred dinars in it! I'll give fifty dinars to the person who returns my wallet to me!' he said. At that, the stupid man thought, 'I've lost my sheep, worth one dinar. If I can come up with the wallet, I'll be rich!' And he took off all his clothing, handed it to the thief, and dove into the well himself. He searched that well for an hour and didn't find a thing, and when he came out, his clothes were gone too."

Domrul's present state reminded him of that ridiculous one. His original act had been idle and empty-headed, and when all his conscious thoughts met up with that emptiness, every act left to him was just as pointless and vain. Domrul's master Shaykh Nozim had also shown his amazement, time after time. "For shame! In this world, we are all fishermen, only we're chasing a whale! And we pay no mind to the tadpoles it eats!" he used to say.

Domrul was struggling to gather his thoughts about the tadpoles of these recent days. The white marble sculpture of Gaia Mangitkhanovna had thrown him into a real state of chaos, and though he did not reveal that to Kuyuk-baxshi, he regretted having listened so indifferently to his stories about Goia. Tadpoles, tadpoles, tadpoles . . . Like the beady mole on her back in the sculptor's studio!

When Domrul recovered a little and let his eyes fall on another little statue hidden among those stones, he remembered how much his heart could sting. It wore that certain kind of wrap favored by old Meskhetian Turk women. Domrul felt as if he had disrobed it—was it an old woman, or was it Death, her wings spread wide?—a woman with two children under her wings. Now as Domrul rode in the jam-packed metro back to Kuyuk-baxshi's house, when he thought about it, he realized the old woman's bat wings had spread out black as flame. As if once more experiencing the very depths of his pain, Domrul's heart was throbbing. He would absolutely have to meet that sculptor. Distracted by other things, he had never had a chance to ask his name. All right, as soon as they left the crowded subway, he would ask. It was a small world, wasn't it? Maybe that sculptor had met Domrul's father at some point. After all, his father had been well-known, famous not just in the valley, but in the capital, too, according to what Domrul's aunt had told him.

But his thoughts, like so many tadpoles, refused to be gathered together. He too, like Jonah the Prophet whom Shaykh Nozim used to cite as an example, had been swallowed by a whale. Emer, Emer, Emer . . . What should he do? She was suffering so much, and she was so badly frightened! What if they had raped her? Domrul ground his teeth together. Apparently his jealousy was mounted up and ready to ride again. Or had

Kuyuk-baxshi, with his stories over tea from the olden days, always meant to pull his thoughts in that direction?

Inside the whale it was bad, inside the whale it was dark, and once you are swallowed by the whale, your prospects of rising up out again are in God's hands alone. That evening, the sleepless Domrul descended into another type of terror. What if they caught him and threw him into jail too? Look, a car had stopped right there, outside the window. Kuyuk-baxshi was gone at a wedding until morning, so he was all alone. There was nobody who could help him. Any minute now four armed men would burst inside, truss up his arms and legs like a sheep, toss him into the car, drive him out to the city limits, and hurl him into some old well.

All those fears meant that in the morning, when the attorney Rustakhezova let Domrul know that the head investigator was summoning Domrul to come see him, all alone, Domrul decided to dispatch Kuyuk-baxshi with a message when he went for his interview at the British embassy. Domrul told him to tell the British consul, when they met, that he had been called in to visit the chief investigator. "If anything happens to me, I want them to know where I am!" he added.

The usual red tape seemed to have an unusually terrible tone to it, this time. Just before he walked into the building, Domrul cast a glance outside, into the open air, with a sense of longing, and from the threshold he sent a bismallah out into the universe. Standing next to the police officer at the entrance was the director himself, with his grin. "It's a shame I don't even know his name. When I spit in his face because of his dirty tricks, I won't be able to curse him by name!" thought Domrul, despairing. They walked upstairs to the director's office.

The director showed Domrul to an armchair, then drew the curtains shut on the window. Unlike in the room downstairs, here, a chandelier hanging from the high ceiling lit the room bright as day. "Must be so he can torture me in privacy!" thought Domrul, panicked. But the director sat down in his own chair behind the desk and offered Domrul a cup of hot tea. "Even their torture methods involve bewitchment!" thought Domrul, suspicious.

"So, younger brother!" began the director. "These are the type of people you are closely connected with? You are . . ." (Here he arched his eyebrows toward the ceiling, knowingly or not.) "The *consort* of such people!" (What a perfect word he had found, thought Domrul.) "And you didn't even tell us!" Not understanding where this conversation was going, Domrul hesitated. If he was playing some sort of trick, this man ought to have started by saying something else!

"As we said," he went on, arching his eyebrows upward again, "we have had the high honor of petitioning *them*, because of *you*. Now don't worry about that side of things, I've just summoned our girl." (Yes, that's what he said, "our girl"!) "You two can have a chat, and I'll go have a word with the chiefs and then give you an answer!"

The director pushed some sort of button, one of the double doors swung open, and the secretary's head appeared.

"Is she here?" the director asked.

"Yes," the secretary answered.

The director nodded his head, and a moment later, Emer walked into the room. The director ushered her in himself, sat her down across from Domrul, put the tea kettle and cups in front of them, and disappeared behind the double doors, which closed softly with a click.

They both stayed silent for a bit. Then Domrul could bear it no longer, and he leapt up from his chair and came to Emer's side. He took her into his arms. Emer was sobbing. "They—they—" She wanted to say something, but Domrul pulled her closer to him, and he started to kiss her weeping eyes and her lips, as they struggled to shape the words. So much had he longed for this frail, miserable girl, and he felt himself a real hero before her. He was her rescuer, her brave warrior. At that moment, nothing could possibly stop him. And Emer—broken, bruised, and alone as tumbleweed in the desert—seemed to have found her protection, her bulwark, and she hung tight onto Domrul, forgetting herself entirely.

Even now, back in reality, the two of them did not truly realize where they were or what they had just done.

One of them whispered to the other, "I've come to take you home."

And the other one responded, in a whisper, "Never leave me alone again!"

At that moment, the bright red telephone on the desk rang, jolting them out of their dream and back into the light of day.

◆

Maybe because of how wrapped up in that "carer" she had become, Gaia had no wish to stay by herself at home. The old blind Beryl had gotten on her nerves, so much so she was ready to go anywhere with Antonina Ivanovna, restless as an ant—if not to London, then just to cruise around Eastbourne itself. At midweek Antonina, in her own particular way—like a timber falling down from a roof—invited her to go to a flea market. Any other time, Gaia Mangitkhanovna would have been unimpressed, but this time she agreed to go easily.

The usual rain was falling outside, but fortunately the market was not far from Gaia Mangitkhanovna's building, just a couple of streets over. Did Gaia Mangitkhanovna have any need for somebody else's stinking, rusting, molding old things? That being the case, maybe she and Antonina could go to some café and sit for a while, and just relax, which is why she had decided to join her at all . . . How buried these people were in all their little things! Maybe it was because they lived on an island. Because their grandparents had been sailors and had to save every needle, nail, and button they ever had, because all around them there was nothing but the sea, and they'd never find another one!

Thinking those thoughts, Gaia Mangitkhanovna walked along, watching Antonina Ivanovna tinker around among the bric-a-brac. Yes, all these English people were apparently here to find something particular, but what was Antonina here for—to search out a piece of manure? All of that vain, hollow, Russian curiosity.

Almost an hour had passed wasting away time like this. Gaia Mangitkhanovna was beginning to lose patience. But there was still one aisle they hadn't yet walked down. When she came to the top of that aisle, Antonina had her eye set on a little box covered in some sort of fake mother of pearl, and while she stared at that, Gaia Mangitkhanovna's eye fell upon a knight in steel armor, standing in one corner. But it wasn't exactly a knight. It was body armor suited for a long-haired woman. All at once she remembered her ant queen costume from so long ago. This armor, this helmet, were just as fine, just as alluring, as her costume. Gaia Mangitkhanovna was transported back into her own past in a flash. She especially remembered the two little jaws set in the mouth of the helmet, perfect for cracking someone's neck in two. Gaia Mangitkhanovna was perspiring in excitement, but she said nothing, not to Antonina and not to the long-haired, short-skirted English tramp selling it.

The next afternoon, she came back to that market on her own, and she bought that steel suit.

❖

When the director came back into the room, they looked guilty and huddled down again into their own chairs. "First time I've seen people making love in such desperate straits," said the director, seemingly down-hearted. Emer, naturally, did not understand his words, but Domrul, who did, was a bit confused again. Were they watching the whole time? What if they were planning to punish them for this too? Had he really just said that?

But the director strode over to his own chair, his mood now happy as ever, and looked at Domrul. "As I was saying earlier, you have nothing to worry about now. The case has basically been settled. You tell our girl she can calm down too. But just so that there's no needless fuss, make sure you understand, please, this is a delicate matter, and we'll need to proceed quietly, without making a mess, and wrap things up carefully," he said. "After this, we'll have some doctors check her out. She needs to get herself together a little," he added, grinning.

"You don't need to translate all of that for your girl here. Maybe you can tell her that you'll be strolling through that famous Hyde Park of yours a week or two from now. And don't forget to invite us all to the wedding! We'll tell them"—and here the director raised his eyebrows to the ceiling again—"it would be a good excuse to make a pilgrimage." Domrul was damned if he'd understood a thing the man was talking about.

But as the director had urged him to do, he translated to Emer what he had said about London. Emer sighed heavily in response.

"Say your goodbyes for the time being. From now on, your girl will be under my personal protection!" the director declared reassuringly. Dom-rul, still confused, bade Emer farewell. Emer started to cry. The director called his secretary. "Look after our girl here!" he told her, and now he took Domrul by the elbow and steered him toward the door.

"Don't leave me alone!" begged Emer, choking out her words.

A demonic thought nagged at him. "Go back! Go save her!" it told him, but the director was now holding his arm tighter.

"They really may release her this week," Domrul thought, "and maybe his eyebrows going up again meant the British embassy, or the Foreign Office." Meanwhile, the director led Domrul outside.

The director whispered a few things into his ear, which the police officer at the door could hear but Domrul didn't listen to, because in the depths of his heart he was remembering the gullible fool who had lost his sheep and gone down into the well. "Now it looks like I've been trapped in the whale's belly, too, or stuck in a concrete cell!" thought Domrul, walking, in fear, all the way outside.

Free, now, out on the street—where he had so longed to be just a short time ago—Domrul felt as if he had just woken up, uncertain whether everything that had happened to him today was a dream or reality, and he was pinching himself over and over again, right there on his arm, which still bore traces of the director's tight hold.

◆

Kuyuk-baxshi returned from the embassy full of good cheer. Not only had they given him the visa that Emer had requested, they had also told him that Emer would soon be free. The ambassador himself had even suggested they might be able to fly out together. That made Domrul remember the director's expressive eyebrows and attribute them completely to the embassy, and he told Kuyuk-baxshi what he and the chief investigator had talked about.

"That settles it! Today we shall celebrate!" said Kuyuk-baxshi, and he took Domrul off to a tiny, cozy café in the center of the city.

We called it a café, but it wasn't really; one difference from the cafés in London was that this one sold alcohol. Before they ordered their drinks, Kuyuk-baxshi told Domrul a tale he had learned from his master Yo'lli-baxshi. The story went that when Mavlono Rumi was still sitting at the skirts of his master Shams Tabrizi, the master had assigned him three tasks. The first was when he was trying to fatten his sheep on walnuts, and he said to the kids hanging around him: "Stone me! Whoever throws the most stones, to him I shall award the most walnuts!" When Mavlono had done that, his second task was to walk from neighborhood to neighborhood, knock on every door, and demand that the man of the house come out and ask forgiveness. Mavlono completed that task as well, and then he was given his third task: to go into the Jewish quarter, and come back with wine. Mavlono hesitated a great deal, but finally said, "Bismallah!" and went into the Jewish quarter, to the house he had been told to go to, and from the half-dozen noble-looking, gray-bearded old men there, he brought back some wine.

Shams Tabrizi handed the wine back to Mavlono. Mavlono drank the wine and found it was no ordinary wine, but a wine as splendid as that drawn from the fountains of heaven. He drank it, and he achieved perfection. Kuyuk-baxshi finished his story, offered up a blessing in the name of the masters, and then recited these words:

A drunken nightingale took this road, a land of flowers it found,
On it went with a flower, goblets and good cheer did abound.
Finally it spoke the truth; in my ear I heard the sound,
Saying the sorrow was gone now, but still no peace could be found.

They drank, and their hearts rejoiced. Domrul remembered that he had not managed to give Emer the bad news about her mother, and he mourned a little. The drunken Kuyuk-baxshi revealed a secret about this secluded place to him. "Younger brother!" he told him. "Do you see that tall building across the street? When Qimbat-guppi and Bo'riboy-marqa were in prison, she used to go to that very building. Here, they say, a mad fortune teller used to cast his healing gaze. He called himself a 'healer by sight,' and just by staring at your hemorrhoids, he could screw them back up into your ass. That's the kind of fellow she used to visit, my friend! As for me, I used to sit at this window, looking, hoping to catch a glimpse of her. Sometimes my sculptor friend waited with me. You know, little brother, if I were to see her one more time, my heart would surely grieve."

"Who?" asked Domrul, completely drunk now.

"Who do you think, my brother? Goia, Goia."

◆

Kuyuk-baxshi's endless tales of his Goia, and the works of art Domrul had seen in the sculptor's studio, brought his thoughts around to Gaia hanovna again. With astonishment, Domrul realized he had never thought of Gaia as *Gaia*, the Greek goddess of the Earth. In one of his anthropology courses, he had read quite a lot about the myths and legends of those ancient Greeks. Back then, when Domrul heard anything about the Greeks or Romans from his professors, probably because of his name, he would compare them with Turkish stories. For instance, there was Gaia, who emerged from the primitive Chaos, the shaper of the Earth. Then, to cover herself on every side, Gaia made the starry heavens, called Uranus; and he posed that story against the Turkish one about Kök Tengri and Earth and Water. And then the professors read, from Homer or Hesiod, about Gaia and her husband Uranus, whom she had created herself:

> She hid her son in ambush, and put in his hands
> a jagged sickle, and revealed to him the plot.
> And Uranus came, bringing on night,
> and he lay about Gaia, full of passion,
> and spread himself full upon her. And her son stretched forth his left
>   hand
> from his ambush, and in his right took the great long sickle
> and swiftly lopped off his sinful father's
> member, and immediately hurled it away . . .

Domrul compared this, as well, to Erklik's revolt against Tengri, and how in that revolt, Yer Mag'us—or was it Yel Mag'us or Yalmog'iz, the Witch?—appeared, rising up from the surface of the earth.

Now, when he thought about it, whether he took the Greek tales or the Turkish ones, Gaia Mangitkhanovna's life in fact turned out to be just like those stories. Domrul even wondered, suddenly, whether he was living his own life or a myth, as he lay awake at night. Maybe Kuyuk-baxshi, with all his endless tales about Gaia, was really a Homer or Hesiod? Maybe Time had returned, and now was the time that would be the opposite of Time's beginning? If the lives of the Greeks had been mixed up with their eternal myths, maybe now it's the opposite; maybe now those myths were building the lives of Domrul and everyone he knew? And maybe Gaia's unbridled lifestyle that we have described here is exactly the fate of the Earth, or Gaia, or the planet itself? Maybe the Mad Domrul of Turkish myth is wrangling with death—those already overcome, the ones still being over-come, and the ones yet to be overcome—and yet not understanding the point of these stories?

When Erklik's rebellion against Tengri came to nothing, and he was not able to become the master of man's spirit, Erklik created the mythical beast Yer Mag'us, or Yalmog'iz, the Witch. That beast extended its great tongue up from the sea to swallow any human beings who were nearing the shore. The khan of the middle world, Taran Misqay, said, "I shall slay this beast!" And he came down to earth from the heavens and joined with a woman named Erka-Shudun and turned into a child named Toma Taran. He came to the edge of the sea, and Yalmog'iz the Beast stuck her tongue out for him, wanting to swallow up the child; but the child was no child, but Taran Misqay, and he grabbed hold of the beast's tongue and pulled her that way to the shore, and the sea overflowed onto the land. Not wishing the land to sink, Toma Taran began drinking the water, and he swallowed down the entire sea. Then Yalmog'iz the Beast was left dry, and she trembled. Toma Taran lifted her up and cast her to the ground. The beast's blood splattered across the rocks. (Ever since that day, rocks have been all different colors.) Toma Taran bent the Beast like a rainbow and broke her into tiny pieces. And from those pieces, ants and insects, bugs and beetles, spread throughout the land.

What was this? Domrul wondered, in the bluish dawn. A legend or fairy tale? Or real life today, for him and Gaia, for Emer and Kuyuk?

◆

The next day, Rustakhezova also confirmed that Emer would soon be given her freedom, but made it known that it was due to her own selfless, zealous service. "It was hard, but we pulled it off!" she said. "Now they've taken your fiancée to the clinic, Sangorodok. They don't let anyone in there. The doctors will bring her back to normal, and you'll be able to take her home in a week or so." Then she said, very seriously, "Do not forget to pay the dowry."

When Domrul heard about Sangorodok, he was plunged into uncer-tainty once more. Wouldn't they torment Emer even more there, or infect her intentionally with some disease or other? Thinking those thoughts, he got into a taxi and rode straight up to the gates of Sangorodok, but he took one look at the dozens of abject human beings standing outside the door and his heart broke even worse than before, and he returned to Kuyuk-baxshi's place. With Kuyuk-baxshi, he went to pick up the paperwork that he had submitted to the local police department when he arrived from London. After that they went home, and they sat together, telling each other of their grief, keeping up the conversation.

After another five days (meanwhile, Domrul went with Kuyuk-baxshi to every wedding in the vicinity), Domrul was again summoned, through Rustakhezova, to the chief inspector's building, and he brought them together to his office, and there, his blue eyes sparkling, he spoke. "Well, my bridegroom!" he began. "There's no way we can outdo you in keeping secrets, but now you've outdone yourself! You hid your sugar mama from us, and that has been revealed"—again he raised his eyebrows up high—"and you've also been hiding from us that your girlfriend is about to be a mama, too, is that right?"

Domrul may or may not have really heard those words, and he did not understand. What had this blue-eyed devil just said? Be a mama? Or did he just mean to say "sugar mama" again?

The director was continuing. "If that's the case, it's a shame, because if *you* had told us at the start, rather than the doctors, you could have already been in London with your fiancée! And it would've been a lot easier for us with the *protocol* side of it." Again his eyebrows went up.

As soon as he had finished delivering this mild reproof and rebuke, he pushed the button for his secretary, and with no additional instructions the secretary entered, leading Emer. Emer held her backpack, and she looked like ordinary Emer again. Domrul stood and walked toward her. He hugged her. The director made no move to stop them. On the contrary, he cautiously walked toward the door, locked it for some reason, winked one blue eye, and took out an elegant bottle of cognac from the shelf beside the door, and four little crystal cups, and poured cognac for all of them. "In the name of the old generation"—and he raised his eyebrows once more—"we drink to the new generation!" And he raised his glass.

◆

Early the next day another of Kuyuk-baxshi's followers drove his master, and Emer and Domrul, to the bar association office. There, Domrul paid

Rustakhezova a handful of cash for her services, and then they all took the road straight to the airport. With the good news of the new life that had appeared between Domrul and Emer, Domrul could find no way to give voice to his bad news; he wanted them to get away from that place safe and sound and then talk, he told himself, putting it off.

At the airport entrance, while the police officer inspected them, they felt on alert again. But they looked and saw everyone else was being inspected too. They went and checked in. The agent looked over their passports and turned to Domrul. "You were born here, weren't you? But you have a British passport. When did you move there?" Her question, made out of ordinary curiosity, seemed to Domrul, that moment, like an interrogation. As if she were stopping them all, telling them, "The game is up! Now back to the way it was before!" Domrul felt that trouble was just one step ahead of him.

Emer was still stunned, and she understood nothing, not where she was or what was happening, and she was making no effort to understand it either. Only Kuyuk-baxshi was still joking with everyone, tossing out an old saying here, an old story there, and making everyone around him laugh.

They went on to customs. The customs officer looked at Domrul's declaration form. "That's a lot of wealth to leave here, buddy!" he commented, making Domrul sweat again. Could they really know who he had given money to? Would they finally catch him now? No, Kuyuk-baxshi was telling them stories too!

In the aul I drank *kumiss* by the glass,
Then I came to the city and scratched my ass!

He walked right by them, too, goofing and giggling all the way. After that came the border guards, and then, going through passport control, Domrul broke out in a black sweat again. Apparently he had not registered with the local police station within three days, but only on day four of his stay. Domrul didn't know what to do, and he was just about to offer a bribe when Kuyuk-baxshi interrupted, and with his wisecracks helped even this solemn border guard understand how things were. "Younger brother, you know, foreigners . . . they don't know our ways of doing things, and the passport lady wrote down her payday there out of spite! Here, use my phone, if you want. Ask her yourself!"

Finally they were past all obstacles, and they walked outside to get on the plane and sat down in their seats. Then Kuyuk-baxshi's cell phone rang. "Yes, friend! Is that you? You said you were coming to the airport? Are you here? Where are you? You see our plane?" Now one of the flight attendants strode over to Kuyuk-baxshi and told him to turn off his phone immediately. Kuyuk-baxshi made an obedient face, switched off his telephone, and looked at Domrul sitting next to him.

"Our friend the sculptor is here . . . There he is!" he said, gesturing out across the tarmac toward the terminal's roof.

Domrul took a look and saw a man with one hand in his pocket, his other arm flailing around and around wildly, and his heart leapt into his mouth.

"My . . ." he whispered.

"Yes, funny, isn't he! That's our O'rhon!" exclaimed Kuyuk.

"My father!" whispered Domrul to himself, and he would have risen from his seat, but the plane was just starting to move.

Fire and Air, Earth and Water

All the way to Istanbul, Domrul felt just as stunned as Emer. Kuyuk-baxshi tried to engage him in pleasant conversation every now and then, but Domrul didn't hear one word. His insides were brimming over with unbridled trepidation. Could he share his grief with Emer? But how could he bring up his newly found father in the face of her newly dead mother? Kuyuk-baxshi, smart and sensitive as he was, had also realized nothing. "They seem so tired, and understandably! They don't even have the strength left for a private conversation, let alone for entertaining me," he thought, and he dropped off to sleep.

What could Domrul possibly do? He could not go back again once they reached Istanbul, because his visa had run out; they'd either arrest him or ship him right from the airport back to Istanbul. Maybe he could call from Istanbul? Yes, maybe . . . But when he imagined making that call, it set him thinking some more. Whatever the case, he would have to talk on the phone in front of Emer, because he couldn't take Kuyuk with him and leave Emer all by herself!

But then again, maybe Emer actually wanted to be left alone now? To gather her thoughts, to put her feelings in order. Up till now, she had suppressed all the turmoil inside her, forced away all the thoughts in her brain, as if by doing so, she could purify her heart all at once, and clearly explain to herself, once and for all, everything that had happened in this whole crazy nightmare. Some people, caught up in this kind of debauchery, this kind of disaster, would end up going to a therapist or a psychoanalyst for years on end. But Emer yearned just for one hour of solitude, and in that one hour, she felt she could toss off the heavy links of the knotted chain that wrapped around her soul.

Stand aside for a moment and ask yourself, honestly, where should she start? With which injury or insult, what blow? Her pregnancy or humiliation, her detachment or desolation, her seething soul or her empty heart? Even just one hour of solitude, one hour of quiet, just one hour outside of time . . .

Kuyuk-baxshi, his eyes drooping, his thoughts roaming restlessly, thought he might fall asleep, but he turned his head to the icy window, and now he was distressed not over the two people sitting beside him, flying from his past into his future, but to the shade flickering somewhere up ahead: Goia. All of humanity was like a weaver who stumbles across a spool of yarn in the dark. The more threads he weaves, the more confusion he creates. Finally, when day breaks, he sees he needs to either throw away the spool or cut away all the knots in the string, and he gives up:

> Lots of jewelers in the *souq*
> Embroiderers and coppersmiths too,
> Do not harbor much hope, Kuyuk,
> Others may find the way too.

◆

Nothing happened in Istanbul. They ate some Turkish kebabs, then got on the plane for London. Though Domrul did learn, during the course of conversation, that Kuyuk-baxshi's sculptor friend O'rhon was married and had children. Emer did not open up either. She tried to smile, as much as she could, at the incessant courtesies of the two men by her side, but her smile was the smile of a person offering thanks while eating unripe, sour apricots.

Everything happened during their approach to Gatwick in London.

By the time they announced that the plane was descending, Domrul could stand it no longer. Suddenly he spun in his seat to face Emer. He placed both his hands on her forearm. "Emer. I'm sorry. Please forgive me. I should have told you this before, but I didn't have the strength. You . . . while you were in prison, your mother . . . passed away."

Emer had been expecting yet another simple kindness, and she had readied her face for another phony smile. But these words must have penetrated into her consciousness, shattered as it was. Her eyes stared wide in fright, her mouth opened in a silent scream, and she suddenly started from her seat and began to yell. Domrul held on to her with all his strength, wanting to stifle that screaming against his chest, but two flight attendants were already rushing toward them, and panic seemed to explode all around them.

Someone shouted for help, someone else was holding his head in his hands, and Emer, still buckled in her seat, was bleating like a sheep being slaughtered. "I need to get out! Let me through!" she begged, flapping her arms over and over again.

One of the flock of flight attendants asked another, "What's wrong? Is she drunk?" And the second was trying to press Domrul and Emer to their seats.

Kuyuk-baxshi, not understanding what was going on at the other end of the row, did not know what to do. He sat there with his mouth open, confused.

"You come over here!" ordered the stewardess who was pressing Emer into her seat with all her weight, and she called Domrul into the aisle, forcing, pressing them together, and she put Emer in Domrul's old middle seat, steering her in, and fastened her seatbelt tight.

Emer was sobbing like a child, her breath catching tight in her throat. "I hate you! I hate you!" she was shouting, pouring out all her pain— maybe to Domrul, maybe to all of them.

The plane touched down. Before the passengers could disembark, two airport police officers climbed aboard. They cleaved their way through the crowds of standing passengers until they reached the row they were looking for. "Miss Finnegan? We have some questions to ask you about the ruckus you caused on this flight. Please come with us."

❖

No, Emer was not put in jail. She, Domrul, and the cabin crew were all interviewed separately and set free with a scolding. When Emer walked out of the airport police station, Domrul and Kuyuk-baxshi were there waiting outside, with their suitcases and other luggage. Emer's face was white as cotton gauze, and her nerves were woven about as tight. She picked up her backpack, which had been sitting on top of a suitcase, said not a word, and walked away toward the exit.

Domrul shoved all the other things at Kuyuk-baxshi and ran after her. "Emer! Emer!" he called. Emer was rushing toward the trains, not looking back.

Finally Domrul caught up with her, and when he took her by the arm, she jerked abruptly away, and when Domrul said "Emer!" one more time, she shouted back at him, "Fuck off!" and she walked on faster than before.

Domrul was immediately dumbstruck. He had expected plenty of things, but he had not expected that. And coming from Emer, after all was said and done! From the Emer he had rescued. He was furious, and he was bitter, and he was mad as a little boy. "Phoo!" he spat, and went back to Kuyuk-baxshi.

Poor Kuyuk-baxshi was wondering whether he had brought all these bad things upon them, and not knowing what to do with himself, he was still sitting there, having found no place to hide. If he could find someone or other to help him get back on that plane . . . Could he ask Domrul to find someone and ask him to see him off?

Domrul came back, picked up his suitcase, and barked, "Let's go." And he started off, not in the direction Emer had taken, but toward a different door. Kuyuk-baxshi tagged along after him like a child. Being a guest of someone else means you are a burden, but being a burden to someone who was already having trouble . . . He felt like just another suitcase clunking and clanking as it rolled along behind Domrul. No different from the suitcase that was stuffed with Kuyuk's old, worn-out clothes. When they stepped through the door into the famous rain of England, that suitcase stepped right in a puddle, stood in line for a taxi, got drenched by the driving rain, and got flung into the back of an old cab—that's what happens with the guest of someone in trouble!

I went out as best I could,
I frowned my eyes as best I could,
and in the place where I frowned my eyes,
there was a never-blooming flower and bud.

❖

Another time Domrul might have taken a train or a bus, but in his bitterness, he hired a cab and took Kuyuk-baxshi to Eastbourne. He had spent as much money on Rustakhezova, so why couldn't he take a taxi fifty or sixty kilometers now?

On the way, Kuyuk-baxshi spoke of his younger days and of his master Yo'lli-baxshi. He wanted to distract Domrul without him knowing it. Domrul didn't offer any resistance. The car's rumbling and the constant sound of Kuyuk-baxshi's voice combined to provide an interesting calm, helping him to gather his thoughts together. One needs to be forgiving, his mind was telling him, and let Emer cool down, let her understand everything. But his resentful heart was still whining, "What did I ever do to be treated that way?"

They drove into Eastbourne along the sea. The rain, which whipped them hard all the way, was left behind in the evening darkness; Kuyuk-baxshi felt the sea more than he saw it, and he brought his stories to an end, turning his ear to the waves.

They walked into Domrul's building. Somehow, in this damp place, dust had appeared from somewhere to settle on the shiny table and chairs in the kitchen. Domrul put the kettle on. They shared the bread that Kuyuk-baxshi had brought with him, and they snacked on raisins and almonds. Over tea, Domrul read his mail. One letter read: "At the end of your first six months caring for your client, in order to assess the results of those six months . . ." So he would have to take Gaia Mangitkhanovna and go to London.

Having been a bit distracted by his tea, Domrul now felt quite uncomfortable again. He saw that Kuyuk-baxshi's eyes were starting to close, due to the time difference, and he made up his own bed for his guest and got himself ready to go take a walk. When he found out, Kuyuk-baxshi wanted to go with him. "Sleep? In the grave, we'll have nothing to do but sleep. We need to see the ocean!" he insisted.

The rain had calmed a bit, and tiny clusters of stars were sparkling on the surface of the sea. And the sea, playing gently with its waves, was sending the light from the street lamps flashing back up to the sky. There was nobody else at the shore, and Kuyuk-baxshi filled his lungs with air, and he started to sing. Domrul walked off toward the hills looming black in the distance. As Kuyuk-baxshi put all his pleasure into that song, Domrul thought of his last happy night here, on this shore, with Emer, remembering it not so much with his heart or his head as with his tongue and his lips. He could taste the flavor of those mussels boiled in seawater.

They had agreed to walk to the hills, but Kuyuk-baxshi suddenly stopped short. "Brother, let's not walk that direction. My heart is somehow resisting. It has gone heavy as a rock," he said.

Jetlag, thought Domrul, and he led Kuyuk-baxshi back to where they had come from. How could he have known, then, the old saying? "A baxshi can see what is bound to be."

The next day, the sun sparkled so brightly that even the bald and the blind, as Kuyuk-baxshi would say, could see that spring had come to Eastbourne. Domrul took advantage of the opportunity and left Kuyuk-baxshi and his dombra for the afternoon with Antonina Ivanovna and Elizaveta Petrovna, the old Russian language and literature professor she had under her care, while he himself rushed out to attend to Gaia Mangitkhanovna, thinking of the letter he had received the day before. As the baxshi might have predicted, when he got to the begum's place, she and her neighbor, blind old Beryl, were sitting together on the balcony, sipping red wine.

The warmth of springtime might just be enough to melt someone as standoffish as Gaia Mangitkhanovna, and she called Domrul over to her side, as if to introduce him to Beryl, and then she brought a third glass from the room and offered some wine to Domrul as well. Domrul stated his business. He explained to her that today they absolutely had to travel to London.

But Gaia Mangitkhanovna was unimpressed. "They can wait, those disgusting little paperpushers! It's our donkey. If we want to, we ride, and if we don't want to, we stay," she said.

After that she addressed her words to Domrul again. "Now, shall we celebrate your girlfriend's freedom?" she laughed, and filled a glass and handed it to Domrul. "To our blue-eyed Tatar!" she pronounced, staring Domrul straight in the eye.

Then Domrul's flesh trembled, and he understood everything. In front of his eyes loomed a vision of that chief inspector, his eyebrows raised all the way up to the ceiling, his blue eyes winking and winking. Yes.

That's what was going on. Domrul did not clink his glass against hers. He just drained it completely.

Beryl had no idea what was going on around her. "Cheers!" she proclaimed happily. Now Domrul noticed that their once-full bottle of Burgundy was half finished.

Gaia Mangitkhanovna stepped away once more. Instead of a toast, she told him, "You go and see those leeches yourself. Tell them I'm satisfied with you. If they need proof, you can bring them to me! I'm not about to let them spend my money in vain!" After that command, she raised her glass.

Again, Beryl offered a "Cheers!" and drank, and Domrul quickly drained half his own glass.

"Fine. I'll go," he said, and walked out.

He went to London that very afternoon and held the meeting and the interview. Then, after hesitating a bit, he dialed the number at Emer's mother's house. After five rings, Emer picked up the phone. Domrul did not say hello, he did not say her name, but only told her, his voice dry and formal, "Come and get your Kuyuk-baxshi. You invited him here." Since Emer didn't hang up immediately, Domrul pressed on.

"By the way, it wasn't really the British embassy who got you out of jail. Gaia—" But the words caught in his throat.

Emer, without a word, hung up the phone.

Domrul returned home before sunset. England's fickle weather seemed to have struck again. The sky, which had shined so nicely all day, was again besieged with black clouds, and the thunder grumbling from far off was again stirring up a commotion in his heart. Thinking he had better check on Kuyuk-baxshi, Domrul called Antonina Ivanovna, and it turned out the three of them had become such great friends that they wanted to go to the local theater that evening, and Antonina Ivanovna asked Domrul politely if afterward he'd like to come over to Elizaveta Petrovna's place, not that it was so splendid a palace, but compared to his gloomy little rooms, surely Domrul would understand . . .

"And also, Elizaveta Petrovna was just saying now that you should come have supper with us too!" Domrul was supposed to call them later, after they got back from the theater.

Outside, it had started pouring as hard as yesterday; the thunder rumbled, and the lightning flashed and crashed noisily. Domrul thought of Emer again. When he thought of Emer, he missed how happy his heart had been just the other day, in the warm springtime of that other country. Then his thoughts turned to his father. Should he call him? What would he say to him? What if he did something to bring old wounds to the surface again? If his father was married, and he had children . . .

Suddenly weary of all the many things that had happened to him over the past days and just recently, and wanting a rest from the ceaseless thoughts that were burying him, Domrul, not stopping to shed his clothes, threw himself down onto the bed he had made up for Kuyuk-baxshi. The thoughts he also could not shed were becoming all mixed up in their multitudes, and he didn't want to hang on to any of them. He lay there feeling lost for a while, until finally, without noticing when or how, he fell asleep.

The loud, shrill buzzing of the doorbell woke him up. As if having just arisen from a deep sleep, feebly, without the strength to really open his eyes, Domrul tottered to the door. Not understanding where he was or what was happening, he opened it. The gusting wind and rain came in through the open door. Domrul shuddered at the blast of cold. Emer was standing on the threshold.

"Where's Kuyuk?" she asked, sounding more Irish than usual when she asked.

"Want to come in?" asked Domrul, rubbing his eyes. Emer demurred a second, then gave up her post in the doorframe. Domrul shut the door, which had been so blasted by the cold.

Emer asked again, "Where's Kuyuk?"

"At the theater," Domrul answered, and then added, in a way he himself hadn't expected, "With Gaia."

"Again you're lying!" said Emer, her voice cold and without feeling. "I've just come from her place. Your drunken old whore told me *everything*." Emer was still standing by the door, as if any second now she'd open it, then slam it shut in Domrul's face and fly off forever.

"I . . . I . . ." Domrul could only stutter. ("Told her everything . . . Told her everything . . . That old bitch!" is what he was thinking.)

"Don't call her that! She's the person who freed you."

"The person? She's no person!" Not only was Emer now given over to her rage, but her words, cold as ice from the air outside, thrust deep into Domrul, one after the other. "So listen, then! Her son was in that same Sangorodok place that I was. With tuberculosis. He was dying. Do you know who put him in prison? Your old prostitute! She riled up her son to rebel against her husband, and then she sold him out. And did you know about her daughter? She's rotting in jail too! That Gaia is no person! She's a witch, carrying around death wherever she goes. Now, where is Kuyuk-baxshi?" demanded Emer, returning to her original question.

"At the theater. With Antonina. I meant to say Antonina."

"So now you're getting your old women mixed up?" scoffed Emer, her sarcasm grating at his ears.

"Emer!" Domrul pleaded. "As long as you've got my child there in your belly . . ."

Emer revealed no feeling, neither on her face, nor in her voice. "And how do you know it's *your* child, eh? Maybe they raped me," she said.

At that Domrul, without really understanding how it happened, slapped Emer's face and yelled, "Shut up, you whore!"

Emer placed her own hand against her face, and in disbelief, she pulled the door open right in front of Domrul's nose and left, out into the windswept, rainsoaked street.

In remorse, in agony, Domrul called into the darkness. "Emer!" That shout was all he had left in him.

Domrul felt despicable. At first he wanted to go chase after Emer, but her completely hopeless tone of voice, and especially her last words, had made Domrul's flesh crawl and frozen his heart into a millstone. "That old bitch told her everything!" he thought again. But had the old bitch actually told her everything? Domrul really did not know what to do with himself. His thoughts were all over the place. Domrul was completely perplexed, not even knowing where to direct his wrath or on whom to take his revenge. At himself? Or at Emer? Gaia? Kuyuk-baxshi? Antonina? Or that far-away chief inspector? At that moment, he cursed the whole world. Suddenly he was back again in his childhood, inside that basement, facing death, wrapped up in his aunt Sakina's skirts, holding his breath . . . He had to talk to his father. He had oceans and oceans of complaints, oceans of wrath, seas full of sins and regrets.

His fingers were twitching violently, but he started to dial the number he found written on a tiny piece of paper. The connection broke up before he finished. He dialed again. Again, he dialed only half the number. He dialed and dialed again. The lament that had been caught in his throat suddenly burst to the surface, and he sobbed. Murky tears from his eyes dripped down onto the telephone. On the third, or fourth, or fifth time, as he sobbed, came the ring on the other end, like a moaning welling up from across thousands of miles, thousands of dark nights, through so many distant decades. One, two, three, four . . . Domrul was shaking, sobbing, breathing hard.

Finally, the annoyed voice of a sleepy woman answered in Russian. "Hello?"

Domrul responded in the same language. "May I speak to O'rhon, please?" he asked.

"Who is this?" the woman answered. "Do you know what time it is?" She left no doubt as to how annoyed she was.

"I'm sorry! I'm calling from England!" was all Domrul was able to get out. There was a long silence. Domrul's sense of calm disappeared again. What was happening? What was he going to say now?

"Yes, hello?" came a strong voice.

"It's me, Domrul . . . Your son."

"Domrul? My child! I knew it! I could feel it in my heart! Where are you, my son, my dear boy?"

"I'm calling from England."

"When Kuyuk spoke of you, my heart skipped a beat! But when I asked your name, he told me what was in your passport. You changed it, did you? Oh, and why didn't you come and find me when you were here?"

"We went to your studio."

"Yes, the studio, the studio . . . Why couldn't I have stayed in town that day! Oh, my son, my dear soul." Now the father began to sob. "I knew that you were alive! And that whore pretended you were dead—"

"Who?" asked Domrul, quietly. He too was unable to keep his tears from falling.

"Who else? That bitch, Goia, of course. Be careful of her, my son! She was the one who had your girlfriend put in prison too."

◈

One time in sixth or seventh grade, Gaia and Sakina's history teacher, a war cripple named Ruben or Rubin—Gaia Mangitkhanovna could no longer remember—had suddenly gone into a fit of hysterics, cursing the Germans and the Chechens, the Crimean Tatars and the Meskhetian Turks. "They're all motherfuckers, traitors, and turncoats!" he yelled, the spit flying out of his mouth. "Now they want to purge the black mark from those villains' names! It's not a pardon they need. They all need to be snuffed out, every one of them!" he fumed. Sakina, Maisie, Sapiyat, and a few other girls jumped and looked as if they wanted to crawl inside their desks. Fortunately, the bell rang, and class was over. Otherwise, the furious Ruben just might have exposed each of them, one by one, and torn them apart limb to limb.

Whether the studious Gaia wrote down those words in her notebook to remember them always, or whether she herself repeated those words just as frankly during some other lesson, her friendship with Sakina, and later with the other girls, was battered and broken for good. Gaia's outcast of a teacher urged her on even more. "Don't trust a single thing they say!" he said. "They'll sell you out! They'll betray you for a penny and make an effigy out of you. Look, every one of them has a sharpened dagger hidden under her skirt to stab you with!"

Sakina, Maisie, and Sapiyat would have been bad enough, but now she was in the full flush of puberty, and Gaia seemed to have secretly given her heart to Sakina's brother O'rhon. Every time she went to their house, ostensibly to visit Sakina, or out in the fields, or whenever she saw O'rhon, that fueled her adolescent lust a little bit more. Now she wasn't speaking to Sakina, so she had lost touch with O'rhon as well.

Gaia took it out on her own mother, flinging onto her all the bitterness that had built up in her over the years. After that, this girl, a staunch Leninist-Stalinist Komsomol member, got her degree, and when she went off to study in Saratov, O'rhon, as if also betraying her, married one of her cousins.

And now Gaia truly trusted nobody in the whole world.

◆

Gaia Mangitkhanovna had finished everything she needed to do. She had written her will and filled out the euthanasia paperwork. She had paid off all her debts to this life. Now her last task would be to make that slug-gard Domrul take the last step and be done with it! From now on, all her remaining days were a gift, a luxury, or in other words, a feast. She spent all day lazing in the warmth of the sun with old blind Beryl. Tomorrow she'd have to call Antonina. True, no matter how much you put your life in order, as long as you're still among messy human beings, somebody is bound to burst onto stage unexpectedly. They'll come right in and stomp all over your clean, tidy room with their boots and shoes, blackened with mud and filth. Just like a swarm of ants. (Actually, guess what she had just seen in her kitchen—ants all over the jar of cherry jam in her pantry. Not flies, not maggots, not cockroaches—just insipid, tiny, yellow ants. Where under the heavens had that calamity arisen from? Had they been signal-ing to her about the mad Domrul's arrival in the morning, or were they a sign of how that shit of a girlfriend of his had been about to storm in here earlier this evening?)

In she stormed, not in Russian, but in English, which is something she'd never understand! "Djidju save mi?" the girl must have asked a hun-dred times. What was she trying to say? Then she tried Russian. "You— savior?" she asked, pointing her finger. If she meant to ask whether *she*, Gaia, had saved her, then the answer would be yes. If Gaia hadn't inter-vened, she'd still be rotting away in there in a pile of her own shit! Either in Karaul-Bazar or in Jaslyk, the worst of those places.

"Yes, yes, yes!" How angry she got when I said that! She is a puke, isn't she!

On she went jabbering away, and pointing her finger at me again. "Yosan! Yosan!" she roared incoherently. Did she mean "yo'q-san"? As in, "destroy-you?" Is that what she wanted to say? No woman has ever borne a child who can destroy me, girl! You're in the palm of my hand, birdie! Look, that blue-eyed Tatar took all the pictures I needed, you little whore!

Let him send them here, and then I'll show you your Domrul, and you too! I told her! Whether she understood it or not, I told her everything! How the blue-eyed one peeped through the hole in the door, and how Domrul humped over you like a dog . . .

Too bad I wasn't there myself then, like before, to peep through that hole with my own eyes . . . Or the way I crushed my husband and his whores, would that I could have caught *you* two! What a shame! But still, I showed her my true self. Well done! Now she'll start to panic, the filthy bitch! "Now get out of my sight!" I told her. "Don't you ever show yourself around here again!" And she disappeared.

Ants need to be destroyed, too, whether with lime or with boiling water. If you don't destroy them, they'll swarm all over you, head to foot.

◈

When Domrul burst into Gaia Mangitkhanovna's apartment, it was just a little past eleven o'clock. But Gaia Mangitkhanovna had apparently not yet gone to bed, and she sat wrapped up in some kind of metal suit on the couch in the living room, watching television, the wine she had opened for herself there in front of her. Domrul came in, extremely agitated, and paying no attention to her bizarre getup, he demanded, "Did Emer come here?" He was yelling.

"Yes, she did," said Gaia Mangitkhanovna without turning around. There was not even a hint of passion on her face or in her voice.

This is who she must have learned it from! thought Domrul, enraged, and he tossed his wet coat toward the door. "Did you tell her?" he shouted.

Gaia Mangitkhanovna took no offense at his tone, just waited in a good-natured way. In his tone, there was something like a son's threat against his mother.

"I suppose I did tell her, assuming she understood. Couldn't you have taught her Russian?" she asked, just like a mother scolding her son. And rattling the metal, she picked up the glass next to her, and as if having forgotten her ridiculous outfit, she gulped down the wine.

As devastated as Domrul had been before his recent talk with his father, now he felt even worse. His fury, once so inflated, suddenly lost all its steam. "What language did you two talk in, then?" he asked, moving in Gaia's direction.

"In whatever ones we knew."

"I spoke with my father," said Domrul, that fury inside him growing larger now. Gaia Mangitkhanovna said nothing. "A man named O'rhon Vaysal."

Domrul waited for her answer. Not a wrinkle moved on Gaia Mangit-khanovna's face. She was still sitting there, as if expecting a story. Except that one hand had started stroking the metal helmet that sat by her side.

"Do you know him?" asked Domrul, raising his voice a little more. Gaia Mangitkhanovna did not move a muscle.

"A sculptor," Domrul continued. Gaia Mangitkhanovna, still apparently waiting for the story to continue, reclined backward elegantly.

"Is your name Goia?" Domrul asked the woman reclining there, making one last effort.

"It's Gaia," she whispered. Then she was caressing Domrul's cold hands, which pressed upon her steely face. "Gaia Mangitkhanovna to you!" she hissed at him.

Domrul started to weep, to sob, like a young child. Now for some reason he was butting his own head against Gaia Mangitkhanovna's metal costume, while his hands tore rudely at the loosely fastened armor, and pulled at the hem of her robe; and then Gaia tossed her metal helmet aside, and pulled Domrul's hand up under her robe, and stroked Domrul's head. Now she noticed her drunkenness, which had been collecting so uselessly all day long. Now everything she had sown in this world, in this life, knowingly or unknowingly, was wrapped up in this idiot right here. Fine. She would not snap his neck in two, but perhaps she would take him up again inside her, into her womb, melt him in the wine she had drunk, take him again with her whole self for the last time, on one last trip, with no return.

Never had her lust been so entangled with her feelings, never had it drowned in those feelings . . . And Domrul! He had a look about him that said he was going to rape, and pummel, and strangle this witch to death. He was turning into the boy who had never emerged from under his aunt's skirt, hiding from the world that was hunting him, hiding from life, and now he would bury all his physical desire, his whole body, as deeply as he could into this pit of a refuge.

A son of the Turks, around thirty years old, was lying in bed with an old woman two and a half times his age, and he wiped the cold sweat off his back with a swath of linen cloth, truly hating himself. Through the open window, the sea breeze carried in the ceaseless shattering sounds of the waves on the gravel, and those lustful noises increased his misery, and he did not know whether to get up or to go on lying there wrapped in his disgust. Whatever had he done? Did he have any sense at all, to be propelled toward this shame? They'd fire him for sure! Or things could get even worse. Now the young man thought of his own, distant love: how could he ever look her in the eye now? Shame, shame, shame! What if he just strangled the old witch to death right here? That thought hitting his brain was enough of a blow to make the young man tremble. Was the old woman even alive? When the fluids of passion were still spilling onto the white sheet, had she yelled her lust out loud and choked herself dead? There was a slight trembling in her clumpy, frumpy henna-dyed hair. Or was that just the breeze? Her crotch barely covered by the sheet, and the beady mole on her scrawny waist, still seemed to be trembling. Or so it seemed to him. She really had moaned, wheezed, in agony.

The young man was in torment. Now what was he going to do?

Police sirens were wailing somewhere in the distance. On the television, not shut off this whole time, the local news was jabbering on about another tragedy near Beachy Head, reporting how rescue teams had recovered the body of a young woman from the shore. The cell phone lying on top of the television was also going into hysterics, jumping in all directions, shrieking nonstop, as if Kuyuk-baxshi, who had seen and heard everything in that midnight world, had been torn away again from all his jokes and his stories, and meant to store them all away inside himself.

καὶ γαῖαν αὐτήν, ἧ τὰ πάντα τίκτεται,
θρέψασά τ᾽ αὖθις τῶνδε κῦμα λαμβάνει

And to Earth herself, who gives birth to all things,
nurtures them, and then receives that fruit of her womb back into herself.

THE END

Credit: Dani Ismailov.

Hamid Ismailov was born into a deeply religious Uzbek family of mullahs and Hodjas living in Kyrgyzstan, many of whom had lost their lives during Stalin-era persecution. Yet he received an exemplary Soviet education, graduating with distinction from both his secondary school and military college, as well as attaining university degrees in a number of disciplines. Though he could have become a high-flying Soviet or post-Soviet apparatchik, instead his fate led him to become a dissident writer and poet residing in the West. He was the BBC World Service's first writer in residence. Critics have compared his books to the best of Russian classics, Sufi parables, and works of Western postmodernism. While his writing reflects all of these and many other strands, it is his unique intercultural experience that excites and draws the reader into his world. His novel *The Devils' Dance* won the 2019 EBRD literature prize.

Photo courtesy of the translator.

Shelley Fairweather-Vega is a freelance translator in Seattle, Washington, with a special interest in the intersections between culture and politics. She has been translating scholarly and creative works from Russian and Uzbek since 2005.